For This Christmas Only

CARO CARSON

———

HARLEQUIN

SPECIAL
EDITION

Recycling programs for this product may not exist in your area.

ISBN-13: 978-1-335-89497-7

For This Christmas Only

Copyright © 2020 by Caroline Phipps

This edition published by arrangement with Harlequin Books S.A.

For questions and comments about the quality of this book, please contact us at CustomerService@Harlequin.com.

Harlequin Enterprises ULC
22 Adelaide St. West, 40th Floor
Toronto, Ontario M5H 4E3, Canada
www.Harlequin.com

Printed in U.S.A.

"Either they're very excited to see us holding hands," Mallory said, "or you gave them a really big tip."

"I wanted us to be all set for refills the rest of the night. We can trade gloves and hold a hot cup with our other hands next." Eli gave her hand a squeeze, a move as casually intimate as that wink.

Next. It wouldn't be a short night.

For a few more hours, she could be the real Mallory, before she went back to pretending that she already knew how to make her life go the way she wanted it to.

"Let's get out of this crowd," Eli said. "We're going to get bumped and spill our drinks any second now. It's dangerous."

It was dangerous. Mallory had just forgotten what was real. This woman who held Eli's hand as they laughed at their near misses with other strangers couldn't be the real Mallory. The real one lived her life as a fledgling businesswoman who followed the rules. This was only a fake date.

Fake dates meant fake kisses, and Mallory didn't do fake kisses. On the other hand, she'd broken half of E.L. Taylor's rules tonight.

Before she returned to reality, why not break one of her own?

* * *

MASTERSON, TEXAS:
Where you come to learn about love!

Dear Reader,

Do you enjoy meeting strangers? The holiday season usually includes a lot of socializing with new people, whether they are coworkers' spouses at an office party or your neighbor's relatives visiting from out of town. This book's hero and heroine meet as perfect strangers at a holiday festival. For very different reasons, they'd each rather be alone, but the best way they find to do this is by being alone, together—which, of course, means they are no longer alone in the end!

I finished writing this book as the worldwide pandemic made us all be alone, together. We may have stayed in our homes alone, but emails, video meetings and phone calls kept us together. In such a serious situation, it was harder to get lost in my writing, but it also made me grateful to immerse myself in a world where the good guys always win in the end. I write books with happy endings because I enjoy reading books with happy endings. I hope that reading this book brings you hours of joy.

Although you and I might be perfect strangers, we already have this love for happily-ever-after novels in common. I would enjoy hearing from you. You can find me easily on Facebook, or you can drop me a private note through my website, www.carocarson.com.

Happy holidays,

Caro Carson

Despite a n̶̶
West Point grad̶
sales executive, **Car**̶ background as a
the happily-ever-after of a goo̶ officer and Fortune 100
a RITA® Award–winning Harlequin auth̶ always treasured
delighted to be living her own happily-ever-after w̶ novel. As
her husband and two children in Florida, a location
that has saved the coaster-loving theme-park fanatic
a fortune on plane tickets.

Books by Caro Carson

Harlequin Special Edition

Masterson, Texas

The Bartender's Secret
The Slow Burn

American Heroes

The Lieutenants' Online Love
The Captains' Vegas Vows
The Majors' Holiday Hideaway
The Colonels' Texas Promise

Montana Mavericks: What Happened at the Wedding?

The Maverick's Holiday Masquerade

The Doctors MacDowell

Doctor, Soldier, Daddy
The Doctor's Former Fiancée
The Bachelor Doctor's Bride

Visit the Author Profile page
at Harlequin.com for more titles.

perfect strangers
This book the people who did their best
is dedicate pandemic to protect their families,
d.
their friends, their neighbors and, perhaps most
generously of all, perfect strangers. Thank you.

Chapter One

Never meet your heroes. Wait until they are
your equals.

—How to Taylor Your Business Plan
by E.L. Taylor

It was her twenty-ninth birthday, and she was sinking in quicksand.

Literally.

Mallory Ames flailed about, trying to keep her balance as wet sand sucked her into its depths. Had this been a movie, a handsome and heroic Harrison Ford might have come out of the darkness and tossed her one end of his bullwhip to pull her to safety. But no—this was Mallory's real life, which meant she was flailing about like an idiot in a town park while a children's choir chirped Christmas carols and a massive Yule log burned brightly in the black night. At least she was flailing on the fringe of the crowd and not detracting from the little choir's moment of glory.

Because this was not a movie, she stopped sinking. After one more wild windmill of her arms, she stood upright, breathing heavily from the sudden exertion. She tried to lift her right foot free of the wet sand. Her rain boot didn't budge.

"Damn it, damn it, damn it," she hissed under her breath as she kicked her right foot back and forth, back and forth, a quarter inch in each direction, trying to get loose. She couldn't vent her frustration any louder than that, not with all the tiny tots running around the park with their eyes all aglow.

It was a big family night here in Masterson, Texas, home of the Masterson University Musketeers. The Yule log was always lit by the mayor on the first Saturday of December. This park had a huge, square sandpit. For most of the year, it was used for volleyball courts, but in the cool December weather, the nets were taken down so a massive tree trunk could be laid across the sand. A bonfire was built under one end for the celebration. Each night, the bonfire would be lit again, a couple of feet farther down the log, until the last of it was burned on January sixth, the traditional date of Twelfth Night and Epiphany. The university's spring semester would begin, and the regular rhythm of life in a college town would resume.

For safety, the fire department had soaked the sand with a gazillion gallons of water for tonight's kickoff.

With great, purposeful strides, Mallory had walked right into the deep, wet sand on the dark side of the pit. She was stuck now in mid-stride, each of her boots mired in the muck.

Back and forth, back and forth, she kicked. Her foot slid around inside her rubber rain boot, but the boot itself was still firmly stuck, shin deep. "Damn— *darn* it. Darn it, darn it, darn it."

"Hey, beautiful. Got a problem?"

Because this was not a movie, the person who stopped on the edge of the sandpit was not a sexy, rugged man. He was an overgrown boy, undoubtedly one of the university students, because he wore an athletic team's burgundy hoodie with the crossed sabers of the Masterson Musketeers printed in white on the sleeve.

He threw his arms open wide as if he were revealing an S on his chest, but it was only the university's initials, MU. "I'm your solution, baby."

He was the problem. She'd been hoping to lose him and his two buddies when she'd started walking with such confidence toward the Yule log and the temporary stage.

She'd come to the park for the anonymity offered by the night. On one side of the Yule log, Christmas lights sparkled, the temporary stage glowed, and rows of booths sold holiday crafts and treats. But on this side of the Yule log, there was no artificial lighting and people were sparse. Mallory wanted peace and privacy to watch the yellow flames while she thought through her plans for the new year ahead of her—only ahead of her. She wouldn't look back.

These blockheads had spotted her as she'd leaned against a pecan tree, alone, and they'd started with the "hey, beautiful" type of catcalls. Nothing to do but ignore them, she'd thought at first.

When their comments had gotten more persistent and they'd begun to zero in on her, she'd decided the best course of action would be to lose them by blending into the light and action on the far side of the Yule log for a little while. But, as she'd started skirting the wet volleyball sandpit, she'd taken her eyes off her goal to look back over her shoulder.

Never look back. Whatever you left behind is of no benefit to you now.

It was one of her favorite maxims from her favorite book by her favorite hero, the multi-millionaire entrepreneur E.L. Taylor. Two Decembers ago, she'd received *How to Taylor Your Business Plan* as a birthday gift from her godparents. Her godmother had looked at Mallory's online wish list and gotten her something she genuinely wanted.

Her brother had given her a gift more typical of the rest of her family, a pillbox with Bluetooth technology that reminded one, through cell phones and smart watches, to take their medicines. Mallory didn't need any medications; her brother had explained that it was a gift for her, because it would make her role as their grandfather's live-in caregiver so much easier.

Their grandfather. *Her* role.

Pill dispensing wasn't her passion. Business was.

Profit and loss statements, fixed and variable assets, supply chain operations—all of it fascinated her. She had finished her junior year at Masterson University's College of Business when her father had been seriously injured, his leg crushed in an accident. She'd been asked to take the next semester off to go back to Ohio to live with him, to dress his wounds, to cook his meals, to clean his clothes and his house, since he'd lived alone after her mother had moved out.

He'd been expected to recover within six months. That December, Mallory had spent her twenty-first birthday driving through an early Ohio snowstorm, chauffeuring her father to the clinic, counting the days until the spring semester began in January and she could go back to Masterson University and the mild Central Texas winter. The doctor, however, had crushed those plans. He'd confirmed what she'd suspected, what she'd been hoping wasn't true: her father's leg hadn't healed enough yet for him to regain his mobility—and for her to return to college.

After his appointment, her father had directed her to drive his car through Sonic for milkshakes to celebrate her birthday. He might have thought she'd wolfed down that milkshake in happiness, but she'd been binge eating ice cream for her heartbreak.

Six months had turned into two years. Her father had regained his health just as her great-aunt had fallen ill and required in-home care. Mallory's entire family had looked to her. Her final year of college, her dream to climb a corporate ladder to a position of respect and financial security—all of that could wait, her family reasoned. She was still so young, and Aunt Effie had *cancer*. What were a few college classes in the face of her battle?

By the time Aunt Effie had gone from surviving back to living, another relative had needed care. Mallory had become the *de facto* choice at that point. After all, as it was pointed out to her, she wasn't doing anything else, and she had so much experience now...

She'd received her crisp, new hardcover copy of *How to Taylor Your Business Plan* two years ago on her twenty-seventh birthday. Once she'd started reading it, she couldn't stop until she'd finished the whole book in the middle of the night. When she'd turned out the bedside lamp, she'd lain in yet another spare bedroom in yet another relative's home, and she'd admitted the truth to herself: she was an unpaid laborer assigned to ill or aging relatives, not their cherished daughter or niece or cousin. Somehow, one delayed semester at a time, one relative in dire straits after another, six months had turned into six and a half years.

When despair had threatened, she'd turned the light back on and picked up her book. The chapter that began with *Never look back* had saved her sanity. E.L. Taylor had been so confident that she, his reader, would succeed in the business world if she followed his advice, regardless of her past. In firmly worded prose, he told her to keep looking forward to her goals, so Mallory had created a plan, mapping out the steps she needed to get where she wanted to go. This September, she'd finally returned to Masterson to finish her bachelor's degree.

This was, finally, December of her senior year. She should have been turning twenty-one. Her family obligations had stopped her life in its tracks as surely as this quicksand had stopped her boots, so instead, she was turning twenty-nine and spending her birthday kicking her way out of a mess of her own making.

Never look back.

Yeah, well, she'd looked back tonight, physically taking her eyes off her goal. That hadn't been what E.L. Taylor meant, but it applied: she'd caved when she'd been faced with a tiny moment of insecurity, and she'd blundered right into this sucking-sand situation. Served her right. She should know by now not to ignore any *Taylor-made* advice.

"I'll be your knight in shining armor." The ringleader of the trio struck a pose, punching one fist in the air. It was Superman's pose, nothing like a knight's, and only when Superman was about to fly away. If this guy wanted to fly away from the scene, that was fine with her.

The other two told him to stop being such a dick.

Charming heroes, all three of you.

"There are children everywhere," Mallory said in her most motherly tone. She was dressed like a student—bright blue ski cap pulled over long hair, jeans tucked into colorful rain boots—but she felt old enough to be their parent.

The second boy, surly in corduroy, sneered at her parental tone. "Like I give a flying f—"

"*Dick* isn't a bad word," said the third. "Relax. You're a pretty girl. Smile."

She kicked her boot a little faster, back and forth, back and forth, *darn, darn, darn.*

The one who'd posed with his fist in the air still fancied himself a hero. He stood on the grassy edge of the sandpit and reached for her. "Give me your hand. We'll get you loose and go party."

"No, thanks. I'm almost loose. Go enjoy your party. Don't worry about me."

He grabbed the sleeve of her pink peacoat and started hauling. She clutched at his forearm as he pulled her off balance.

"Stop! Stop. I was almost—" Her right boot chose that moment to finally pop free from the sand.

Did the hero catch her?

Of course not. Real life was never like the movies. He kept pulling, so onto her butt Mallory fell. Her rear end landed on the cold, grassy edge of the sand court, but her left foot was still stuck in the quicksand, so her left ankle was stretched to its absolute, painful limit.

"Damn it!"

"Watch your language," the corduroy-wearing dude sneered. "There are children everywhere."

"Let go of my arm."

The ringleader finally realized that he'd done more harm than good. "Oh. Sorry. Yeah. Here."

He let go of her, then reached over the wet sand and snagged the top of her left boot. He pulled it free. Since Mallory had been pulling hard herself, the sudden release sent her own knee banging into her chin.

Her teeth clacked together and she fell back, but she didn't curse this time.

"Sorry," the ringleader said again.

Mallory lay on her back in the grass while three dudes who didn't know their own strength leaned over her, looking almost comically confused at how she'd gotten there. The one who'd told her to smile now offered his hand. When he pulled her to her feet, he pulled her knitted mitten all the way off her hand.

"Whoops," he said, laughing.

When she grabbed for her mitten, he held it over his head. "I'll give it to you when you agree to come party with us. It's for your own good. You need to have some fun."

"I'll buy you a drink," the ringleader said.

Mallory held her hand out, palm up, for her mitten. "You can't. You're not even twenty-one."

They all seemed faintly surprised at her statement. Offended, too. "We've got plenty of booze at our house."

The ringleader narrowed his eyes and studied her face a little more closely in the faint light from the too-distant bonfire. "How old are you?"

"Old enough to buy my own drinks." Or she could, if she had the spending cash. She made another quick grab for her mitten, but she wasn't fast enough. *Damn, damn, damn.* The mitten was a blue cable-knit, like her hat. She wanted it back, but she wasn't going to beg while they watched her jump for her own mitten.

"Come with us. We'll show you a good time."

The stage, the crowd—light and anonymity—were at her back. So was the ringleader. The other two were in front of her, nothing but darkness beyond them. It galled Mallory to have to be polite to them, but she fell back on one of the little white lies women used in these situations. "No, thanks. I'm meeting my boyfriend here."

All three scoffed at that. Apparently, they knew the game better than she'd thought.

She pulled her ski cap down firmly over her ears. "Really, he'll be here any moment."

"Bring him, then. Where is he?"

The ringleader walked around her to join Corduroy Boy and Mitten Stealer, so the three stood shoulder to shoulder with their MU letters on their puffed-up chests. They'd called her bluff, and they knew it. However, with the three of them in front of her, she could now back up freely. She glanced back over her shoulder.

Never look back.

Yeah, well, she was playing a role here. She pretended to spot her boyfriend in the crowd behind her. "I think I see him. Gotta go."

"Aw, don't be that way."

She turned her back on them and walked fast, heading toward the light and the crowd. One guy called out, "Your mitten will be at the Kappa Lambda house. Come and get it, beautiful."

She didn't look back until she'd skirted the sand courts and reached the stage. The children were filing off. The university's string quartet members were climbing up, cellos and violins in hand. She'd lost the trio of athletes, but now she was surrounded by other people's families, other people's holiday happiness, so much noise and chaos when she'd craved some time alone.

A line had formed in front of the Yule log. People stopped at a card table, scribbled their hopes for the coming year on little pieces of paper, then waited for their turn to throw the paper on the burning log. Their wishes for the new year were carried by the smoke up to the stars.

The fire department had erected a waist-high fence to keep anyone from getting too close. Little pieces of evergreen were tied to the paper notes, so the paper could be tossed more easily into fire. Some people were throwing hard, trying to hit the actual Yule log, but most of the papers were falling short, landing in the bonfire.

A little boy threw his note, but it barely cleared the fence. One of the firemen quickly used a fire iron as a golf club to chip-shot the little folded paper into the bonfire. "Close enough for a Christmas wish," the fireman assured the little boy.

Mallory would aim for the Yule log, just to be certain.

A donation jar sat on the table amid the clutter of paper slips and stunted golf course pencils. Its handwritten sign indicated which charity the money would go toward. *Donations requested but not required.* Not required meant free.

Free was right in Mallory's price range—temporarily. She made a mental note of the charity. She would donate to them when she started making money. She merely had to stick with her plan. *Never look back*, never this, never that. There were a lot of *never*s in a Taylor-style business plan, but if she could just follow them all, financial security would be hers.

It was working. She was here; that was proof. Her very first step had been to reconnect with the Masterson University admissions office by signing up for their email newsletter. Because of that step, she'd seen an announcement that their esteemed alumnus, entrepreneur E.L. Taylor, was going to be the Executive-in-Residence the next academic year. He would spend the spring semester as a guest professor for the university's College of Business. *Her* college.

That had seemed like fate. It had ignited a fire under her, at any rate. She'd accelerated her timeline to free herself from the endless family obligations and win readmission to MU. Parts of that had been painful, but she'd started her senior year this September. She had just one more semester to go. When it began in January, E.L. Taylor himself was going to arrive on campus, and she was going to be here to meet him. Before her graduation in May, she would take the next-to-last step: she was going to ask him to look at her Taylor-inspired business plan.

And then, Mallory Ames was going to execute her final step. She was going to ask E.L. Taylor to invest in her first business venture.

He would, because he'd be impressed with her business plan. He just had to be, for she'd followed his book precisely. She would present it with the confidence he'd assured her she deserved…unless her nerves killed her first.

Not nerves. *Anticipation.* The anticipation was killing her. What if he said no? What if he laughed at her plan?

What if her hero didn't even like her?

Mallory picked up a pencil stub and a blank slip of paper, one with a tiny pine cone attached by a ribbon. She refused to blush as the woman to her left and the man to her right each dropped dollar bills into the jar and gave her pointed looks for not doing the same.

Mallory knew her coat made her look more affluent than she was. She'd found it in her grandmother's closet. Peacoats never went out of style, and although the color was a Paris Hilton pink from a previous decade, the hand-me-down was high quality. Let the locals judge her for being cheap tonight. Someday, her donation to that charity would dwarf theirs.

She'd barely finished scribbling a single sentence when she heard Corduroy Boy's unwelcome voice.

"Well, well. Look who's here."

She stuffed the paper and its mini pine cone into her pocket. She wasn't going to wait in line, getting harassed the entire time by three meatheads who didn't know the difference between flirting and pursuing someone relentlessly. She headed toward the opposite side of the park, where hundreds of square hay bales were stacked three high, far enough away from the Christmas festival that no spark from the Yule log would be carried on the wind to ignite them.

As the crowds came nightly to enjoy the Christmas lights, the hay would be spread to keep the field from turning to mud. During Mallory's first three years as a Masterson Musketeer, she'd watched the stacks of bales get shorter and shorter as the holiday break had gotten closer and closer. She'd associated the smell of fresh hay with Christmas and college, anticipation and excitement, every year that she'd been away.

What would she answer if Mr. Taylor asked her about that huge time gap between her junior and senior years? *I never look back*, she'd say with confidence, and then she'd move on to her business plan. It would be the right answer. It was the only possible answer she could give him.

E.L. Taylor would never invest in Mallory's ideas if he knew the truth. She was practically thirty and definitely broke. What kind of person let herself be told what to do, where to live, with whom to live for so many years? A weak person. So weak that three young men had instinctively singled her out as their easy target tonight.

They'd stolen her mitten, and her hand was cold—and all of a sudden, she was fighting back tears. She shouldn't feel like crying over something as trivial as a stolen mitten, but it was the only pair she owned.

Since those guys could afford luxury extras like fraternity fees, they probably had parents supporting them. They were athletes, so they probably had sports scholarships covering the cost of their dormitory and dining hall. But Mallory? Familial caregiving paid nothing. She was poor enough to qualify for a work-study job that helped pay her tuition and gave her a dorm room at a reduced rate, but it hadn't covered her textbooks or the mandatory meal plan for those who lived in dorms. This one year of room and board had eaten up her meager savings—her *minimal assets*, in business lingo—and her hand-me-down car as well. Those rich boys couldn't imagine how valuable that mitten was to her.

Did life have to always be so unfair?

Never expect life to be fair. You must continue to play when the game isn't fair, or you'll never win.

E.L. Taylor was right, but Mallory was losing the game tonight, sinking into despair as surely as she'd sunk into the quicksand—and all over a mitten.

With her cold hand, she wiped hot tears from the corner of her eye before they had a chance to fall. In the future, when she wore a sharp suit and high heels and sat behind an executive desk that would be polished to a shine, that mitten would be insignificant. Therefore, it was insignificant now.

Dry-eyed, she left the crowd behind her, determined to find a quiet spot to watch the Yule log's flames in peace. That had been her plan, and she was sticking to it. *Never abandon a solid plan.*

She squinted at the hay bales. There was someone out there. A man? He was standing so still, she wasn't certain she was really seeing a person in the shadows.

She didn't take her eyes off him as she got close enough to see that he was real—and definitely a man, arms crossed over his chest, shoulders filling out his leather jacket. Alone in the night, he made a compelling figure. Had this been a movie, she would've assumed he was the brooding hero, reluctant to get involved but capable of saving the day if he must, Bruce Wayne on a dark sidewalk, a soldier off duty in a civilian dive bar.

The golden light of the Yule log's flames touched his profile. His features were strong, his expression fierce. He hadn't shaved for a day or two. His hair was thick and a little too long, only a shade less dark than the night. He might make a better villain than a hero, a young Rickman in a bank vault, Tommy Lee Jones on a battleship, the kind of anti-heroes that had made her father's favorite action movies pleasurable to watch with him.

But this wasn't the movies. This was real life, so Mallory didn't know if this man was a good guy or bad guy. Only one thing was certain: this was no college boy.

From behind her, three specific college boys sounded too close. "Don't be like that. Wait up."

Leave me alone.

The angry man ahead of her looked like he felt the same way toward the whole world. He glared at the fire, looking a little feral. Unapproachable.

The trio behind her started to sound more irritated than amused. "We know you can hear us."

Never look back. Everything that mattered was ahead of her.

"What's the problem? Boyfriend didn't show up, huh?"

"Boyfriend," the mitten-stealer said in a voice

meant to carry. "As if someone would want a bitch like her."

So much for *Smile, beautiful.*

Mallory kept pretending she didn't hear them, but her bare hand was clenched into a fist of frustration. It was always the same, wasn't it? If a woman didn't act flattered by a random man's attention, then he assumed she had a problem, not him. Mallory had turned twenty-nine today, twenty-*frigging*-nine. Was there an age where she wouldn't have to deal with this kind of crap? She lengthened her strides as best she could in loose rain boots on poorly lit, uneven ground.

Behind her, they laughed. "Is she trying to run away? From what? A party?"

Mallory kept her eyes on the man ahead of her. There was arrogance in his stance. If Mallory's anger made her look as forbidding as he looked, no college boy would mess with her.

They wouldn't mess with him, that was for certain, which would make him an excellent pretend boyfriend for the next ten minutes or so. She just had to stand next to him and make a little small talk, get him to smile politely in response.

Actually, he didn't look like he knew how to smile. A nod, then. A few polite words from her, a nod from him—that would be enough to convince those three jerks she wasn't alone. They'd turn away, she'd tell the angry man to have a good night, and that would be that. She could return to the pecan tree and ruminate on her future in peace. It was an excellent plan.

Her future boyfriend was winning his staring contest with the Yule log. Mallory wasn't even two steps away from him now, so close she could see the flames dancing in his eyes, so close she could see—

Her boots dragged to a stop as if she'd stepped into quicksand again. The fine lines in his face, the grim set of his mouth, those eyes—

Nothing anyone said or did would faze this man. He wasn't arrogant. He was…hardened.

She chickened out.

But as she took her first step past him, the book's maxim roared inside her head: *Never abandon a solid plan.*

She spun to face the flames, standing shoulder to shoulder with the man she'd chosen.

Chapter Two

Never show your doubts to the world.
　　　　　　—How to Taylor Your Business Plan
　　　　　　　　　　　by E.L. Taylor

The man was so damned intimidating, this close.

That was precisely why Mallory had walked up to him, though. She took a few silent, calming breaths through her nose, the way every free online yoga class had taught her to do.

He didn't acknowledge her existence.

After a few seconds, once Mallory was certain that she wouldn't sound even the tiniest bit alarmed, she made a polite observation. "The Yule log is a real giant this year. That must have been some tree. I heard it was uprooted by a tornado this summer."

He didn't respond with so much as a flicker of an eyelash.

She leaned forward just far enough to peek past him. The three guys were still making their way toward her, hollering and fake-punching each other, practically buzzing with all the heady power of being young, financially secure, and free to raise hell on a Saturday night.

Mallory tried a little harder, smiling her friendliest smile at the man—or rather, at his profile. "Chilly tonight, isn't it?"

The man might as well have been a statue.

She was left smiling in his direction like an idiot, feeling as stupid as if she'd stuck her hand out to shake and he'd just left her hanging.

She leaned back this time, just enough to look past his shoulders toward the frat boys. They'd slowed down, but now the ringleader was ducking and weaving around his friends, imitating the way Mallory was peeking around someone to see them.

Mallory wasn't playing peek-a-boo, damn it. She put her bare hand on the stranger's sleeve, her cold palm on colder leather that had nothing but hardness underneath. Of course, a statue's arm would be hard. "I've got sand in my boot. Can I just use you for balance for a second?"

Without waiting for a reply that wouldn't come, she stood on one foot, clinging to his sleeve as she started to push one boot off. Then she thought better of it. She'd keep her boots on in case she needed to take off again. Instead, she brushed the sand off the outside of her boot, an operation that got sand stuck in the knitted wool of her remaining mitten, but at this point, it hardly mattered since—

"Who are we trying to make jealous?"

She hopped in surprise. *The statue speaks!*

"Is he sufficiently jealous yet?"

She quit slapping her boot and stood on two feet once more. "Who?"

"The man you're looking for while you force yourself to talk to me."

How he'd seen her look anywhere was anybody's guess, since he still hadn't taken his eyes off the fire. The corner of his mouth had twisted into a sort of mocking smile to match the disdain in his voice, but Mallory didn't let go of his arm. Not yet—not while she could see Corduroy Boy out of the corner of her eye, smacking her mitten against his palm, making her feel like she was twenty, not twenty-nine.

Never expect life to be fair.

"I'm not trying to make anyone jealous," she said.

He scoffed at that, a shocking amount of derision packed into a short snort. He thought this was a joke, just like the boys who were currently treating her mitten as their toy.

They would treat her like a toy, she was sure, if she were stupid enough to go to their party to get her mitten back. They were the kind of young men who'd be utterly, genuinely surprised when a girl yelled no and pushed them away. They wouldn't have had any idea she hadn't been willing to accept the attention of popular athletes—why would a girl object to that?—and they'd act shocked that she hadn't appreciated being pushed off the dance floor into a corner, so the one she'd been dancing with could grind his hips against hers, just a little fully dressed public foreplay, so his bros would know he was a stud who'd be getting laid later that night. In the movies, every girl understood Sandy pushing away Danny at the drive-in.

But real life wasn't the movies. When her no made him look bad, they'd all get mean. They'd call her a tease as she walked out of their keg party. They'd make fun of her every time they saw her on campus for the rest of the semester.

Mallory had been through it all. She'd been labeled a bitch at a party on her twentieth birthday, then jeered at on Tuesdays and Thursdays the next semester, when she had to cross paths with one of the guys in her microeconomics class. She'd gone to the student services center to see if there was some school equivalent of a restraining order, but the boys hadn't been violent at the party. They hadn't tried to stop her from leaving when she'd so boldly said no and walked off the dance floor, and they weren't making threats when they saw her in class. They were just loud and rude.

It hadn't mattered in the end. Her father had fallen off a ladder and shattered his leg and pelvis, and Mallory had needed to leave campus, anyway.

She'd let her hands freeze solid rather than put herself in that kind of situation again. She was worth more than a million mittens. She'd known it then, and she knew it now.

She let go of the leather jacket. Her uncooperative fake boyfriend uncrossed his arms and straightened his sleeve with a tug on his cuff, as if she could wrinkle a bomber jacket made with leather so high quality, James Bond could have worn it. The man might have been like her grandparents, investing in one quality piece of clothing every decade or so, but his hands were leather-clad, too, in driving gloves that looked painted on. His dark jeans fit exactly right over boots that looked as perfectly made as his jacket. Even his hair was stylish despite being shaggy, evidence that it had been cut very, very well in the past, and no doubt would be again.

Money.

This wasn't a movie, but in real life, there were people made of money. He was one of them.

Mallory stuffed her hand into her coat pocket, wrinkling her paper wish, and wriggled out of the sandy mitten. It was better to look like she hadn't bothered with gloves at all tonight than to look like a beggar who had only one.

She wasn't a beggar. She was this rich man's equal. She just hadn't built her own company yet. Every trait she needed to do so was already within her, as her book had so wisely pointed out. When Mallory Ames was the CEO of her own company, she'd be the same person she was right this minute.

So, she returned the intimidating man's scoff with one of her own. "That's an incredibly high opinion you have of yourself. You're certain that being seen just standing next to you is enough for a woman to make any man jealous."

Finished with his cuff, he crossed his arms over his chest once more.

Mallory crossed her arms over her chest, too, but not to imitate him. She just wanted to tuck her hands under her arms for warmth. "It's more likely a man would feel sorry for the woman standing next to you, with the way you're giving her the silent treatment."

"I'm not giving you anything."

"I noticed."

"You walked up to me for a reason," he said, still watching the fire. He had yet to spare a glance for the peon beside him. "It wasn't because you had a sudden desire to talk about the weather. Then you leaned on me instead of a hay bale to get the sand out of your boots, yet you didn't take them off. You barely bothered to brush off one. It's obvious that you wanted someone to see you touching me. Once he did, you stopped. We're done. Take your sandy boots elsewhere."

Her mouth fell open at his rudeness.

After a moment of silence, he spoke again, sounding weary. "Did you think you were the first woman to try this with me?"

Beyond him, the ringleader broke away from the other two and started walking toward her, shaking his head at her like she was a disobedient puppy. Her ruse hadn't worked. The stranger beside her was too obviously not interested in her as a human being.

Damn it, damn it, damn it. It looked like she was

going to spend her twenty-ninth birthday just like she'd spent her twentieth, yelling no and pushing away a college boy who'd then go tell his entire team what a bitch she was.

She didn't bother trying to hide her frustration. "I'm trying to fend someone off. Fend them off, not toy with them. Not make them jealous."

Out of the corner of her eye, she saw the ringleader hesitate. Arguing made her look like she knew this stranger well, didn't it?

The irony wasn't lost on her, but it only fed her irritation. She shouldn't have to play these games. "You know, if I could help out another woman just by letting her stand next to me for a few minutes, I would. I *have*, more times than most men seem to believe is possible. All you had to do was say, 'Nice weather. Not too chilly.' That was all that was being asked of you." She raked her gaze over his oh-so-casual, oh-so-expensive clothing, from his shoulders to his boots. "Would it have hurt you to spare so little?"

At last, a reaction: he clenched his jaw. "You want someone to think you have a male protector?"

She blinked. "That's kind of a medieval way to put it, but yes."

He finally looked down at her. His eyes were silver, startling—a mirror that reflected the flames. In one smooth motion, he uncrossed his arms, placed his hands on her waist and picked her up high enough that her head and shoulders were above his. She squeaked in surprise and grabbed his shoulders for stability, but he dropped her onto the stack of hay bales, leaving her sitting five feet off the ground with hay poking her rear right through her jeans.

Oh, she didn't have to fake an argument now. "What are you *doing*?"

"You wanted safety. Done." His gaze dropped to her feet as they dangled above the ground like a child's. "And your boots won't get any sandier."

"You idiot. Now I'm sitting up here where anyone I'm trying to avoid can see me."

"He'd already seen you, had he not?"

She threw her hands up. "What now? I'm supposed to wait here until he comes to pull me down? You've made me more helpless. All you had to do was act like I'm your girlfriend, not a bale of hay. Really, was that so difficult for you? *Really?*"

The fire framed him from behind. It gave him a dark-angel kind of appeal, a sinfully handsome Lucifer with striking eyes. She glanced toward the last spot she'd seen the trio—they'd stopped and were huddled over one glowing cell phone screen—and back at him.

He turned around. She thought he was going to walk away, but instead, he leaned back against the hay bales. *Her* stack of hay bales—so she wriggled back and pulled her right knee out of his way. He rested against the hay bale, its edge just below his shoulder blades, which meant she now was sitting with a man's shoulders between her knees.

Mallory gaped at the back of his head.

"But—" she started.

She stopped. But what, really? With his shoulders

between her knees, it certainly looked as if they knew each other well.

Fine, then. She rested her forearms on top of his head, like he was that executive desk she'd have someday.

"What," her desk asked, sounding furious, "are you doing?"

"I'm acting like you're my boyfriend."

"You've never had a boyfriend, have you?"

She stuck out her tongue at the top of his head. "You've never been one, have you? You seem to think sticking me on a pile of hay bales and turning your back on me is a normal thing to do on a date, but let me tell you, it's not."

He spoke through gritted teeth. "There wasn't time to buy you flowers."

She snorted, unwillingly amused, even as she kept an eye on the trio. They were all looking at her once more, clearly shocked that she hadn't lied, although she had. They turned to go, but first, the ringleader hit his hero pose, holding her mitten up high in one fist, then flipping her the bird with his other hand.

She stayed cool, even blasé, as she lazily raised one hand and flipped him the bird right back.

She was hoping he'd be so incensed, he'd throw her mitten down. *Step on it, leave it the dirt, I don't care. I can wash it. Please, leave my mitten behind. Please, please, please...*

They left with her mitten. She'd lost the game. It was utterly unfair.

You must continue to play when the game isn't fair, or you'll never win.

She had to come up with a plan for replacing that mitten.

From across the sandy courts and the open field, she heard the string quartet playing "Good King Wenceslas." Mallory knew the lyrics by heart, of course. *When a poor man came in sight, gathering winter fuel.* She knew how the poor man felt, hoping he could find what he needed for free. If she could find a pair of mittens on the ground...

That was it. Tomorrow, she'd check the lost-and-found box in her dorm building. A set of gloves or mittens could have been there long enough that they were now free for the taking. If not, she'd check the lost-and-found box in the College of Business's main building, where she worked. If not there, then she'd check every building on campus until she found an abandoned pair. The stolen one had matched her ski hat, but she'd have to take what she could get now. Beggars couldn't be choosers.

A beggar.

Her plan was to beg for mittens. The truth of it weighed her down. She'd never impress E.L. Taylor or any other investor. She was worse than a beggar; she was weak. She'd spent the better part of her birthday evening letting three guys dictate where she'd go. Make that four guys—she hadn't decided to sit on these hay bales.

The violin notes carried on the night air. One tear

broke free from Mallory's lower lashes, making a warm run down her chilled cheek.

That fourth man grumbled up at her. "How much longer is this date going to last? It's like having a damned bird nesting on my head."

She chuckled despite herself, but the sound hic-cupped and ended with something like a sob.

"Are you—are you *crying* on me?"

She shook her head no, which made a few more tears roll down her cheeks, but he couldn't see that. He could only hear her voice, and since her voice would give her away, she stayed silent.

Never look back. She'd pushed so hard to be here. She'd suffered through lectures from her brother and his wife. Gotten guilt trips from every other relative. Driven from Ohio to Texas in a hand-me-down car, then sold it to buy the annual meal plan at the college dining facility.

She'd burned all her bridges.

And for what? The coming Executive-in-Residence had sent his preferred schedule to the business college this week. The only courses Mr. Taylor would be teaching were exclusively for MBA students, not for those finishing their bachelor's degrees. Not for her, the woman who'd hugged his book to her chest in the middle of the night and vowed that she would be a success someday.

Her plan hadn't accounted for the possibility that she'd be denied access to Mr. Taylor as a professor. But her plan hadn't totally failed her, either. She'd seen Mr. Taylor's schedule because she worked in the

administrative offices of the College of Business. She
had that job because she *hadn't* been weak.

The financial aid she was receiving required her to
work on campus. She'd been assigned a job bussing
tables in the student dining facility. Collecting dirty
dishes didn't fit any of her plans, so she'd gone over
her financial aid contract with a businesswoman's
sharp eye. The work-study program was ostensibly
designed to give students experience related to their
field of study, and she'd found a single sentence in
the document that stated students could suggest their
own jobs. So, dressed like the young and successful
CEO she would be someday, Mallory had walked
into the College of Business's administrative offices
to ask where she could best help them.

They'd created a position for her, an assistant to the
administrative assistants. A secretary for the secretar-
ies, essentially. She wanted to believe they'd hired her
because she exuded that Taylor-coached confidence,
but she suspected the permanent admins had merely
been happy to get a student as old as she was. Maturity had, for once, been an advantage.

Maturity and confidence were getting harder and
harder to hold on to. A minute ago, she'd just flipped
off the mitten-stealing trio.

*Because I had a plan. I wanted them to be so
angry, they'd throw my mitten down.*

So many plans. So much stress. But if she hadn't
had a plan, then she wouldn't have pushed herself to
scramble for her office job. If she hadn't done that,
she'd have zero opportunity to speak with E.L. Tay-

lor this coming semester. She couldn't take his class, but she could leverage her job to gain access to Mr. Taylor. She'd look for opportunities to deliver his messages or print out his lesson plans. She'd stay alert, she'd hustle, and she'd *make* those opportunities happen.

Just thinking about it made her feel exhausted.

Two years of hoping and planning had really been two years of running into obstacle after obstacle. The cost of the textbooks and the dining plan, for example, had been a staggering five thousand dollars. Since practically everything in the town of Masterson was within walking distance from the campus, selling her old car had been the right solution. Now, she never had to fear where her next meal would come from, three meals a day, seven days a week, not until after she received her diploma. She hadn't run into that obstacle. She'd *surmounted* it. That was what E.L. Taylor would want her to tell herself.

But…

But, just for tonight, as she stared at the flames of a Yule log, she wanted to stop trying so hard. She wanted to stop pretending she was unfazed by every obstacle. She had doubts. Doubts about her plan. Doubts about her future. Doubts about herself.

The man she was resting on looked like he'd weathered so much, nothing could faze him. Were all these disappointments and worries, her self-doubts and stolen mittens, weathering her, too? Making her hard? Did she want to become that tough?

The alternative was to let her life be steered this

way and that at the whim of others. That hadn't been a happy life, either, and she'd chosen to leave it.

Never look back.

The stranger didn't ask her anything else. He just stood there like a rock, so she kept leaning on him, not like a child sitting on her father's shoulders, not like she was getting a piggyback ride, just…leaning on him as she sniffed back her tears and did her calm yoga breathing.

He took off his gloves and held them up. "Here."

Surprised, she took them, wiped her cheeks, and gave them back, dangling them in front of his face.

"Put them *on*." He sounded like he couldn't believe he had to spell it out. "Your hands are freezing."

She sat up straight, embarrassed that her freezing fingertips had been brushing his forehead. The gloves were like a second skin on him, so they weren't too terribly loose on her. Her fingers slid into the luxurious warmth gladly.

Now that her arms were off his head, he ran his hand through his hair, as if that would restore order to the untamed layers. He turned just enough to look at her out of the corner of his eye. "How much longer are we going to be here?"

She rubbed her gloved hands together. "You should have asked me that a minute earlier. I'm not really incentivized to send you and your warm gloves away now." She leaned to the side a bit, so he could see her expression and know that she was only teasing.

He remained serious. She felt a moment of concern for him. Poor man, so grim. Hardened.

Relax. Smile. You need to have some fun.

On the other hand, maybe he was content just as he was. If he didn't want to smile, he didn't have to smile.

She sighed as she sat up straight again. "I'm just kidding. You were a very effective imaginary boyfriend. They've gone."

He faced forward once more.

She frowned at the back of his head. Maybe he thought she needed more time to compose herself. It was embarrassing to realize she probably hadn't fooled him about the crying any more than she'd fooled him about getting sand out of her boots. Only a few tears had actually fallen silently, rather attractively, like an actress's single tear in a black-and-white movie. At least Mallory hoped so. At any rate, she'd sniffed most of her tears back, not sobbed them all out. If he assumed she needed more time to pull herself together, he assumed wrong.

"They actually left a little while ago." She didn't want to admit that being tossed onto a haystack had done the trick. "I didn't mean to keep you this long."

"I know."

She waited, but that was all he had to say.

She rolled her eyes behind his back. "So…should I leapfrog over your head now, or would you care to move aside, so I can jump down? Take your time deciding. My fingers aren't warmed up yet."

He stepped to the side, but before she could wriggle to the edge of the stack to drop to the ground, he kicked the heel of his boot back into the hay to make a step and hoisted himself onto the stack next to hers, a six-foot-something man landing right beside her. Had this been a movie, she would have been Debbie Reynolds, aghast that Gene Kelly had just dropped out of nowhere into her convertible.

This man had such a physical presence. He was big, and he was *built*. He had a body that vaulted to the top of a tall stack effortlessly, a body that had picked her up like she weighed no more than a bag of sugar. A muscled, masculine body.

Bodies. It had been so long since she'd thought about bodies as anything but frail. Injury, cancer, extreme old age—she'd worried about those bodies for so long. It had been the career she'd fallen into, easing their aches and pains, finding ways to get them to eat when they weren't hungry and drink when they didn't thirst, to walk when walking hurt.

At the university, she was surrounded by bodies that were so jarringly at the other end of the scale. Barely out of adolescence, they filled college classrooms with more energy than they could contain, boisterous bodies that could withstand the abuse of all-night study sessions and day-long keg parties.

The man beside her was neither of those extremes. He had strength and control, a man who had a body that he could rely on to perform. Need to lift a woman over his head? Done, without thinking twice about it. His demeanor wasn't arrogance, perhaps, but confidence that he could handle whatever physical task he needed to.

She let her eyes roam over his shoulders, his

thighs, his hands. The confidence that made him look untouchable to men would make women wish he wanted, *needed*, to touch them. Mallory had no doubt he knew how to handle that kind of physicality, too. Some people just had sex appeal, and they never really lost it, Paul Newman with silver hair and laugh lines.

Her fake boyfriend had it in spades, but no silver hair, not yet. Not for a while. He looked to be in his early thirties, a body near the same age as her own. He was just right for her.

For me?

What could she possibly do with a man whose body was…oh.

He turned to her, and it was a fresh little shock to look him full in the face. His days-old beard looked rough and dark, his hair fell forward after he'd pushed it back, but he was undeniably handsome. Had this been a movie—

He smiled at her, a polite, practiced, obligatory stretching of the lips, and she felt a little déjà vu.

Strange. If she'd seen him before, she wouldn't have forgotten him. No woman would. Yet there was something vaguely familiar about his stiff smile, except nothing about this man fit the word *vague*.

"You must want to get back to the festival," he said, a surprisingly courteous hint for her to be gone. "Your family or friends must wonder where you've gone. Your real boyfriend, perhaps."

Now he wanted to make polite small talk? She was used to him being all broody and curt. Her sudden sexual awareness of him—of her own body—made her broody and curt, too. "If I had a real boyfriend here, I wouldn't have needed to borrow you, would I?"

His smile became just a tiny bit more real at her comeback.

She looked away, hoping this flushed feeling inside wasn't a visible blush on her face. She was a grown woman sitting next to a grown man, not a flustered teenager who didn't know how to respond to a cute boy in class.

"I came by myself tonight," she said, determined to sound her age. "There's nothing at the fair for me."

It all costs money.

She'd planned for that. This evening, she'd been one of the very few students in the cavernous dining hall for dinner on a Saturday night, as usual on the weekends. She'd celebrated the start of the holiday season with one of those foil packets of instant cocoa, reconstituted with the hot water from an institutional coffee brewing machine.

She hadn't come to the park for food or cocoa, because she could get those on campus. She'd come for the rest. The Yule log was free. The music was free. Reflecting on one's future under a pecan tree was free. Maybe the powdered instant hot cocoa wasn't as tasty as the hot chocolate she remembered buying here years ago, but it had been prepaid. Beggars couldn't be choosers.

She squinted at the distant booths as if she wanted to read their colorful signs much more than she wanted to look at an appealingly rugged man. "There was some amazing hot chocolate over there, if memory serves. I don't see it from here."

"You come every year?"

"No, it's been a while. I went to college here." She left it at that. It was embarrassing to have gone to college but have no degree. Even worse to be living in a dorm on her twenty-ninth birthday. "How about you? Do you come here every year?"

"No."

If she rolled her eyes at yet another curt answer, he'd see her do it, this time. She rolled them, anyway. "So, what brings you here this year? Did you go to college here?"

"Of course."

That could be the reason behind that déjà vu. They might have had a class together—or she could have just admired him from afar. He must have been eye-catching at nineteen, too.

"When did you graduate?" she asked. "Maybe we were here at the same time."

"Don't you think you would have remembered me?"

Her mouth fell open again. Hot body or not, the man had an ego the size of Texas. "Do you think you're so amazing that I would remember if our paths had crossed between classes?"

He scowled at her.

She held up her hands and laughed a little. "I'm sorry, but you really do have an astonishingly high opinion of yourself."

It could have been a trick of the flickering fire-light, but he looked almost confused.

"It's okay," she said. "I envy you, actually. It's better than being full of self-doubts. Trust me."

"I find it hard to believe you harbor a single self-doubt," he said, with a very clear, very arrogant scoff.

She'd imagined that look. He'd probably never been confused about anything in his life.

He elaborated. "You say anything you want to say, fearlessly. You're confident that you have the right to tell me what's wrong with my own opinion of myself. Don't pretend now that you've been quaking with fright in your sandy boots for even a minute."

This time, her laugh was directed at herself. "Wow. I must be doing a good job of behaving the way I wish I already was, all fearless and what-not." She clapped her boots together to send some dried sand showering down, but it was a halfhearted effort, and she gave it up after a few tries. "Honestly, I'm second-guessing myself all the time. If I fooled you, I must have that whole 'fake it 'til you make it' thing down pat. That's something, I suppose. Some kind of achievement."

Sitting side by side, they fell into silence as they stared at the bonfire. From the stage beyond it, the string quartet began "O Come, O Come, Emmanuel." It was a slow and haunting carol, a song of yearning for someone to come and change a hard, unhappy world. Such longing for things to get better, someday...

Someday.

Never show your doubts to the world. If you must indulge your doubts, do so alone. You will be con-

*fident when your plan succeeds. Eliminate the pos-
sibility of having witnesses to any earlier version of
yourself.*

"Fake it 'til you make it," she repeated quietly.
"What happens if you never make it? You'll have
spent your life being a fake. Maybe being the real
you, flaws and all, would have been better than pretending to be something you never became. You'll
have missed the chance to find out."

Every inch of the body beside her went still.

"Sorry," she said. "I don't expect you to stay and
talk philosophy with me. I just came to see the Yule
log and debate my future with myself. I didn't expect
to have a human to talk to."

Not that the human was talking back much, but
still...

*Eliminate the possibility of having witnesses to
any earlier version of yourself.*

She shouldn't have admitted her doubts out loud.
But did a stranger she'd never see again count as a
witness to her weak moments?

Her book would say he counted. E.L. Taylor hadn't
even made exceptions for family members. When
Mallory's brother had snooped out her plans, she'd
needed to pretend she was confident that she'd be re-
admitted to MU—and that she'd win the financial aid
her brother informed her he would not be providing,
although she hadn't asked. If she'd admitted she was
worried, her brother would have been even harder to
deal with. As usual, her book had been right. *Never
show weakness.*

Mallory sighed. "The real me isn't usually so maudlin. It *is* my birthday, though."

"That makes you sad?"

"My twenty-ninth birthday."

"Ancient."

"You sound like every smug, grouchy octogenarian in my family. 'You're young. You have plenty of time.' Easy for them to say. Every single one of them, from my great-aunt to my brother, was married with a job and a house at my age."

Her fake boyfriend lapsed back into silence. It irked her after his sarcastic *Ancient*.

"You must think you have plenty of time, too," she said. "You don't look very domesticated yet. No offense."

"I have the house."

Mallory shrugged. Of course, he did. *Money* meant ownership of real estate, almost always. When she had money someday, she'd invest in property, too—a house, a townhome, a condo. Anything. She couldn't wait.

"And the job?" she asked.

"If you want to call it that."

Don't ask, Mallory, don't ask, don't ask...

"And the marriage?"

He slid her a very knowing look.

Okay, maybe she had been fishing for information. "Since I'm wearing your gloves, I see you have no wedding band."

He didn't bother to confirm the obvious. Mallory was happy she hadn't imposed on someone else's husband to stand in as her fake boyfriend; that was the reason she felt a little relieved that he was a bachelor. Not that she would ever begrudge another woman the space to stand next to her own husband someday, if that woman needed shelter. In fact, her future husband would have to be the kind of guy who'd help out any person who needed help.

Not that she was looking for a husband. First things first. She didn't have her bachelor's degree yet...at almost thirty.

Never look back.

It was hard not to on her birthday. The mournful Christmas carol was killing her. She'd lost so much time, waiting for her degree, waiting for her real career to happen, waiting to have her own home and—well, if not her own husband, at least a madly passionate relationship. Waiting, for years, for everything, while she'd traveled down the caregiver detour that she'd never seen coming.

She fell back to lie on the hay bale and stare up at the night sky. The smoke from the Yule log made a little plume of gray in the distance, but the stars above were bright in the clear night, white sparks of infinity that obeyed the laws of physics, not wishes.

She didn't need a Christmas wish. There was no mystery to the way her life was unfolding. Her path was the result of her own decisions. Why wasn't she where she'd expected to be at twenty-nine? The fault lay not in her stars, but in herself.

"I let too many birthdays slip by," she explained to the night sky. Maybe to herself. Not to the stranger's back. "I won't let that happen again. Every year will be a milestone year from now on. I'll make every single one count."

The string quartet's next song was more lively, all Santa Claus and toys and childhood, a better melody for tonight's crowd.

Mallory sat up again. She swung her rain boots in time to the children's song.

The man next to her did not. He didn't seem to have anything childlike left in him.

"Are you waiting for someone?" she asked.

He was silent.

"I'm just trying to make conversation so that I can wear your gloves a little longer."

More silence.

She didn't have to worry about him being a witness to her weakness. He'd never say a word to anyone.

She took her time as she took in his strong profile, the grim set to his lips. *Stoic* was a good word for him. Stoic, the way her grandfather looked when his body hurt and he didn't want to admit it was holding him back from some task he still expected himself to do, like hunkering down to put air in his car's tires. *I can do that for you, Grandpa. Let me help you stand. That asphalt has to be hard on your knees.*

Mallory tried again. "Why are you out here, staring at a fire by yourself?"

"Not because I'm sad." *Unlike you*, she practically heard him say.

"Hey, don't judge. Odds are, it's not your birthday."

He didn't smile at her flippant comment, not exactly, but his mouth sort of relaxed.

She picked at a piece of straw. "I'm not sad that I'm twenty-nine. It's just that, each birthday, I have an appointment with myself to stop and evaluate if I'm where I want to be."

Never allow your actual timeline to lag behind your projected timeline. She could hardly admit she was letting a business manual direct her entire life, could she?

"This time two years ago, things were not good in my life. I listened to a—a—"

A book.

"To a friend, and I made changes. Hard ones."

My book gave me the resolve I needed to object to my family's plans and make my own.

"So, this birthday, I'm actually right where I had always wanted to be. Finally."

"Congratulations." His tone was somber. The sarcasm was missing, for once.

"Yeah. Thanks." She laced her fingers together, warm now in his gloves, and let her hands rest in her lap, palms up, cupping…nothing. "I just thought I'd be happier once I'd gotten what I wanted."

She could feel the intensity of his gaze.

She kept looking at the gloves. "Do you know what I mean?"

The music stopped. She looked up from her hands to his unsmiling eyes.

Yes, you do. Poor man, so grim.

The quartet pushed chairs aside to place their instruments into black cases. In the absence of music, the crowd got louder. Families were talking, friends were meeting up. So much noise. So much connection.

The only connection Mallory had made tonight was with a stranger who barely spoke. She decided to fake some confidence—it really had become a habit in the past two years—and make him a little less of a stranger. She held out her hand to shake his. "My name is Mallory, by the way. What's yours?"

He didn't take her hand. Just as she'd suspected when he hadn't returned her first friendly smile, he was the type who'd leave somebody hanging if they approached him while he wasn't in the mood to be bothered.

Well, she was bothering. She kept her hand out, ready to shake, and raised one eyebrow at him in challenge.

"Eli," he said, and waited.

For what, she didn't know.

"Well, Eli, it's nice to meet you." She grabbed his hand with both of hers and pumped it up and down a few times. He let her, watching their hands as if she were performing some exotic ritual from another civilization.

But as she let go, he abruptly adjusted his grip so he was shaking her right hand properly. His handshake was firm, decisive. All of his physical confidence translated, unsurprisingly, into an impeccable businessman's handshake.

Or not.

He didn't let go.

Chapter Three

Never let anything take you by surprise.
  —How to Taylor Your Business Plan
    by E.L. Taylor

The woman had no idea who he was.

E.L. Taylor let go of the hand that was wearing his glove.

She dusted her hands off on her jeans. "Well, now that I've been a Debbie Downer, I should get going."

Not Debbie. *Mallory.*

Mallory was the first person in at least two years who hadn't recognized him. She hadn't even started with the *Don't I know you from somewhere?* line of questioning he got from strangers who needed an extra moment to place him.

Yes, they knew him from somewhere.

From birth, Erasmus Leonardo Taylor had been well-known. Announcements had appeared in all the right places. From the first private kindergarten class, everyone at each of his prep schools had known whose son he was, students and faculty alike. He was called Eli by his immediate family, because Erasmus Leonardo was an asinine name for a child. He was called Taylor by everyone else, but he wasn't plain Taylor. He was *Taylor, Harold and June's oldest son—yes, the Dallas Taylors, the ones with the summer estate outside Galveston; you know the ones*. For the first eighteen years of his existence, everyone in his world had known who he was.

Then, he'd come to Masterson. The town was small, but the university was large. Thousands of students were not from Dallas, thousands had never spent their summers in their family's oceanfront vacation home in Galveston, thousands had never played the traditional round of golf with their father's business partners on their sixteenth birthday. Most had never played a round of golf at all.

He'd loved it.

He'd kept *Eli* a secret and ditched the ludicrous *Erasmus* entirely, using E.L. Taylor on every term paper, signing *E.L. Taylor* on his first legal contract, which had been his dormitory agreement. One of his many-greats grandfathers had founded one of the fraternities in the mid-1800s, guaranteeing his progeny membership in perpetuity, but Taylor had ignored that legacy and chosen a fraternity that none of his ancestors had ever belonged to, then been elected president of it. He'd aced his classes while leading the men's record-setting crew team, rowing in the first seat, the man with the most power, the man who led the team.

The end result was that everyone at Masterson University had known him by the time he graduated. Everyone in the world of collegiate crew had, too, and he'd attracted the attention of Olympic recruiters for rowing. To fly across the surfaces of rivers and lakes around the world, using his own body to power the fastest, cutting-edge racing shells... That would have been something.

However, Harold and June's son was not expected to spend two years training for any sport at an international level. He'd been named after two legendary geniuses. From birth, Erasmus Leonardo had been expected to have a brilliant mind and to nurture it, so that he would, one day, bend numbers and legalities to his will and become master of his own fortune. A gentleman's competence at sports was expected, but to devote oneself entirely to a physical pursuit was not.

So, he'd done what he'd been raised to do. He'd graduated from Masterson and gone to Harvard for his MBA. Harvard had an outstanding rowing team, as well as an infamous policy that barred all graduate students from competing in varsity sports. With that temptation out of the way, he'd mastered his master's degree, allowing himself one physically challenging outlet by returning to the fencing he'd first learned at his prep school, competing only at a club level, not intercollegiate. Not international.

He'd graduated and promptly invested in a winning array of stocks and real estate. He'd performed as spectacularly well as expected, accruing his first few millions, but he'd been in his mid-twenties, a little reckless. Tracking the stocks of long-established companies wasn't as thrilling as taking bigger risks in unknown start-ups. Instead of holding a stock that increased by a mere tenth of a single percentage point, he could invest in companies that grew by one thousand percent or more.

Most start-ups failed, however, becoming money pits until they finally dissolved, but Taylor had a good eye for new products and an even better judgment when it came to predicting which fledgling entrepreneurs would grow into successful CEOs of new companies. His millions had turned into tens of millions. Everyone in the world of venture capital knew him.

Fortunately, the world in general did not. He'd always been able to ditch the suit, don a leather jacket and ride a motorcycle across Texas like any other man. Stop and get gas without being photographed. Stop for a plate of barbecue without giving an autograph. He'd been able to stop being E.L. Taylor whenever he wished to.

Then, he'd written a book.

It had given him name recognition outside the world of high-stake investments and black-tie charity galas, so a few television producers had come to call. He should never have agreed to be a guest millionaire on a few episodes of *Shark Tank*. It had made his face as recognizable as his name, so a famous female recording artist had come to call—and come to his bed. He should never have agreed to escort her to the Grammys. The added exposure had sold more books. Their breakup had sold even more.

Taylor could not go anywhere or do anything without being watched, pointed at, photographed, whispered about. Anyone who had attended Masterson University during any part of the four years he'd been there invariably recalled that they'd been close friends.

This fall, Taylor had found himself on a private airstrip with one of those alleged school buddies. The man had proudly pointed out his private plane, a two-seater with a single propeller. It was laughably small compared to Taylor's personal jet, the equivalent of a go-cart next to a Ferrari. On that unimportant evening in September, Taylor had been inconvenienced by a change in plans and was impatient for his jet's return. The man he barely recalled from college had been happy, even eager, to take him from Houston to Dallas. *I'll fly; you buy*, he'd offered. He'd wanted Taylor to pay for the fuel, less than $150.

E.L. Taylor had spent that much on his lunch that day. The whole idea of returning to Dallas in a hobbyist's prop plane had been absurd, but it must have appealed to Taylor on some level. For whatever reason, Taylor had tossed the pilot a couple of hundred-dollar bills, and they'd taken off.

The plane had crashed.

There'd been a harrowing emergency landing into a lake rather than a residential street, an attempt to spare the people on the ground from being killed. Taylor had gotten out alive. The pilot, who'd only been flying to Dallas because Taylor was famous, was still in the hospital three months later.

E.L. Taylor wished he'd never written that book.

"Maybe I'll see you around town, Eli." Mallory started pulling at the fingers of one of his gloves to take it off. "If not, have a nice holiday."

Incredible. She didn't want to hang on to him. She was leaving, as if he were just any stranger at the park, and she didn't care if he remained a stranger.

He never went by Eli publicly, but he'd given her the name just to see if she'd raise that eyebrow and chastise him for being untruthful. *Oh, come on, we both know that's not your name.* That was what he'd expected her to say.

She hadn't. Had his appearance changed so much since the crash? He'd pulled all the necessary strings to ensure the world didn't know he'd been in a crash, so no one would have a reason to look for any changes. His physical and mental health couldn't be questioned, or the stock value of the companies he oversaw could fall. He was unrecognizable to himself on the inside, but he hadn't thought the world noticed any difference at all.

Mallory pulled off one glove and started on the next. Whether he liked it or not, she'd hop down and be gone in seconds.

He didn't like it. "Where are you going?"

That comment did earn him one of her raised eyebrows, and he realized he'd asked it as if she needed to account for leaving his boardroom in the middle of a meeting without being dismissed.

He made an effort to modify his tone. "To get that hot chocolate, I assume."

She stopped tugging at the glove. "I doubt the same church is still selling that particular hot chocolate."

She spoke softly, sadly—absurdly so, given the circumstances. By her own admission, she had whatever it was she'd worked hard to have. She did not have nightmares of oil burning on the water's surface as she struggled to get free of the wreckage of a plane. She had no idea how much worse life could be. Sure, she'd said she wasn't as happy as she thought she'd be, now that she'd gotten what she'd wanted, but *not as happy as I thought I'd be* was different than *sad*.

"What is so sad about hot chocolate?" he asked. Or tried to ask. Perhaps he'd said it more like he was demanding that she explain it to him.

"I haven't been back to Masterson for a long time." She paused as if she needed to steel herself against something. "I never graduated. I came back this fall to complete my senior year."

His first impression had been correct: she was a college student.

"Do you think that's dumb, to come back after so long? To be a twenty-nine-year-old woman living in a dorm? They put me in the dorm that houses foreign students, since they tend to be older, and there are a few graduate students going for their MBAs and PhDs, but I think I'm still the oldest. I'm definitely the only one taking bachelor-level classes. No one has any classes with me. They don't even study in the same library."

He didn't know what to say. He was only three years older than she was. He couldn't imagine the humiliation of moving back into a dorm.

He shouldn't say that.

You didn't face death in a plane crash.

He shouldn't say that, either.

She jerked her head away, like his silence was criticism, a little blow. He felt badly about that, but she recovered quickly enough, sitting up and tugging her cap lower on her forehead. "It doesn't matter. Everything is going great. I just mentioned it because it's been eight years since my last Yule log lighting. I'm not going to waste my time on a futile hunt for the hot chocolate of my youth. I planned to do something else tonight."

"Masterson's a pretty small town beyond the university," he began, trying to be reassuring. "I doubt any new churches have been built in the last eight years. I'm certain none have been knocked down. There's a good chance your hot chocolate is still there."

What am I doing? I don't cheer people up.

He shrugged—at her, at his thoughts, at his uncharacteristic attempt to make conversation when the subject wasn't business. "You should at least walk over and take a look, if it tasted so good that you remember it after eight years."

"Yes. Um…yes. You did me a favor tonight, so I do owe you a cup."

This was a novelty. A woman was going to buy him a cheap cup of hot chocolate at a small-town festival.

She ducked her chin, a little bashful. "But I'm afraid I don't have any money with me at the moment."

Ah, so she did know who he was.

Every light dimmed, inside him and out. He didn't bother to hide the derision from his voice. "No, of course you don't have any."

He knew women, and he knew this routine. She wanted him to buy her something. *Just look, Taylor, isn't that the most adorable set of earrings? I wish I had my credit card with me…but I don't.* He'd have to be a tight-fisted Scrooge not to pick up the tab. He'd never miss ten thousand, and women knew it. Men did, too—who else but E.L. Taylor should buy the round of overpriced, under-the-table Cuban cigars on the golf course? Women, men—everyone knew it, including Mallory.

"You don't have to sound so sarcastic." She pulled the empty glove through her bare hand slowly, no doubt gauging the value of the supple leather. "I just meant—"

"I know what you meant."

Did you think you were the first woman to try this with me?

He should never have told her his name was Eli. That was private, a family nickname, one only his sister and brother still used. If word spread that E.L. Taylor went by *Eli*, then business associates who wished they knew him better than they did would try to call him *Eli*. It would become a constant reminder that he'd been a sucker at a stupid Christmas fair.

He pushed off the edge of the hay bale stack and dropped to the ground, then turned to Mallory. He'd stuck her up there. He'd get her down, and then she could remove herself from his vicinity—and no, he wouldn't pose for a selfie with her before she went.

He reached for her denim-clad hips and pulled her to the edge of the hay bale.

"Hey—I can get down on my own."

She pushed him with her hands on his shoulders, but he'd already lifted her off the edge, so instead of landing on the ground, she ended up sliding down his front, her chest in his face for a moment, followed by a puff of her body heat escaping from her coat at her throat, then her smooth cheek brushing his unshaven one. A few strands of her long hair caught on his lower lip as she landed with her boots between his and her ski cap soft against his neck.

Sex.

Two seconds of accidental contact, and his body suddenly woke up from months of hibernation. Hips, waist, heat, hair—hair that would trail across his chest when she purred her way down his stomach.

Sex.

He stayed as he was, his hands on her waist, her hands on his shoulders. She tilted her face up to him, their gazes locked, and her indignation changed to something else. Her lips parted on a little intake of breath, her eyes went wide as she focused on him, on his mouth.

Sex—she was thinking it, too.

The sensation swamped him, as foreign as if he'd just now discovered how primal desire could feel. He'd had no interest at all since the crash, none whatsoever, but if there was anything good about being recognized as multi-millionaire E.L. Taylor, it was that any woman he wanted would happily come to his bed—and this woman, he wanted.

"Goodbye, Eli."

That was a laughable thing for a woman to say.

"Goodbye? This is the end of our date?" He kept one hand on her waist and braced his other on the hay bales by her head. His arm blocked the light of the bonfire from reaching her face, but the sight of her wide eyes and parted lips was already burned into his mind. He leaned in, bringing his mouth closer to those parted lips. "Then it must be time for the good-night kiss."

"This was a fake date. You didn't even buy me flowers, remember?"

He stopped cold. "I need to buy you something. Of course."

He should have pushed himself away from the hay bales, turned his back on her and walked away.

Instead, he drew her closer. "Kiss me nicely then. Prove to me I should spend my real money on my fake girlfriend."

Her sudden little breath wasn't arousal. It was—

she was—*laughing* at him as she leaned back on the hay bales, putting space between them. "You really think you're God's gift to women, don't you?" She started jerking off the remaining glove, pinky finger, ring finger, middle finger.

He scowled. The woman was not lingering over the middle finger. Surely not.

She moved on to her index finger as she made her point. "You don't know anything about women. We don't like to be dropped on hay bales, and we don't like to be told to perform before you decide whether or not we're worthy of your time or your money. You have no idea how to date a woman at all. No wonder you're so grouchy."

"I'm not dating you. You're the one who demanded that I be your boyfriend."

"I know, and you did me a favor. I understand why you were hinting that I should buy you a cup of hot chocolate in return. I owe you. I get that."

Hinting? He didn't hint about anything. Ever.

"Trust me, I would love to be able to buy you a hot chocolate. I'd love to be able to buy anybody a hot chocolate, but I don't have any cash in my pocket. I was going to offer to do something different for you, instead."

Skip the kissing, straight to bed? He could work with that.

"But you're being so rude, forget it." She pulled off the second glove and slapped the pair against his chest. "Take your gloves and move, so I can go do what I'd planned to do before all of this."

He didn't attempt to take his gloves. "What, exactly, was that?"

"I'm going to find myself a nice, out-of-the-way pecan tree where I can brood about my own life in private." She stuffed his gloves in the open collar of his jacket. "And not watch you brood about yours."

She stepped right around him and walked away.

Taylor stared at the hay bale where her face had been. She truly did not know who he was. She hadn't wanted him to buy her anything. She was just an attractive woman in a ski cap who'd wanted to stand next to him for a few minutes. Nothing more. And now, she was gone.

He turned around. He didn't want to brood alone by these damned haystacks. He wanted to brood in the company of—

"Mallory."

He barked out her name in the only tone he knew, the one that demanded a person drop everything for him. It worked on his staff. It worked on everyone's staff, every place he went. It even worked on his little sister.

Mallory kept walking. She waved her hand by her ear in annoyance, flicking away his command like it was a pesky, harmless bug.

How dare she?

He had power. It had nothing to do with the bedroom. He had power where it mattered, in boardrooms. He could bankrupt a company by voicing a doubt. He could kill someone's career with a word. If E.L. Taylor told anyone to stay, they stayed without question. Did she not know with whom she was tangling?

She did not.

She thought he was Eli, and the part of him that was Eli desperately wanted to be with the woman who had no idea who E.L. Taylor was.

"Mallory, wait." But his words still sounded like an order, and she kept walking.

He yanked the gloves free from where she'd stuffed them in his jacket and started after her.

Chapter Four

Never let an opportunity pass you by.
　　　　　—How to Taylor Your Business Plan
　　　　　　　by E.L. Taylor

Taylor caught up with Mallory easily.

He was taller, so his strides were longer. He also wasn't hampered by clunky rubber boots. She plodded along in a fairly silly way, looking from behind like all the nineteen-year-old girls on campus who favored cheap, colorful rain boots. He'd assumed she was one of those girls when she'd first grabbed his arm and started babbling about sand in her boots.

She'd gotten serious quickly. He'd heard the unmistakable experience in her voice when she'd talked about fending off a man. In his peripheral vision, her long hair and ski cap had reminded him of his little sister. If his sister had needed to stand next to a stranger in a similar situation...

With that mindset, Taylor—*Eli* Taylor, the big brother—had put Mallory behind him, where no one could reach her without going through him first. But, as he'd lifted her to the top of the hay bales, he'd looked at her face full-on in the firelight. He'd realized immediately she was no college student.

She was a woman. He was a man. Since the dawn of time, that was how trouble began.

Trouble—for example, there was no reason for him to feel this stupidly compelled to fix her first impression that he was a jerk.

He caught up to her and matched her stride, trying to think of the right thing to say, trying to figure out what he even wanted to say. This compulsion to make things right wasn't trouble; it was a nuisance. Annoying. Uncomfortable.

She stopped abruptly. "What?"

He stopped, unprepared. "What?"

Her hands made a few random, angry gesticulations. "This. You. Following me, all broody and silent. What do you want from me?"

"I want..." He didn't know what he wanted. She fascinated him, that was all. Her face was so expressive, even prettier in the brighter light, now that they were closer to the bonfire. He could see more details. She had very feminine, feathery eyelashes. He liked the little dip in the center of her upper lip.

She threw her hands up and started walking.

So, he walked. "My first impression was that you wanted to make somebody jealous. My conclusion was that you wanted to spend the night with me."

"Sheesh. Your ego. Amazing."

It wasn't ego when it was true. Most women his age did want to spend the night with him. Younger women, too. Older women. That didn't mean he slept around casually. He was too damned busy at work. He was too damned picky at leisure. But he'd always known an interested woman when he saw one—until tonight.

"It was my mistake. I've been…" He was not going to say he'd been a celibate recluse the entire fall, which had apparently made him lose his accuracy when it came to picking up on the signals that a woman wanted him. "I've been misreading everything since the moment you first walked up to me, and I apologize for it. You don't owe me a cup of hot chocolate. I owe you one."

She clomped along beside him in silence.

He couldn't blame her.

He did possess the social graces expected of Harold and June's son; he just so rarely needed to be charming to anyone, anymore. This was one of those rare occasions. Mallory would be gone in a moment if he didn't change tactics.

"If you don't want to have a cup with me, you could tell me which church sells the good one you remember. I've been making an ass of myself all night, and I need to drown my sorrow for screwing up a fake relationship with a genuinely interesting woman."

"St. Margaret's," she muttered unwillingly—but she stole a look at him.

That tiniest of victories made his heart pick up speed unnecessarily. "If you don't want to drink hot chocolate with me, I'd still like to pay for your cup."

"How? You'd give me cash? Don't do that. It's weird to pay a woman who wouldn't kiss you. Almost as weird as demanding she kiss you before you paid for anything."

"I meant we could do what every college student does. You fly, I'll buy."

As soon as the words were out of his mouth, the memories flashed. Oil burning on the water's surface. Wreckage. Fear.

She laughed. "I haven't heard that all semester. Everyone in my dorm must be broke. Lots of us willing to fly, but nobody to do the buying. So, you'll give me the money, but you expect me to bring you back a cup for each of us?"

No one will face death, here on the ground. A chill slid down his spine, anyway.

"Plus, I'd bring you the change, naturally."

He shoved down his past and focused on the here and now—on Mallory's expressive face. He had her full attention now, no more sneak peeks. "Correct. Then we can find a couple of pecan trees, and we'll go back to brooding alone."

"Alone, while we drink hot chocolate together? Am I getting this right?" She looked amused, even while doing that imperious lift of her eyebrow.

"Yes. We'll drink the same thing at the same time,

side by side, but under separate trees, so we won't be obligated to exchange ridiculous niceties, like 'gee, this hot chocolate is delicious.'"

"What's ridiculous about that?" she asked.

"It's a given. Hot chocolate is never bad. There's no need to state the obvious."

She stopped at the edge of the sandpit. "True. I'm tempted."

His heart had no reason to beat so strongly.

"But I'd be getting the harder part of the bargain," she said. "I'd have to wade through a crowd of families with rowdy, cranky children, looking for a booth that may or may not be manned by the same chocolate-loving nuns I remember, and then I'd have to carry two cups all the way back here without getting bumped and spilling anything."

He didn't want to go into the crowd. He was afraid he'd be recognized, and that would be the end of Eli's anonymous night and the resumption of the rest of E.L. Taylor's unsatisfying life.

Mallory didn't want to go into the crowd, either. She was afraid she'd get bumped and spill her drink.

Not the same thing.

She had no idea how lucky she was to be able to strike up a conversation with a perfect stranger who didn't assume they already knew everything about her. No idea how lucky she was that every single person she met didn't expect her to make their financial dreams come true, from ten thousand dollars in jewelry to a million dollars in venture capital—or even

$150 in plane fuel. How lucky that she hadn't learned to avoid strangers like the plague, the way he did.

Lucky…except the only reason she'd struck up that conversation with a stranger tonight was that she'd needed Eli—or any stranger—to discourage another man's unwanted attention. That was why she was going to say no to hot chocolate. She was afraid she'd run into the person she'd tried to fend off before, and this time, the fake boyfriend who'd helped her would be out of sight, waiting under a pecan tree.

She gave him that no. "The hot chocolate probably only costs a dollar. Sorry, Eli, but that's not worth the amount of time and effort I'd have to put into it. Besides, the hot chocolate would cool off too much by the time I got all the way out to the pecan trees. It's pretty cold tonight."

Finally, he was prepared. That was not the real reason she was declining, and he knew it. Her need outweighed his, hands down.

"In that case, we'll have to go get the hot chocolate together. We don't have to talk. I'll drown my sorrows in silence."

"If we're going to do that, then we might as well find a seat over there in the pavilion. We can brood alone, together, there, instead of wasting time looking for the perfect pair of pecan trees while our cocoa gets cold."

"Sharing a bench is problematic. I have it on good authority that everyone would feel sorry for a woman by my side, if I gave her the silent treatment. It might look like our date is going badly, if we don't speak."

It would also keep them in an area where there were more people, more chances of him being recognized. But her lips were twitching; he'd made it hard for her not to smile at him, which made it hard for him not to smile back.

"Okay, then," she said. "We'll talk just enough to make our fake relationship look realistic. Deal?"

"Agreed. And you're right, it is getting colder. Put these back on." He handed her the gloves. The satisfaction he felt as she slipped her hands into their protective leather was unreasonable.

Woman. Man. Trouble.

This wasn't trouble. This was a cup of cocoa with an attractive stranger, a half hour out of his life, at most, until the novelty of being Eli, of being with a woman who called him *Eli*, wore off. She'd muse a little more about her birthday; he'd listen. It couldn't possibly lead to trouble.

They skirted the wet sand easily as they began their quest to find the chocolate-loving nuns of St. Margaret's.

This was the quietest date Mallory had ever been on, real or fake.

Eli hadn't been kidding when he said they'd talk as little as necessary, without exchanging any banalities like *gee, this hot chocolate is delicious*. They sat a polite distance apart on a park bench under the pavilion in silence.

"Gee, this hot chocolate is delicious," she said.

Eli continued scrutinizing everyone who ventured near their bench.

"Those nuns are absolute connoisseurs of chocolate," she said. "Cocoa sommeliers."

Someone drifted their way. Eli raised his cup for a drink as if he were using it to hide his face.

"Am I your fake girlfriend?"

He lowered the cup and frowned at her. His stunning eyes weren't silver, but blue, now that they were in better lighting. Paul Newman blue.

"You appointed yourself to that role," he said.

Paul Newman blue, minus the laugh lines.

"No, I appointed you to be my fake boyfriend. Are you now using me as a fake girlfriend?"

He had to be using her as a decoy or defense of some kind. That made so much more sense than buying her hot chocolate as an apology for being rude. She was the one who'd imposed on him, after all, barging in on his privacy by the hay bales.

She didn't mind being imposed on in return, particularly because she had no objection to sitting beside the sexiest man she'd ever seen in person—which made him the sexiest man she'd ever seen, period. Sex appeal could be so strong that it jumped right off the silver screen—or off the television screens in various bedridden relatives' homes. But when it was coming from a man with a powerful body—a living, breathing man who had strong hands that had warmed up these gloves—the appeal was magnified a thousand times. This evening was a little birthday present to herself, a chance to play make-believe for a while, with herself cast in the starring role as the object of adoration for six feet of glowering gorgeousness. He needed to do more adoring to make anything look plausible, though.

"Don't get me wrong. If you think I'm enough to make a woman jealous, then I'm flattered. But you might want to look at least mildly interested in me instead of constantly looking for her."

"There's no *her*."

"Who are you looking for, then? Am I helping you fend off a whole group of women who might start begging for your attention, otherwise?"

"Something like that."

"No kidding? Tell me more. Is some sorority determined to descend upon you and make you their mascot—I mean, their official sweetheart?"

"God, I hope not." He looked somewhat appalled at the idea of being attacked by a flock of nineteen-year-olds. That was a point in his favor.

The fact that she was the one doing all the talking was not. She held her disposable cup of hot chocolate in one hand and used her other to start counting off his words. "'There's no *her*. Something like that. God, I hope not.' That's ten. An even ten words. I don't know who you're on the lookout for, but she's not going to believe this setup if you only start talking to me after you spot her. Or the group of hers. Or whatever."

Without taking his eyes off the crowd, he slid closer and put his arm across the back of the bench, just behind her shoulders.

"Happy?" he grumbled.

"Eleven."

He smiled around the edge of his cup before closing his lips to take a sip.

Do that again.

She was fascinated. When he didn't have that grim set to his mouth, his lips looked softer, especially in contrast to the heavy black stubble around them. She'd never kissed a man with a beard. It had to be rough. A high school marathon make-out session would surely leave a serious red rash on the girl's face. Good thing most boys in high school couldn't grow a beard.

But this man had left boyhood behind long ago. A big, solid body like his would be so thrilling to snuggle into. If this were a real date, her hand would fall naturally to settle on his thigh. She'd feel more through denim than leather; his thigh would be as hard as his arm. She'd turn her face up to his, and he'd kiss her, chocolate kisses, hot kisses. Eli, her fake boyfriend with kissable lips—

"You're staring."

"Twelve and thirteen." She kept her chin up, faking confidence despite her embarrassment at being busted for staring. "That's some peripheral vision you have. You never look at me, yet you keep track of where I'm looking and what my hands are doing." She realized her hand was resting mostly on her thigh, but her pinky finger had drifted to his jeans, a touch of authenticity to her fantasy. She moved it quickly.

"When my hands are brushing sand off my boots, I

mean. You kept track of how many boots you thought I had to brush off to make a man jealous." She could feel her cheeks heating, which he probably could also see with his super side vision. "Which isn't what I was doing, because there's no *him*."

"One," he said.

It took her a second. One boot, he meant.

"Fourteen," she answered.

He smiled again at her word count, a lift of just one corner of his mouth, which made her wonder what it would feel like to be kissed by him.

You could have found out by the haystacks.

With a sigh, Mallory straightened up and refocused on the holiday scene. A high school choir had taken the stage. Their director was conducting them with intense motions, ensuring each *fa* and *la* cut off on the beat. An overabundance of little children, most still wearing the construction-paper reindeer antlers they'd worn onstage, crowded around the fence in front of the Yule log to throw their wishes on the fire.

Wish after wish was hitting the sand. An indisputably handsome fireman was using a fire iron to whack them into the fire as he made each child laugh. If that guy wasn't already married, then a dozen single women who dreamed about white picket fences were probably drooling over each swing. He looked like he'd make such a good dad someday—a handsome one, too. All in all, it was a wholesome little vignette, *It's a Wonderful Life* if George Bailey had been a hot hunk.

Was it bad form to notice a hot fireman while on a fake date with a fake boyfriend?

Her fake boyfriend was certainly scowling at the fireman as if he were a rival. Eli had nothing to worry about. The white picket fence wasn't Mallory's dream. She'd spent almost all of her twenties living behind everyone else's white picket fences.

He's not jealous of a fireman, Mallory Ames. This isn't a real date.

Eli simply scowled at everything, even sweet little children and their hero.

"Isn't it cute how the kids' faces light up when the fireman talks to them? Did you ever want to be a fireman when you grew up?"

"No."

She waited a moment.

"Fifteen," she said.

Nothing, not even a flicker of reaction as Eli stared hard at the bonfire scene.

She nudged his knee with hers. "Hello? Anybody home?"

He frowned a little—or rather, his usual frown deepened a little—but he closed his eyes, turned his head away, and resumed scanning the crowd.

She tried again. "It looks like he's as much of a hero to them as Santa Claus. That's good, since you can't aspire to be Santa Claus. You can aspire to be a firefighter. If your hero is real, you can make a plan to become just like him."

Just like she had. It was only a matter of weeks now before she'd arrive at work to find the office down the hall, which had been empty all fall, occupied by none other than her very own hero.

She knew what he looked like, of course. In the black-and-white photo on the back of the book jacket, he was handsome in that clean-cut, prosperous way, with short hair and a cashmere sweater over a button-down. The photo had been taken outdoors. He looked a little bit impatient. She imagined he'd paused for that photo on his way to a polo match, or perhaps just before he'd boarded his yacht. It was hard to picture a multi-millionaire like him in the administrative offices of the business college, even in one of the private offices—but he'd be there. Soon.

It was unnerving.

"Have you ever met one?" she asked Eli.

"I try to meet as few firefighters as possible."

Mallory had meant heroes, not firefighters specifically, but Eli's aversion to them struck her as odd. She'd assumed everyone admired firefighters, if for no other reason than they raised money for good causes by posing for calendars with kittens. Eli would probably just stick a kitten on top of a hay bale and consider the job done.

"I guess nobody wants to meet a fireman who is working. That would mean your house is on fire."

She paused.

"And you actually own a house, so is that why you avoid them?"

Still nothing.

She sat back with a huff, which would have knocked his arm off the edge of the bench's back behind her, had he not been as unyielding as a statue. "You know, if I were your *real* girlfriend, I wouldn't put up with this cryptic crap. I'd be talking to you all the time. You'd have to talk to me."

"How very fortunate that you're only my fake girlfriend, and therefore we are brooding in silence together, talking only as much as necessary."

"Was that a complete sentence? You're positively witty when you use a complete sentence." She batted her eyelashes. "I have faith in you, Eli. You can get the hang of this if you keep practicing tonight. Maybe you'll go on a real date someday, and you'll just knock her socks off with your complete sentences."

His smile increased from a sexy half to two-thirds. Good God, the man was devastating when he smiled. So far, *she* was the only reason he'd smiled at all tonight, which made that sex appeal factor go off the charts. A dark and dangerous man whose smiles were exclusively for her? *Happy birthday*.

Maybe if he'd smiled at her like that when they'd been by the hay bales, she would have handled that almost-kiss differently. When she'd slid down his body, he'd looked at her like he wanted to make her his, right there in the night, consequences be damned. He'd given her permission to kiss him with a level of breathtaking arrogance, the kind an alpha-male bad boy would have in a woman's fantasy.

In a fantasy, Mallory could take what she wanted from a man like that. In reality, there'd been an undeniable thrill in being seen as sexually desirable, but the chance to indulge in a moment of pure lust had been too much for her. In a split second, she'd chickened out, stepped back and laughed. After all, who would kiss a man in the flickering firelight, just because he was drop-dead gorgeous and intensely focused on her?

Not Mallory Ames, apparently.

Never let an opportunity pass you by. Of course, E.L. Taylor hadn't been giving her advice about carnal indulgences, but she'd missed the opportunity to be kissed the way she'd fantasized about, by the kind of man she'd fantasized about.

She'd gotten a free cup of hot chocolate, instead.

E.L. Taylor would not be impressed.

Mallory watched the fireman pose for a photo with a little boy in reindeer antlers. That boy was no worse off for having met a hero. Then again, he was a child, and no one expected him to be his hero's equal.

Never meet your heroes was her hero's crystal-clear edict, and his advice hadn't been wrong yet. On the other hand, he'd also said to never let an opportunity pass her by. She had to seize the chance to learn from him in real life. She couldn't obey both *never*s.

"Tell me something, Eli," she said. "Have you ever met one of your heroes?"

Chapter Five

"Never."

Eli said the word with finality.

It sounded like the perfect way to say out loud what E.L. Taylor wrote. The inflection was exactly right: he knew best, end of debate, move on to the next chapter. If Eli narrated the audio version of Mallory's business book, she'd probably fall asleep in the dorm with it playing in her headphones every night.

She wanted to hear him say it again. "Did you say *never*?"

Eli gave her that look out of the corner of his eye,

the one that meant he didn't answer unnecessary questions. She'd asked, he'd answered, and he knew she'd heard him. Move on.

It was so deliciously bossy, it made her a little weak in the knees, not that she'd want him to sense that. *Never show weakness.*

"'Never' isn't a complete sentence." She pulled off her ski cap and shook back her loose hair. "Everyone has a hero at some point in their life. You must have had one as a child."

"Never." He said it differently this time, quietly, nothing like E.L. Taylor at all. This poor stranger. He really was too grim.

She angled herself on the bench to face him more fully. "Didn't you have a favorite teacher when you were little?"

"They were all excellent."

That could have meant he'd had dozens of hero teachers. Instead, it sounded like he'd had none.

"What about a coach?"

"No."

"Hey, Eli?" She leaned in close and waited until he looked up from his hot chocolate. "We're having a conversation here. Don't make me start counting again."

After a moment's staring contest, Eli smiled maybe a tenth of a smile, just a crinkling at the corner of his eyes, a look as devastating as…well, every other expression he had. She was getting used to this feeling, though, being constantly but pleasantly flushed beside him, all of her senses jazzed up by this physical awareness of him.

"I don't need a lot of words," he said. "In this situation, I can describe you in only one. *Fearless*."

Her heart contracted. Those half smiles were sexy, but this, *this*, was her undoing. A confident man, admiring her confidence…which was, unfortunately, fake.

"If I were fearless, I wouldn't be so nervous to…" *Kiss you.* "To meet my hero."

"Don't meet her," he said, the voice of authority once more. "The timing isn't right to meet her if you're uncertain. It may never be right."

"It's not a *her*. How would you know whether or not I should meet mine, if you've never met yours? You can't know whether it would be good or bad."

"Touché."

He said it curtly, quickly, *toosh*. He said it like he was impressed with her counterpoint, which made her feel so light she might as well be full of champagne bubbles instead of hot chocolate.

But she pointed at him. "I wasn't trying to score a point. I'm proving to you that you are wrong. What about family? What about your dad? My brother idolizes our dad."

Displeasure touched his face. "We're talking more than necessary to keep up appearances."

"No, we're not. This is what a real girlfriend would do, you know."

"No, it isn't."

"Seriously, it is. You're not supposed to toss your

date onto haystacks without warning. You *are* supposed to talk to her over drinks, even nonalcoholic drinks. You truly have never had a girlfriend, have you?"

He gave her the *unnecessary question* look again—with a good dose of that alpha arrogance.

Right. There was no way this man was an untouched virgin.

"Fine," she said. "Then what kind of weird girlfriends have you had? What do you even do on a date, if you don't talk?"

He gave her a look: *Really?* Then he sat back and let his gaze roam over her hair. Without the ski cap, her hair had to be messy, even a little wild. He took his time, studying her hair from the crown of her head to where she'd tucked it behind her ear, tilting his head as if he were deciding whether or not he was satisfied yet with how wild it looked.

Yet. If not, he'd undoubtedly take her for another tumble to get her looking thoroughly debauched. He'd probably start by whispering a sexy something into her bared ear.

Mallory felt naked without her hat. If this was how he looked at a woman's hair on a public park bench, how would he look at a woman in his bedroom, when she was all his and completely exposed to his gaze?

Eli's gaze glanced over her heated cheeks, before he raised an eyebrow. *Any more questions?*

"In the park?" she asked, incredulous.

Silence.

"On a bench?"

He gave her the hint of a purse of his lips, the faintest imitation of Zoolander, spoofing a supermodel.

Mallory burst into laughter. "How many of your dates end by being jailed for public indecency?"

He couldn't sustain the smolder. She caught the twinkle in his eye just before he looked down at his cup, but his shoulders gave him away.

"Eli, is that an actual chuckle? Are you laughing? You are." She poked him in the chest. "You are trying so hard not to smile."

He caught her finger mid-jab and pressed her gloved hand to his chest. She tried to pull her hand back, but he held tight.

She reversed course and pressed her hand into his chest. "Is that a heart I feel beating? You do have a heart, Tin Man. You've just gotten rusty when it comes to smiling. You need an oilcan, that's all."

"You do have a brain, Scarecrow. You just need the diploma, that's all."

Oof. Mallory had walked herself right into that one. In the movie, the Scarecrow hadn't really needed a diploma, but it had been part of his happily-ever-after.

She didn't let her confident façade slip. "They just hand them to you in Oz, apparently, as long as you can prove you murdered a wicked witch."

"You'll earn yours."

He spoke like her success was a foregone conclusion. He really would be a great narrator for her book. She supposed a business planning guide would be an odd choice for a bedtime story, but if he were reading it, she'd go to sleep feeling hopeful that she had what it took to change her world for the better, drifting into a night of happy dreams as she snuggled against his chest, listening to that deep voice...

He let go of her hand and slouched a little, stretching his legs out in front of him, crossing his ankles in those classic boots. "If this date requires more talking, then go ahead. Tell me about your childhood hero, instead of demanding to know about my non-existent one."

"My childhood hero? Singular? I had many."

He nodded toward the last remaining children and the firefighter. "Tell me about one you met."

"The first one I remember was when I was six. I met Cinderella at Disney World, and I'm telling you, I thought I'd explode from the excitement. She asked me what my name was, and then she acted delighted to hear it, like it was the most special name in the world."

Eli smiled fully.

Finally.

With Christmas lights and music all around her, and with a handsome leading man beside her, the evening was taking on a magical glow. It felt like a real date, even though she knew it was not. She hadn't forgotten for a moment, but he'd placed her hand on his chest as if he didn't mind at all if she touched him, and now he was relaxed and smiling because he was enjoying their conversation.

This was such a luscious little evening of make-believe. He would smile at her like this when she tossed that bedtime book aside and spread her hand on his chest—on his bare chest.

"You remind me of my little sister," he said.

Ugh. No. Stop.

"I think she was in kindergarten when she met Cinderella. She went crazy, too." He shook his head at Mallory like she was in kindergarten herself. "What is it with you girls and a sparkly blue gown?"

"A gown?"

"That's what girls love about Cinderella. A big, sparkling, blue gown." The authority in his voice edged closer to derision. "It's probably behind the wedding gown mania later in your lives."

His smile was for himself. He was so satisfied with his dissection of a children's hero—worse, a *girl's* hero. It reminded Mallory too much of her brother's visits during his college breaks, as her one semester off had dragged into two. He'd take control of the TV as if only he knew how to operate it. Then he would dismiss her movie suggestions as silly girl-stuff. Her father would agree, although he'd enjoyed all the movies Mallory had watched with him to keep him company while he was a housebound invalid.

She didn't want Eli to be like that. "We weren't excited about a blue gown. It was about the hero who was wearing the blue gown. She was—"

"Hero*ine*."

She narrowed her eyes at him. "*Hero* can be gender-neutral, and that was the most trivial big-brother thing to interrupt me with. I'm not your little sister.

I'm your fake girlfriend." *You're my birthday fantasy. Don't ruin it.*

"All true." He polished off his cup of hot chocolate.

Mallory might have chosen to spend her birthday with a hot guy, but she wasn't going to be patronized as if she were a child, not even by the hot guy. "The reason girls love Cinderella isn't because she wore a pretty dress. Girls aren't that shallow. Cinderella's moment of victory isn't her arrival at the ball in a glass carriage. It's at the end of the story, when she doesn't have a magical disguise. That's when she wins. It's about being seen, being valued even when you're dressed in rags, not only when you're in a sparkly blue gown."

"*That's* what you're thinking in kindergarten?"

"Well, no. I don't mean that kindergartners analyze a hero's journey, but that's when those ideas are being formed. Subconsciously, girls are excited to meet Cinderella in her sparkly blue gown, because they recognize that it's a symbol that Cinderella is a winner."

"You said she wore rags when she won. They sell more dolls in sparkly blue gowns because that's what little girls like, and it doesn't matter whether or not the doll accomplished anything in the blue gown."

"It's not about dolls." Her frustration was real, but she faked being cool. "How about this? Soldiers earn medals when they are filthy dirty on a battlefield, but we dress them up in sharp uniforms and pin the medals on them later, while they're looking their best. Cinderella won when she wore rags, but we like to see her looking her best, now that her battle is won."

Eli leaned in closer, a smile still flirting with the corners of his mouth as if he found the whole awful conversation entertaining. "A handsome prince noticed her while she wore a blue gown, then a second time while she wore rags. Is that a battle victory? It's not much."

"You're right." Mallory didn't have to fake her sarcasm. "Thank you for proving that having a handsome man notice you isn't all it's cracked up to be."

"Touché, once more."

His approval wasn't thrilling now.

"You think I'm handsome, at least," Eli said. "I also fulfilled the requirement to notice you while you were not wearing a sparkly gown."

"I'm not wearing rags." She said it as if it hadn't taken forever to get the mothball smell out of her grandmother's peacoat. It was humiliating to be only a mitten away from scrounging through a lost-and-found box. Mallory could feel a knot of old and new sadness clogging her throat. This whole evening had been terribly emotional, all quicksand and broken plans. "The only reason you noticed me was because I decided you would. I gave you no choice."

"I'm glad you didn't." He raised his cup in a toast. "I would have missed out on some excellent hot chocolate."

With that meaningless bit of polite charm, he ended the subject. He'd torn apart her childhood hero for sport. End of discussion. Move on.

I'm not done. Mallory crumpled her empty cup and threw it at the nearest trash can. It hit the side of the metal barrel and fell to the plank flooring. "Cinderella doesn't care that the prince is rich. The important thing is that he loves her. She'll have an ally from now on. A champion."

Eli looked bemused. "An affluent champion. One who can buy her sparkly blue gowns and put her up in a castle."

"Should she aspire to keep her rags and remain in her family's attic? Do you know anyone whose life goal is to be poor?"

"Yes." He held up his empty cup. "The nuns that made this hot chocolate. Who knew women living in poverty would make something this rich?"

"You're being insufferable." She crossed her arms, rounding her shoulders so that she wouldn't be leaning against his arm on the back of the bench any longer. "You wouldn't know a hero if one sat right next to you. Cinderella, for your information, was a hard worker even when life wasn't fair to her, even when her own family wasn't fair to her. Her prince and her castle and even that sparkly gown were what she deserved. She worked hard, and she got what she deserved after all her hard work."

"Hard work? It was servitude. She was treated like a servant by her own family, performing every chore they didn't want to do themselves."

"I…"

Servitude to her own family…

Eli uncrossed his ankles and pushed himself out of his slouch, a leisurely lion toying with a mouse. "Worse than a servant. She wasn't paid for all that hard work you admire. She got some food and a bed in a room where her family didn't want to sleep."

"I…"

Spare bedrooms and food…her own family…

"She was being used," he said, "and she was allowing herself to be used."

"Allowing it? Where was she supposed to go? A homeless shelter?"

Cinderella hadn't had any options. Mallory understood that. For years, she hadn't been financially free to return to school. Her father had needed to pay for his medical bills instead. Her own savings had slowly dwindled down to nothing. It hadn't seemed right to add something like a bottle of nail polish to Aunt Effie's grocery cart, or even necessities like maxi pads or toothbrushes. Mallory would do Aunt Effie's shopping for her, then purchase her own things separately.

Mallory had been frugal, but her savings couldn't last forever, and she couldn't get a paying job to fill her account back up. Her family wouldn't allow it. They'd needed her with them full-time. Who else would help an invalid get to the bathroom and back, day and night?

Mallory had believed it would be impossible to go back to college without her family's financial help, because they'd said so. Missed semester after missed semester, medical bills and home repairs, new televisions and used cars had taken priority over her.

Worst of all, she'd been lied to by her own father. He'd told her he wasn't getting disability payments from the government any longer, until the month that a paper check had arrived in the mail rather than being electronically deposited. Her father had claimed that he hadn't realized he was still getting monthly payments. If the checks kept coming, he'd be able to send her back to school next year, he'd said, so she should be happy. But her father wasn't a very good liar. She'd only felt betrayed.

She would have still been waiting on her fifty-ninth birthday if she hadn't made her own plan. E.L. Taylor had been right. *Never believe those who say it can't be done. There is always a way to get it done. They haven't tried hard enough to find it. You will.*

"Cinderella is a terrible heroine for young girls." Eli crumpled up his cup and pitched it toward the trash can with just the right arc, just the right amount of force to land it in the barrel. "That story teaches girls to keep hoping all the garbage they're putting up with will magically disappear one day, so they continually put up with garbage. I don't want my sister to believe that the possibility of a wealthy prince in the future is worth putting up with any kind of abuse in the present."

Any kind of abuse...by her own family...

"Prince Charming could be poor, and he'd still be her choice. It's about finding someone who doesn't treat you like a servant. It's choosing your own friends, and making your own family, if you need to. It's having enough respect for yourself to be with people you can trust, instead of people who'll lie to you to keep you where they want you."

None of which she'd done for herself.

Eli's laugh was more like a scoff. "Self-sacrifice and servitude won't help you find any of that, either."

"Stop it." Mallory pushed herself off the bench and took a step away, desperate to put some space between herself and his terrible, horrible opinions. "You don't know what you're talking about. You don't understand anything."

"Mallory?" He stood, too, and had the audacity to look baffled. "We were talking about fairy tales. I was telling you that my little sister—"

"We were not talking about fairy tales." She stalked over to the trash can, scooped her cup off the ground and threw it into the barrel. "We were talking about heroes. *My* heroes."

"Childhood heroes. You must have outgrown Cinderella."

Eli had gentled his voice. He slowly put his hands into his pockets, as if she were a spooked horse, and he didn't want to make any sudden moves to upset her.

Too late.

Eli had been the mirror. Everything Mallory had thought reflected well on Cinderella looked tragic when she saw it on herself. Mallory had been a woman used, letting herself be used, until she'd stumbled from a fairy-tale story to a business manual that had forced her to stop waiting for that magical moment when she'd be sent to the ball—back to Masterson. If she hadn't been given that book as a birthday gift, whose house would she be sleeping in tonight, after she'd cooked and cleaned and administered the medicines, then cleaned up the food one more time when her great-aunt or grandfather was too sick to keep it down?

She thought she might be sick herself. What if she hadn't read that book? What if?

"I've got to go." She whirled around and clomped down the shallow wooden stairs as fast as she could, heading for the darkness, because she was about to bawl and she needed to do it in private. No one could see the worst version of herself. Her book said so, and her book had saved her.

There was no darkness in this part of the park. Everything was bonfires and Christmas lights. Mallory started to jog down the row of booths, weaving around the people in line at each one, desperate to reach the darkness beyond the stage.

"Mallory!"

She didn't want to talk to him. She was sorry she'd ever talked to him. She was—*damn, damn, damn.*

She was wearing his super-expensive gloves.

She stopped in her tracks and fumbled with the gloves, her vision blurring, her chest heaving as she fought to keep the sobs at bay—*not here, not now*—until strong hands, larger than her own, cupped hers together firmly but gently.

His voice was just as firm and gentle. "Please, don't leave yet."

Mallory lost her battle.

She started to cry.

Chapter Six

Never apologize for being right.
> —How to Taylor Your Business Plan
> *by E.L. Taylor*

God, he was an ass.

Eli had known it for some time, but this was terrible, even for him. He'd made this genuinely interesting, expressive, attractive woman cry.

"Don't cry," he said, a stupid command.

"I'm n-not." Tears ran down her face and she was doing something anxious with her hands.

He tried to hold them still. "I didn't realize your feelings were being hurt."

"This isn't about my feelings. This is about *you*, and your lack of feelings."

He had nothing to do with this drama over a fairy tale, but Mallory's face scrunched up as anger warred with sadness. If being angry with him stopped her tears, she was welcome to chew him out. Tears made him uncomfortable. Anger was easy to take.

Best to let Mallory get it over with. He tossed her some easy bait. "I have no idea what you're talking about."

She didn't yell at him to let off some steam. Instead, her tone turned icy. "You're so proud of not having a hero, of not ever having had a hero. You think that makes you superior to all the little girls who have hopes and dreams. I'm here to tell you, Eli, that it makes you worse." She threw her hands apart, knocking his away. "It makes you a man who has no one to aspire to be like, no dream to reach for. You're a man without any inspiration to keep growing."

He dropped his hands to his sides. *A man without any inspiration.* The world hadn't noticed any change in him, none at all. How had she?

Everyone knows women get emotional. She's throwing words around, angry at everything in general. It's a meaningless rant.

But the platitudes and excuses which had enabled him to ignore anyone else's inconvenient feelings had stopped working the same moment a small plane's propeller had stopped working. Mallory knew precisely what she was saying and to whom she was saying it. She'd listened to him tonight, better than he'd listened to himself.

She pulled his glove off her left hand, one clean

jerk. "So, who should I feel sorry for? Little girls who hope that being good will lead to a good life? Or you, a man who thinks he's too good to have a hero?"

He stood there, shocked. Mallory had summed him up accurately and succinctly: compared to hopeful little girls, he sucked.

He should say something. "I didn't—I didn't real-ize your feelings were—" *You already said that. Her feelings weren't doing anything. You are the problem.*

She shook his glove at him. "Here. Take it, take it. I have to go." She gave the other glove a vicious pull, then held the pair out in one quivering fist. "Take them, please. I need to go before I c-cry." But her tears were already falling. She was in pain.

He grabbed her wrist and tugged her close, wrap-ping her in his arms as if he could shield her, but her pain wasn't coming from something he could break or beat or buy. She tucked her chin and pressed her wet cheek against his neck, hiding her face. Sobs wracked her body.

He was appalled. It didn't seem right. It didn't seem fair. This lovely woman who'd demanded his attention, who'd laughed at his sullen silence, who'd spoken to the stars and to a fire and to a stranger, now was genuinely heartbroken. He wasn't certain why.

"P-people are staring. I want to g-go."

"Then, we'll go." It didn't matter *why* she was cry-ing. It only mattered that she was.

He glanced around for a quick escape, then shep-herded her in between two booths, keeping an arm around her shoulders and turning them both sideways to squeeze past a few propane tanks and card-board boxes. The area behind the booths was darker, just a grassy parking area for those who worked in the booths. Quieter, too, because the speakers that had begun playing prerecorded holiday music were pointed away from them. Only a few other people were back here, smokers taking a break, mostly. The tips of their cigarettes glowed orange in the night.

Eli led Mallory in between two parked pickup trucks. There, in semi-privacy, he leaned against the side of one of the trucks and wrapped Mallory in his arms again.

"I'm fine," she said, and then she set her cheek on his shoulder, looking away from him, and gulped in shaky breaths that did not sound fine.

He didn't know what to say, so he said nothing. He had no idea how a cup of hot chocolate had led to this situation. He didn't want to see her cry, but as he held Mallory in her sturdy wool coat, he felt… he felt… He didn't mind being the one she cried on.

Step one is to name your emotions. His thera-pist wanted him to work on that. Eli had consulted a therapist a few weeks after the crash, of course. He was no fool. People who faced near-death events generally needed professional advice to process the experience—and Eli's ability to sleep had been shot.

He'd hired a highly sought-after and very discreet counselor. *Can you put a name to your emotion, Mr. Taylor?* Terror. And in that final second, regret.

Mallory shifted a little, murmuring something apologetic. Eli cupped her head in his hand lightly to keep her as she was, so she wouldn't feel obliged to raise her head and step back if she didn't want to.

She didn't want to; she rested more heavily on his shoulder. He smoothed back a few strands of her hair, which were tickling his nose—a nuisance. Then he put his arm back around her and settled into her as she settled into him, and none of it felt like a nuisance.

Trouble?

It didn't feel like that, either.

When you can identify an emotion, Mr. Taylor, then you can accept it for what it is, no more, no less. As Mallory's breathing grew more and more calm, Eli looked at the stars over the silhouettes of the trees, and he felt calmer, too.

Calm was an emotion. There; he'd identified it. Like any other emotion, even terror, calm wouldn't last. He closed his eyes to soak it in while he could, the feel of another human being in his arms, the feel of having a person to hug.

His eyes flew open again. A hug. He'd almost forgotten it had a name.

There was nothing similar to it in his life. When he greeted his parents, his father shook his hand. His mother kissed his cheek. His brother and sister, twins born more than a decade after him, had turned eight during his freshman year at Masterson University. They'd rarely been part of his life once he'd left home for college.

The touches Eli gave and received were handshakes, firm ones that served the purpose of gauging a person's mindset or sealing a deal. When he made the time, there was contact during evening dinner dates—an arm offered in escort, or a hand on the small of a woman's back—followed by a night of sex.

He was relieved to remember that he'd had sex fairly regularly, before September. Not as often as people thought, but frequently enough. He wasn't some strange creature that existed in a world devoid of human contact.

But sex was not *this*. Sex had a goal. Every touch had a purpose: to entice, to increase arousal, to ramp up the craving for the climax, which then finished the need to touch. A shower. A drink. A civilized goodbye until next time.

He closed his eyes again. After a moment, he tilted his cheek toward Mallory's hair, seeking that tickle, that touch that didn't have any purpose.

At the hay bales, when Mallory had first grabbed his arm for balance, he'd practically shaken her touch from his sleeve the moment she'd let go. But after she'd lectured him, and after he'd seen her face in the firelight, it had felt different when she'd sat behind him and plopped her arms on top of his head. The sensation had been foreign, unexpected, but not unpleasant, in its way.

He'd grumbled about it, but he hadn't moved away. Maybe he'd wanted a touch that was neither business nor sex, without knowing he wanted it. Was that an emotion with a name? Was there a term for that kind of desire?

I like being with Mallory.

That analysis was specific enough for now. He wouldn't move away. He wouldn't shake off her touch.

He'd hold Mallory for as long as she'd let him hold her.

This was the most mortifying date Mallory had ever been on, real or fake.

Nobody wanted to have a big epiphany about the psychology behind their failures. Nobody wanted that to happen while they were at a holiday festival with a handsome man. Nobody wanted that handsome man to be the one who revealed how her old hero had led her astray.

Mallory was so angry at herself. Her hero hadn't even been real. Cinderella was only a character in a fairy tale that had been told centuries before the Brothers Grimm had written it down, yet Mallory had absorbed this nonexistent person's values: suffer patiently, voice no complaints. She'd let them influence her real life, of which twenty-nine years were now gone.

Mallory had been even angrier at the man who'd pointed out the obvious flaws in the fairy tale, but stating the obvious was all Eli had done. When she'd freaked out, he'd come after her. She'd castigated him for not having heroes, but he was holding her right now, anyway, and it felt incredibly good. He was as big and strong as he was broody and gorgeous. The way he glared at the world made her feel all the more protected in his arms.

It was an illusion. The strongest arms couldn't undo her past. Tonight, she could taste the shame and despair she'd felt two years ago, when she'd finished the last page of *How to Taylor Your Business Plan*, turned out the light and seen the truth.

Another shudder went through her. Eli tightened his hug. He didn't say everything was okay. He didn't tell her to pull herself together. He was simply here, holding her, and he didn't seem to be in any hurry for her to dry her tears and move on. She'd insulted him, yet he was being a nice guy…which meant she was the jerk, here.

Never apologize for being right, E.L. Taylor said.

Mallory hadn't been right.

When I know I'm the one in the wrong, I don't believe in making someone wait on my apology. That was what her grandpa would say.

Thoughts of her grandpa were making her homesick now, too. Knowing she'd have to leave the temporary security of Eli's strong arms and return to standing on her own two feet wasn't much of a motivation to dry her tears.

Eventually, they dried up, anyway. "I'm sorry," she mumbled, keeping her cheek on Eli's shoulder.

"Don't be," he said.

"Yes, I should be sorry. I said some harsh things."

"You didn't say anything that wasn't true."

He sounded so matter-of-fact about it, in a resigned way. *I know I'm uninspired.* Poor man. No wonder he was so grim.

"I failed to see that I was upsetting you. I should have recognized that you were defending Cinderella so passionately because she's your personal hero."

"She *isn't*." Mallory hiccupped, miserable on every level. "But she was. I think I've watched every movie version of Cinderella there is. She always keeps her dignity, but she never tries to leave, not until she meets Prince Charming. Her story did shape my thinking, without a doubt. You're the one who didn't say anything that wasn't true. You can't imagine how much I wish it hadn't been true. I wasted so many years emulating that exact kind of servitude to my family. I didn't realize it until it was too late."

"Too late for what?"

She picked up her head and moved back just far enough to look at his face, shocked that he couldn't see the obvious. "For what? Do you really have to ask that?"

He kept an arm around her as he brushed her hair from her wet cheeks. Her shame and regrets and misery built with each strand of hair he smoothed back, until, with an unbearable sincerity, he repeated, "Too late for what?"

The dam burst. Her words came tumbling out over hiccups and tears. "Look at me. Just look at me. I'm twenty-nine. I'm still in college. I live in a dorm. You can joke all you want and mock me for thinking that twenty-nine is ancient, but that's because you aren't in my shoes. You can't understand how it feels to be this far behind. You already have a house, and you have a career, and you could be married if you wanted to be, but you don't want to be, because men don't have to be married to get sex."

His eyebrows rose. "What?"

"It's true." She was talking too fast, but it was too hard to slow down. "It's true, my grandpa says so. He told me that when he was young, if you wanted to have sex, you had to find a wife. Marriage meant sex. It was a big proof of your manhood to have a wife. He says that's why men today don't get married right out of school anymore, because they can have all the sex they want."

"Ah… Okay?"

She swallowed bitter tears. "It never occurs to anyone to point out that women aren't getting married now, either, and it's not because they're home alone, wasting away as spinsters. They have careers, and they don't have to marry to get all the sex *they* want. Women like to have sex, too, you know."

He cleared his throat. "That's excellent news."

A second passed.

Mallory did a quick mental replay of her whole dam-burst. Somehow, Eli had kept a perfectly straight face. *Excellent news.* She gasped a laugh. Sort of.

"Is that a chuckle?" Eli dipped his chin to catch her eye. "You're trying not to laugh, aren't you?"

She gave his shoulder a weak push. "You're mildly funny, sometimes."

"Good." His smile was brief. "But I'm also insufferable, sometimes. I want you to know that if I'd had any idea how important Cinderella was to you, I wouldn't have said anything."

She still had his gloves in one fist. She spread the fingers of her other hand wide, then turned her hand over, looking for signs of all the labors it had performed. There weren't any. She had nothing to show for years of caregiving. Nothing.

"I spent a lot of time trying to please a family that thought I was a convenience for them. Why did I allow that? I kept agreeing to their demands. I was *obedient*."

"Mallory." He brushed her hair behind her shoulder, then gave it a little tug, as if she were his sister. "Why do I find 'obedient' so hard to picture?"

She took the question seriously. Why hadn't Eli recognized that the woman arguing with him on the park bench was the girl who'd let herself get stuck with the work nobody else in her family wanted to do?

Because she wasn't that girl any longer. She'd made a plan for a different life, and it was working. Eli was seeing her at her worst tonight, but her worst wasn't as pathetic as it would have been two years ago. She looked into Eli's silver-blue eyes and saw that the Cinderella reflection didn't fit over her image anymore.

"I wish I'd met you on my twentieth birthday." She longed to reach up and push his hair back, the way he did himself. She wanted to trail her fingers along that heavily stubbled jaw. "If we'd debated fairy tales back then, I might have wised up sooner. In case you were wondering, I have wised up. You might find that hard to believe after this evening, but I wouldn't be here in Texas tonight, otherwise. I'd be freezing in Ohio."

"You said a friend gave you some advice two years ago, and you made some hard choices."

"Yes, he…he did." It was flattering that Eli remembered that. She needed to remember that she'd called a book *her friend*.

It was. Her business plan had saved her from her fairy tale.

"Tell me more."

She'd said that earlier, too. Eli's expression was hard to decipher. When he'd stood over her like this at the hay bales, he'd been looking at her like they needed to risk that public indecency charge. He was focused entirely on her once more, but this time, she wasn't certain… "Why?"

"We agreed to pretend to date your way. Talking."

They weren't in public. They didn't have to talk. He must realize that. "Are you trying to be nice to me because I was crying?"

"Not at all. I'm practicing my complete sentences."

He was more than mildly funny, really. She gave his shoulder another push.

As if she'd actually imparted any momentum, he fell back against the pickup truck and stayed there, settling in to spend more time with her.

"Hard choices?" he prompted.

"That's not a complete sentence." She was being difficult, and not entirely by accident. If she wasn't careful, she'd start thinking this was the beginning of a special something. She, the twenty-nine-year-old coed in rain boots and a pink peacoat, starting something new with him, the silver-eyed man in the pricey bomber jacket who had enough unconscious swagger for ten action heroes.

Not likely. Not even in the movies.

"Allow me a second attempt. Mallory, you made an earlier comment concerning a friend's advice and the resultant hard choices you made for yourself and the direction of your life. Share one or two examples with me, if you would."

"You're such a comedian. Who'd have thought it?"

He waited.

She supposed she could answer his question. If it made her sad, well, he'd already seen the worst.

"I had a long talk with that friend, then with myself, trying to get to the essential, underlying question. It was simple, really. 'Am I going to finish my degree?' Yes or no. I'd been waiting for my family's permission to finish college."

She kept her chin up, but she didn't look into the mirror of his eyes. She knew how weak that looked.

"I did need their money, but only because I'd let them convince me that all of the work I was doing was merely part of being a family member, not actually a job. Nobody else in my family was doing the nursing and caretaking, though. Just me. Was I going to finish my degree? The answer was yes, so I had to draw a line in the sand. I told them I wasn't willing to continue without a salary.

"My friend explained things in an unemotional way. I followed his directions to—" That sounded odd. She tried to cover for herself. "To have alternate in-home care options ready to present to them. I even made an appointment with them for us to sit down and discuss it, like I was pitching an opportunity to invest in a start-up."

"A start-up." The corners of Eli's eyes crinkled just a little, that tenth of a smile.

"I was the start-up. They could invest the money in me and get reliable live-in care at a bargain rate in return, or they could hire someone five times more expensive and I'd find someone else to invest in me. One way or another, the new Mallory Ames start-up was going to bring in some money, then turn it into a diploma."

"Well done."

His smile, his approval, his *interest* in her little tale were each their own champagne bubble. The effervescence was pleasant, but champagne wasn't powerful enough to make her forget the reality of where she was and how she'd gotten here.

"Don't think too highly of me. I meant I'd get a job at the Golden Arches or something. But if McDonald's had invested minimum wage in Mallory Ames, that would have been more money than my family had invested, and McDonald's would have gotten one heck of a burger flipper in return."

"Exactly. Well done."

"It was a bluff." Mallory ran her thumb over the cable-knit hat protruding from her pocket, over all the ups and downs and ins and outs. "If I'd moved out and gotten a job somewhere else, I would have had to spend almost every penny I earned on renting someone else's spare bedroom. To make sure it wouldn't come down to that, I only asked for a salary that would amount to this year's tuition. It wasn't even a quarter of what hiring a stranger would cost.

It was still so hard, though. I had just moved into my grandpa's house to care for him, so he was at the meeting, and his sister, my dad, my brother and my brother's wife. Five against one. But my—my *friend* had gone through every possibility with me beforehand. I was ready when the shouting started."

"Your family shouts?"

"Yours doesn't?"

She'd meant it flippantly, but curiosity made her pause for an answer.

"No."

She made a rolling motion with her hand. *Keep going, that's not a complete sentence.*

His lips quirked. "I haven't tried to hold a business meeting with them. My younger sister can be dramatic, if memory serves."

"My brother always shouts. People hate the noise and leave the room, so he wins that way. It's not a fair way to play the game, but I knew he'd do it. When he threw my paperwork back at me, I wasn't surprised. I'd presented actual contracts from a couple of caregiving services, and he picked out the fact that the professional caregivers were allowed to eat one meal a day away from their patient, but they had to pay for that meal. He acted like that invalidated every other point." Mallory imitated her brother's most patronizing tone. "'Haven't you noticed? You never have to pay for your lunch.'"

Eli made a rolling motion with his hand. *And? Keep going.*

"I told him this meeting wasn't about a sandwich. It was about a salary."

Eli actually made a sound of amusement—and approval. *Pop* went another champagne bubble.

"So, long story short, my dad took over. Instead of shouting, he got all weepy, saying he'd always wanted his little baby girl to be a happy homemaker, not the ungrateful woman before him. I kept pretending I was cool and confident. Once they realized the shouting and tears didn't work, they dropped that and started talking. From that point on, it was simple math. My salary request was so much less expensive than hiring someone to take care of Grandpa, it was an easy decision for them once they realized I meant business."

Eli looked serious in the starlight.

"No pun intended," she added.

He still looked serious. "Why do you describe yourself as pretending?"

"'Fake it 'til you make it,' that's my mantra."

"But why have you chosen it? I haven't seen any evidence that it applies to you."

"You're saying this after witnessing my crying episode, up close and personal?"

He crossed his arms over his chest. "You weren't pretending to cry."

"I know that." She crossed her arms over her chest, too, and leaned her back against the side of the pickup truck behind her. The trucks were parked so that a door could be opened for a driver to get in, but no farther apart than that. They spoke across the width of a truck door like they were speaking across the width of an executive desk. Mallory wanted that type of success, that financial security. Yet here she was, leaning against someone else's pickup truck, breaking rule after rule of her business plan, discarding everything that had worked for the past two years.

This was for one night only. They hadn't exchanged phone numbers or addresses, or even offered their last names. She might have mentioned hers in passing just now, but it wasn't like he was going to memorize every detail about her. He wanted a one-night, fake date, too.

She wasn't abandoning a good plan; she was pausing it. She looked at Eli in the soft, gray night and stopped pretending that she was any future version of herself.

"It's exhausting to keep up this big façade of being an energetic, goal-oriented person. You should see me at work. I've got a part-time campus job where I sit in a cubicle with an outdated desktop computer, and I type up things I'm told to type up. That's all there is to it, but I dress like I'm going to call a team into the conference room for a meeting. I'm faking it because I wish I had a job where I needed to wear business attire instead of rain boots and hand-me-downs." She tugged on the collar of her coat and sheepishly squinted at him through one eye. "I'm vain enough that I only kept the good hand-me-downs. It makes it easier to pretend I'm successful."

Eli remained serious, as if even that information wasn't trivial. "If you have a job that you perform in business attire, then you aren't pretending you have a job where you wear business attire. If your family shouted and cried, and you remained both unemotional and on topic, then you didn't pretend that you were cool and confident. You were."

"On the outside. My heart was pounding in my chest because I was so scared I'd fail. My heart was breaking a little, too. My grandpa was the person who could have ended up in a stranger's care if I'd failed. He was the last relative I took care of, and I enjoyed living with him the most. The irony was that he was the only person in the family who thought I was doing the right thing by threatening to find a job that paid something."

"Is this the grandpa who told you about men and marriage?"

"Yes. He taught me so much about life. I really miss him."

"I'm sorry for your loss." Eli said.

"Oh, he's not dead. He's ninety-three and kicking. He moved into an assisted-living apartment complex in August, just before I came down here to start the fall semester. He did that for me, so I wouldn't feel guilty about leaving him."

She had to pause for another breath. She couldn't cry on Eli again.

"He gave up his *house* for me. I still can't believe it. Before we moved out, he overheard me making calls to find a ride share to get from Ohio to Texas. He gave me his car. He signed the title over to me, so it wasn't a loaner car I'd feel obliged to return. He said he didn't need it anymore, because the assisted-living center provides shuttles to doctors and grocery stores and everything.

"I pretended it all made me as joyful as my grandpa wanted it to make me, but it tore me up inside. I didn't cry, though. I can usually hold my tears. There's just something about tonight that's been getting to me." She exhaled heavily. "I'm sorry you got stuck with all this crying."

Eli shrugged away her apology. "You don't make a very good Cinderella."

That sounded insulting. Cinderella was iconic, the perfect example of how a woman should be endlessly patient, never unkind. Cinderella was beautiful, too, the center of attention as she gracefully entered the palace in her sparkly blue—yikes. Maybe the glamour was a bigger factor than Mallory wanted to admit.

Eli looked stern, like a principal about to lecture a student who was wasting their potential, or a police chief about to dress down the rookie. "Cinderella only went to her ball because of someone else's magic. You're here, in the middle of your ball, because you earned it yourself with your own hard work."

"What?"

He didn't give her the *unnecessary question* look. Instead, he pushed himself off the truck and placed his hands on her crossed arms, cupping her elbows, pulling her up to stand in front of him.

"It wasn't Cinderella's type of hard work, doing whatever chores others dictated she would do. You are the one who determined what needed to be done, not your family. You worked hard on the right things to hit your goals."

That praise sounded excessive. "I wouldn't have managed it on my own, if I hadn't gotten good advice from my friend."

"People get excellent advice all the time, but that doesn't make them successful. You were smart enough to recognize which advice could work for you, and you were dedicated enough to implement it."

He spoke with authority, but there was something in his expression that said she wasn't his underling. She was important. She mattered. It didn't remind her of anyone else in any movie at all. This was just him. Talking to just her.

"Don't cry over Cinderella again. You aren't anything like her. It's very clear that she doesn't measure up to you."

Mallory looked at her leading man under the starlight, and she felt one last tear slip from the corner of her eye to roll elegantly down her cheek like a bit of movie magic.

Eli ran his finger up her cheek, stopping it in its tracks and whisking it away.

"I'm sorry I agreed to this fake date," she whispered.

"Why is that?"

"Because I would kiss you right now, if we were real."

Chapter Seven

Never be afraid to speak the truth.
>—How to Taylor Your Business Plan
>*by E.L. Taylor*

"Nobody wants a fake kiss," said Mallory.

Eli looked at the woman he wanted to kiss more than he could remember wanting to kiss a woman in a long, long time. Far longer than since September.

Mallory bit her lip.

"I'll take a fake kiss," he said.

"It wouldn't feel like a real one." There was a breathless note in her voice that affected him as much as that lip-bite.

Nevertheless, Eli let go of her arms. She'd had

an emotional evening, too much of it his fault. He shouldn't push.

But E.L. Taylor had habits that were hard to break. He could be ruthless when he knew what he wanted. He could also charm when he needed to charm, and he could balance those two things, because E.L. Taylor was a very good negotiator.

So, he let go, but he didn't step back. "In the pavilion, you said I couldn't know that heroes ought to be avoided, unless I'd met a hero in the past. The same logic applies here. You can't know if a fake kiss will or won't feel right unless you try it."

She lowered her gaze to his mouth, so with the taste of victory on the tip of his tongue, he moved a little closer, ready for that kiss. She had only to sway toward him.

Abruptly, she lifted her gaze —and her chin, too. "Who said I've never tried it before, Eli?"

You really think you're God's gift to women. Same tone of voice. No one else spoke to him like that, ever.

His smile wasn't intentional. "Fearless."

"I've got standards," she said.

"So do I. You exceed them all."

"Eli." She shook her head ever so slowly, a dimple appearing as she fought not to smile. "Eli."

It's Taylor.

If Mallory kissed him, she would be kissing an imposter named Eli. He wasn't playing fair. He was withholding information that would surely change the game.

But he *was* Eli. He had been more than half his life,

until he'd come here, to this town. Until, at age eighteen, he'd entered Masterson University and seized the opportunity to be someone else, a man of his own design: E.L. Taylor, the multi-millionaire entrepreneur, the hotshot with the model *du jour* on his arm, the man who had it all.

This September, he'd seen that for the lie it was. He couldn't defy gravity, and when he'd fallen from the sky, he'd known that his life, like everyone else's, could be lost on a dime. If Mallory kissed the real Taylor, she'd be kissing a man who'd nearly died without leaving behind anything that anyone would mourn. His stocks and homes and cars would not have ceased to exist. They would have been divided among his family by a law firm that would've charged an outrageous bill rate. Only Taylor himself would have ceased to exist, and nobody would have missed having him in their lives—not his terse conversation, not his cold companionship, not even his business acumen.

Mallory would be better off kissing the fake boyfriend. The real E.L. Taylor wasn't worth a dime.

"I only give real kisses." Mallory placed her hand on the side of his face, tentatively. He could feel the gentle hold, but not more, not through the bristles that he hadn't shaved in too many days. Then her thumb stroked a little higher, over his cheekbone, and he felt her cool skin touching his. She pushed a few of her fingers through his hair, smoothing back a piece that must have fallen forward, and his eyes closed in reaction, as if she'd stroked him somewhere much lower, much harder, someplace where the touch would have a purpose.

"Since you were kind enough to hold me while I cried real tears, here is a real kiss." She rose on her toes as she tilted his head down, and she placed warm lips just above his left eyebrow, on the spot she'd just bared with her fingertips. "Thank you for being so patient and kind."

She stepped back.

Eli Taylor stayed as he was, head bowed, humbled by a kiss that had no other purpose.

Mallory bumped into the pickup truck behind herself.

She'd done it. She'd touched him, she'd kissed him, and now she'd backed herself into a corner where the only gracious thing left to do was leave with whatever dignity she still had after crying her heart out with a stranger. She gave her cheeks one final wipe with the hand that had just touched Eli's face—his beard, his hair, all real, all warm.

Bodies... She'd spent so many years caring for bodies in distress, she'd forgotten that a touch could be warm and sexy, a touch between two people who were attracted to one another, equally vulnerable— but that wasn't the case here. Mallory hadn't seen any vulnerability in him at all. He was just this alpha male who said the perfect thing now and then.

This birthday party is a fantasy, remember? Time to go back to the dorm, Mallory.

She took her ski cap out of her pocket. The mitten

came out, too, and fell to the ground. She bent to pick it up, although, really, what was the point?

Eli bent to get it, too, so they ended up with an awkward moment, an attempt not to butt heads. His arms were longer, and he snagged the mitten before she did.

She'd been holding his gloves in her fist this whole time. "Here. I'll trade you."

She took her single mitten and slapped it on her jeans a time or two. The reason she'd stuffed it in her pocket when she'd first stood next to Eli was so she wouldn't look like a beggar with only one. She pretended she still had two, but just didn't want to wear them. "This is just too sandy to wear. I'll wash it later."

"You wore only one mitten when you first walked up to me."

So much for that little attempt at fakery.

"That peripheral vision of yours is really something, because you sure as heck didn't even glance at me while I was brushing the sand off my boot. I know, because I was looking at you the whole time, ready to give you a nice, fake smile. Yet somehow you noticed I was wearing only one mitten?"

He was back to the *unnecessary question* mode, apparently. The expression on his face wasn't as supercilious as before, though. It was awfully close to concern.

"Yes, I only have one." She tried to make it sound funny. "You know what they call a single mitten?"

"No."

She smacked it one more time, a mess of blue wool and sand. "A rag."

She'd thought it would sound clever in the context of their Cinderella conversation, but it fell flat. It was too true. One mitten was useless.

"Where's the other one?"

"At a fraternity party, apparently." She stuffed the mitten back in her pocket. "Better it than me."

"Frat boys?" He looked upward, picturing something in his mind. "Three of them, to the left of us. Kappa Lambda on one jacket."

"Is peripheral vision your superpower? I would swear you didn't look away from that bonfire for a second. I thought you were having a staring contest with it. You were winning, by the way."

His frown was so sudden, she thought she'd angered him.

"Is that a bad thing?" she asked.

He shook his head, a single, sharp no. "I assumed you were trying to make one of them jealous. They were frat boys. You looked like a coed. It made sense. But when I picked you up—"

"When you threw me on a hay bale."

"When I saw that you weren't that young, I assumed they couldn't be who you were avoiding. I stopped paying attention to them."

"You didn't see them flip me the bird?"

"Obviously not. I wouldn't have let that stand." He scrubbed his beard in an angry sort of way. Mallory imagined the rasp of those whiskers on his palm was stimulating—or punishing. "It's not an excuse, but I was distracted by..." He fell silent.

"By me? The *femme fatale* in the sandy rubber boots?" She laughed, mostly so he'd stop being so serious about it. He shouldn't feel badly for not challenging three guys who hadn't done anything in his sight.

"By having a large bird making herself at home on my head. If I'd seen them flipping—"

"This is excellent news. Maybe not as good as the other excellent news I clued you into tonight, but if you were that distracted, then you don't know how I responded. Please assume that I was far too mature to flip them off in return."

"Did you?"

"Oh, yes. I was quite brave, hiding behind you. If they'd gotten angrier, though, you could have found yourself in the middle of something you didn't know I was instigating over the top of your head. It wasn't fair of me to risk that happening to you."

He waved off her concern. "It's all part of the fake boyfriend duties. Anytime, Mallory."

And then, he winked.

That wink hit every note that made her body sing. Fun, sexy, confident, *intimate*, a wink meant for no one except her.

She looked away, down the row of pickups, for a breath or two. "You know, you can be really charming when you want to be."

"That's also excellent news. I feel pretty damned rusty."

"Nothing an oilcan can't fix. Practicing could help, too."

Pull me close again. Touch my hair again.

He didn't. She was rusty at the dating game herself, an understatement if there ever was one, but he sure seemed like a man who was into her. Then again, he kept his hands clasped behind his back, a soldier standing at ease, content to look at her and talk, no need to touch.

She had a need to touch, so she reached up to skim her fingertips across the forehead she'd kissed. "You don't have laugh lines, but you don't have permanent frown lines, either. You know how they wonder if a zebra is black with white stripes or white with black stripes? I'm wondering if Eli is an angry man who can be sweet sometimes, or if he's a very nice man who has something in particular to glower about tonight."

"I'm thirty-two," he said. "It's a little soon to have acquired either."

"But which are you on your way to getting?"

"I've smiled more tonight than I have in a year."

"Must be the hot chocolate."

"It's you."

The silence should have been electric, a prelude to more. *Ask me for my number. Kiss me in the starlight.*

Eli remained content to simply look at her. He'd stated a fact. Nothing more.

It was up to her, then. "If you'd like to practice smiling and being conversational, maybe you could come back another night. Or a lot of nights. I live here—I mean, near here, obviously—so I come here a lot of nights. I'll be coming here. I did, the other Decembers that I lived in Masterson. I like the Yule log." Mallory cringed inside. She sounded breathless and awkward, Baby announcing she'd carried a watermelon.

Eli practiced his rusty smile on her, the remote, polite one that gave her that déjà vu feeling. "This is my first and last night in the fake boyfriend business."

Mallory translated that too easily: *I won't be seeing you again.*

"But it's been a memorable night," he said. "Thank you for sharing your twenty-ninth birthday with me."

Goodbye.

Of course. She should have known, she *had* known, that she couldn't stay with a handsome man under a night sky forever. It was time to get back to the real world, back to campus, back to her dorm and its fluorescent ceiling light.

To get there, she'd have to walk down the row of booths where she'd stopped and cried in a stranger's arms. Some people would remember the girl who'd publicly bawled in a hard-to-miss Paris-Hilton-pink coat. They'd be curious as she walked by in the other direction, trying to guess how that had turned out.

She must still look like a mess. She nodded toward the light that came through the space between the booths. "I'm going to sneak over there and take one of their napkins. I need to wipe my face off and get my act together a little bit. You never know if you'll run into a professor or a coworker. I'd like to be able to fake like I haven't spent the evening on an emotional roller coaster."

Eli pulled a crisp white napkin from his back pocket. "Courtesy of the nuns. It came with the hot chocolate."

"Thanks." Mallory wiped her nose and face and tried not to compare the coarse napkin to the soothing way Eli had smoothed her hair off her cheek. The napkin went into her pocket with the mitten and the wish and the mini pine cone. No sense in making both of her pockets bulge out unattractively.

She pulled on her ski cap and did a little hasty hair-tucking, leaving it long down her back. "Okay, how do I look?"

"You look perfect."

She waved away his pat answer. "I mean, is it obvious I've been crying? Are my eyes bloodshot? It's probably too dark for you to tell here, but it will be light over there."

"You look perfect." There was just a touch of that *unnecessary question* tone in his voice. He'd declared her perfect. End of discussion.

She put her hands on her hips. "Seriously? My nose isn't even red?"

"It's cold outside."

"So, yes, it's red."

"You look perfect, Mallory."

"Then you're not a very tough critic."

"I'm a very harsh critic, and I choose my words deliberately. If something is perfect, then no part of it needs to change. You're perfect."

She sighed. "It's just as well this is only for one night. I couldn't keep up this pretense much longer."

"What are you still pretending to be?"

"Perfect on top of fearless, apparently. If you spent more than a few hours with me, you'd realize I was nowhere close to either one. The advice to act like I'm already the person I want to be sounds good, but it has a lot of pitfalls. That might be one thing to discuss with my friend next semester. He'll be here, at MU."

"We've already discussed it," Eli said, and in her fantasy, he sounded slightly jealous that she'd be continuing their conversation with someone else. "You aren't faking anything important."

"Just the business attire, huh? I must look pretentious in my cubicle, dressed more formally than everyone else."

"Only if 'formal' means a ball gown."

She was very sorry the evening had to end. "You're pretty perfect at lifting my spirits, Eli. Thank you for being my fake boyfriend on my birthday."

That seemed so inadequate for an evening that had been full of self-discovery, spent with a man who knew just how to comfort her, whether with a hug or a stern lecture.

Never be afraid to speak the truth.

She looked into his eyes one last time, wanting to see herself the way he saw her. "I hope we run into each other again."

Those eyes narrowed. "You're leaving?"

"I thought... We said this was for one night only."

After an eternal second, he didn't contradict her,

but his answer made her heart take a hopeful hop. "It doesn't have to be a short night."

She should leave. Her brain might continue to remember this was only a fantasy, but her heart just wasn't listening.

No, thank you. I must go. It was firm, decisive, final, and it would protect her vulnerable heart.

Instead, she waffled, gesturing vaguely toward the back of the stage and the booths. "We've done everything there is to do, really."

"The night is still young. What else do people do in Masterson to celebrate a birthday?"

"It's a college town. They hit twenty-one and drink themselves into oblivion."

"I was here for my twenty-first. I know that much. But you're an ancient twenty-nine. This is my first time back since I graduated. Where do the old folks go?"

"Very funny." She tried to be tart, but her heart was feeling bubbly—*The night is young!*—and Eli was jarringly adorable when he tried to be funny, a brooding James Dean breaking character, laughing in an outtake on a blooper reel.

"We could go to the Tipsy Musketeer. They're still the most strict about checking IDs, and they don't sell dirt-cheap booze, so there won't be a lot of college students there. Their live musicians are really good, too."

"I remember the place." But Eli was looking regretful or hesitant or something. "It will be crowded on a Saturday night."

So that was it. She should have put two and two together sooner. He'd chosen to be all alone out by the hay bales. He'd spent their first fifteen minutes on the pavilion bench looking at every passerby as if they were his personal enemy—and he'd hidden his face with his cup more than once. As bold and confident as Eli seemed to be, he wasn't comfortable in crowds.

"Or, if you don't want to walk all the way to Athos Avenue, we could stay here," she offered, giving him distance as an easy excuse rather than whatever his issue was with crowds. "I'm up for another cup of hot chocolate—oh. Never mind. I'm not trying to get you to spend more of your real money on your fake girlfriend."

"The nuns aren't charging enough to break the bank. Besides, we both could use another chance to hold a hot cup to warm our hands."

"You could just put on your gloves."

He began pulling one on. Unlike her, his larger hand needed to ease its way into the tight leather. "You could put on your mitten."

"It's too sandy. I'm not going to look dorky in one mitten and have sand itching me in between my fingers, too."

He fastened his right glove with the snap at his wrist, looking so damned James Bond cool that Mallory barely registered that his gloves must have been custom-made to fit him so perfectly.

"In that case, here." He picked up her left hand and put his left glove on her, like he was dressing a child.

"What are you doing? Are you going to make us both look dorky?"

He held out his bare left hand. She placed her bare right hand in his, and he laced his fingers between hers. They stood together in between the trucks, holding hands. "There. Now we'll both have two warm hands."

"My hand must feel like an icicle in yours."

"Not for long."

That unconscious arrogance, that certainty that he could handle anything physical, like warming up her hand quickly with his own, made Mallory's heart hop and flutter every which way.

Eli started walking toward the booths, holding her hand. She fell into step beside him and savored the sensation of being in sync.

He led her past the boxes and around the propane tanks. They walked into the light, and not one person at the festival looked at Mallory with concern or pity. Only envy followed her on their way to the St. Margaret's booth.

Eli paid for their drinks with a folded bill, which he handed to the nun with a murmured, "Keep the change." As they walked away, Mallory carried her cup in her gloved hand. So did Eli—such a coincidence. He took her bare hand in his once more, and her heart hopped and bubbles popped—not a coincidence at all.

Behind them, the nuns burst into excited twitters, sounding just like her heart.

"Either they're very excited to see us holding hands," Mallory said, "or you gave them a really big tip."

"I wanted us to be set for refills the rest of the night. We can trade gloves and hold a hot cup with our other hands next." Eli gave her hand a squeeze, a move as casually intimate as that wink.

Hop. Pop.

"Let's get out of this crowd," Eli said. "We're going to get bumped and spill our drinks any second now. We're flirting with danger."

I know I am.

Eli was being so charming, it was going to be hard for a real guy to live up to it on a real date. She had a feeling a fake kiss with Eli would set a new standard that any real kiss wouldn't be able to match. It was a good thing she didn't do fake kisses.

On the other hand, she'd broken half of E.L. Taylor's rules tonight.

Before she returned to reality, why not break one of her own?

Get Up To 4 Free Books!

Dear Reader,

IT'S A FACT: if you answer 4 quick questions, we'll send you 4 FREE REWARDS from each series you try!

Try **Harlequin® Desire** books featuring the worlds of the American elite with juicy plot twists, delicious sensuality and intriguing scandal.

Try **Harlequin Presents®** Larger-Print books featuring the glamourous lives of royals and billionaires in a world of exotic locations, where passion knows no bounds.

Or **TRY BOTH!**

I'm not kidding you. As a leading publisher of women's fiction, we value your opinions... and your time. That's why we are prepared to reward you handsomely for completing our mini-survey. In fact, we have 4 Free Rewards for you, including 2 free books and 2 free gifts from each series you try!

Thank you for participating in our survey,

Pam Powers

To get your 4 FREE REWARDS:
Complete the survey below and return the insert today to receive up to 4 FREE BOOKS and FREE GIFTS guaranteed!

"4 for 4" MINI-SURVEY

1 Is reading one of your favorite hobbies?

☐ YES ☐ NO

2 Do you prefer to read instead of watch TV?

☐ YES ☐ NO

3 Do you read newspapers and magazines?

☐ YES ☐ NO

4 Do you enjoy trying new book series with FREE BOOKS?

☐ YES ☐ NO

Please send me my Free Rewards, consisting of **2 Free Books from each series I select** and **Free Mystery Gifts**. I understand that I am under no obligation to buy anything, as explained on the back of this card.

☐ **Harlequin Desire®** (225/326 HDL GQ3X)
☐ **Harlequin Presents® Larger-Print** (176/376 HDL GQ3X)
☐ **Try Both** (225/326 & 176/376 HDL GQ4A)

FIRST NAME   LAST NAME

ADDRESS

APT.#   CITY

STATE/PROV.   ZIP/POSTAL CODE

EMAIL ☐ Please check this box if you would like to receive newsletters and promotional emails from Harlequin Enterprises ULC and its affiliates. You can unsubscribe anytime.

HD/HP-520-MS20

HARLEQUIN READER SERVICE—Here's how it works:

Accepting your 2 free books and 2 free gifts (gifts valued at approximately $10.00 retail) places you under no obligation to buy anything. You may keep the books and gifts and return the shipping statement marked "cancel." If you do not cancel, approximately one month later we'll send you more books from the series you have chosen, and bill you at our low, subscribers-only discount price. Harlequin Presents® Larger-Print books consist of 6 books each month and cost $5.80 each in the U.S. or $5.99 each in Canada, a savings of at least 11% off the cover price. Harlequin Desire® books consist of 6 books each month and cost just $4.55 each in the U.S. or $5.24 each in Canada, a savings of at least 13% off the cover price. It's quite a bargain! Shipping and handling is just 50¢ per book in the U.S. and $1.25 per book in Canada*. You may return any shipment at our expense and cancel at any time — or you may continue to receive monthly shipments at our low, subscribers-only discount price plus shipping and handling. *Terms and prices subject to change without notice. Prices do not include sales taxes which will be charged (if applicable) based on your state or country of residence. Canadian residents will be charged applicable taxes. Offer not valid in Quebec. Books received may not be as shown. All orders subject to approval. Credit or debit balances in a customer's account(s) may be offset by any other outstanding balance owed by or to the customer. Please allow 3 to 4 weeks for delivery. Offer available while quantities last.

Chapter Eight

Never allow yourself to be rushed into a decision.
—How to Taylor Your Business Plan
by E.L. Taylor

They were moving into the adult portion of the evening.

Alcoholic beverages were being drunk. Adult dancers had taken the stage. Eli glanced around the mostly child-free, late-night crowd, shaking his head. The adult portion of anything in Masterson was still shockingly wholesome.

The dancers on the stage were performing German folk dances, a lingering bit of culture from the German settlers who had established towns throughout Central Texas in the 1800s. The stage had been set with a tall maypole, made slightly less anachronous in the month of December by sporting red-and-white ribbons. It was slowly turning into a woven candy cane as men in lederhosen circled in one direction and women in dirndl dresses circled in the opposite direction. The men and women never touched. Wholesome.

Because a large number of Spanish and Mexican people had settled Texas, too, the hungry members of the audience were using their German beers to wash down burritos. And because Texas had been and still was cattle country, those burritos were stuffed with a cowboy standard, barbecued beef brisket. All the facets of Texas blended in a wholesome harmony.

There wasn't much seating available, so the fat branch of a live oak, sprawling low along the ground, was being used by Eli and a dozen other people as a place to sit. He sat closest to the massive trunk, using it as a shield from curious eyes. Eli had the surprising, astonishing Mallory Ames sharing his seat, sitting between his thighs. He'd bought her one-dollar hot chocolate with a one-hundred-dollar bill. He'd hugged her when she'd cried. He'd held her hand as they'd looked for the best spot to sit and talk, because talking was what she did on dates. Nothing that came close to public indecency.

Because they didn't have the tree to themselves, whenever Mallory had something to say, she'd turn her head and murmur it to him. He'd tilt his head to hear her better, and the closeness of her lips to his cheek made him acutely conscious of the possibility that this time, this comment might be the one where the words on her lips became a kiss on his cheek.

Shockingly wholesome.

The bonfire was at his back, so he benefitted from its light, but he didn't have to visually fight the flames. Distance made all the difference, in fire and everything else. Taylor's money was in a bank far away, but Eli had a few hundred-dollar bills in his pocket. Taylor's residences were in Dallas and New York and Monterrey, but Eli was renting a single-family home here in Masterson for the coming semester, a house which had a tree with a rope swing in the front and a porch that overlooked a lake in the back. His superyacht was berthed somewhere along the coast of Greece, but a rowboat lay at the ready by the rented home's dock.

Distance mattered most of all with Mallory, because there was none. *Mallory*—this woman, this incredible person who laughed and cried and talked to him as she made herself at home on his lap—Mallory was the reason he didn't want the night to end.

From the first moment she'd walked up to him, she'd touched him almost constantly. She let him touch her in return, not a sexual *carte blanche*, but he could sit beside her with his arm across the back of the bench. He could hold her hand. He could loop his arms around her waist as she sat on his lap on the branch of a century-old tree. It was so wholesome, so innocent, yet so addictive, satisfying a craving he hadn't known he had.

Can you identify that emotion, Mr. Taylor?

Mallory shifted in her sideways position. Her legs were over his left thigh and her backside was in the vee between his legs, pressing against his inner right thigh. He could feel her muscle flex as she moved, feel her softness against his inner thigh as she relaxed once more. Her denim jeans rubbed and rested against his denim, two thick layers of material that kept their bodies from actually touching. Being denied the feel of her skin, yet being able to feel the intimate motion of her body against his, created an unexpected level of eroticism, here in a small town's park.

She turned to murmur another little something to him. "I think the accordion player has a thing for one of the dancers. He checks her out every time she circles past him, and she's giving her skirt an extra little swirl to show off."

Her upper lip grazed his cheek, a millimeter of her touching a millimeter of him for the space of a single syllable as she spoke. Would this be it? Would this comment end with a kiss?

The distance between them held as she whispered her secret observation, no kiss, not yet—but a fraction of a second before she turned back around, she took a quick little breath. Had that been intentional? Had she snuck in a taste of his body heat, tempted herself with the warmth of his skin?

He'd never in his life wanted to kiss a woman this badly. He'd never imagined it was possible to want to kiss someone this badly.

She wanted to kiss him, too. She'd almost kissed

him a half dozen times this evening, at the hot chocolate stand, between the parked pickups and, yes,
over by the hay bales. He knew her expressions better now, enough to know he hadn't been wrong then.
She wanted to kiss him, but she wouldn't let herself do
it, because she'd told him she didn't give fake kisses.

It wasn't possible for Eli to receive any other kind.
Eli was a fake.

No matter how far Taylor distanced himself from
his real life, he was E.L. Taylor. He always would be,
until the day he didn't narrowly escape death, whether
that happened in seventy years or tomorrow. He was
withholding information from Mallory. He was playing the game unfairly.

Mallory slipped her left arm around his waist,
making herself comfortable. Tomorrow, she would
still be Mallory, wearing business attire to her campus job and studying in her dorm. He would wake up
alone in a six-bedroom lake house and be E.L. Taylor.

Loneliness.

Taylor had spent October and November naming
the feelings he'd known in the years before the terror
of the plane crash: anger, impatience, tension, disgust,
triumph. But he'd overlooked *loneliness*. Even his
expensive therapist had missed it, but it was easy to
identify, now that Mallory had made it go away this
evening. He'd been lonely as E.L. Taylor.

Emotions didn't last forever, not terror, not calm,
not loneliness. But loneliness had been around the
longest, so it was hard to imagine it as temporary. It
wasn't: all the warmth they were building between

them would freeze when he admitted the truth—when he admitted he'd lied. He would be lonely again after this evening.

"Do you see it?" Mallory said under her breath. "Watch."

Taylor—no, he was Eli, for tonight—Eli watched what Mallory wanted him to watch, glad to delay the inevitable. Onstage, the accordion player was looking right through the dancers in front of him for some-one else. A female dancer caught his eye, and she gave her apron an extra swoosh, flipping it up a little higher and showing a little more stocking-clad leg as she sashayed past the oompah band, peeking over her shoulder to be sure that one particular musician had appreciated it.

"I see it," Eli said.

Mallory made that rolling gesture. "Practicing, remember?"

He gave an exaggerated sigh. "Why yes, Ms. Fear-less, I do see it. It's fascinating, like one of those bi-zarre mating dances between two birds. Two very large, very German birds."

She pressed into him harder for just a moment, the tree-branch equivalent of her earlier shoulder shoves. "Very funny."

The idea that anyone found him funny was amus-ing to him, so he had a bit of a smile on his lips when she turned her head toward him and said, "Seriously, you—"

She blinked, a flash of feminine lashes covering a moment of surprise—at what? His smile? Of course he smiled when she was close. With another little catch of her breath, she turned back to the stage to finish her sentence. "You have your moments."

No kiss. Not yet. So close, but they were on a fake date. If he made this a real date, she'd kiss him. He was certain of it.

There was no such thing as a real date with a man who lied about his identity. He was certain of that, too.

Eli silently cursed. If he wanted to make this a real date, if he wanted her to kiss the real man, he was going to have to take her aside after this show, walk with her out to the dark so nobody would recognize him before he had the chance to tell her himself, and then confess that he'd been lying all evening.

Surprise. That would be her first emotion, but then what?

E.L. Taylor was a half billionaire and a half-dozen other things she wasn't expecting. He wasn't a loner; he was popular wherever he went. He wasn't an anonymous guy in a college town; he was a leader in the world of venture capitalism.

Someone farther down the branch got off, making everyone sway for a moment as the tree adjusted to the lighter weight. Between his thighs, he felt Mallory use the muscles in her backside and legs to hold onto him, not the tree. She trusted him not to fall and take her down with him.

She was so relaxed around him, a woman with nothing to hide. She knew which was her public persona and which was her private, and she'd shown him both tonight. He respected her self-awareness.

He wasn't there yet. He had to force himself to dig deeper than surface-level. He wasn't popular; he was famous. The people who looked up to him as a leader were the owners of the start-ups Eli had chosen to invest in. He was resented by those he hadn't helped, feared by those who knew he could buy them, sell them or ruin them at will. He didn't make friends in his line of work.

But he was rich. In his experience, being rich made up for a lot of flaws in every aspect of life. He rarely spent any time with his family, but his parents could live in Monte Carlo because of him, and his siblings, who were twenty-one now, had cars and college degrees and trust funds. He'd heard no complaints about his inability to make Thanksgiving dinner this year. Or last year. Or the year before.

Went it came to girlfriends, being rich was their favorite thing about him. Not being a completely selfish bastard in bed was their second favorite. He couldn't recall a girlfriend having a third favorite thing about him.

You're mildly funny.

Without money, without sex, Mallory liked him. He didn't want to lose that, but the truth would come out. E.L. Taylor couldn't hide on campus for a full semester. She'd see him sooner or later, if only as a face on a poster for the lecture series.

He hugged Mallory a little tighter. She ought to

hear the truth from him, which meant he had to tell her tonight.

The German dancers began turning their circles in the opposite direction, undoing all their weaving. The maypole's ribbons unraveled at a steady, rhythmic pace. Eli's time was running out.

It would be okay. She was going to be angry that Eli had been a trick, even a test, but then she'd be delighted that Taylor was rich. It was always okay, when one had money.

Eli studied Mallory's profile, imagining the way her face would take on that avaricious gleam he was so accustomed to seeing on other faces, the one that let him get away with so much.

He couldn't picture it. When he told her the truth tonight, no greedy glint would come to her eye—but she would know he was looking for it. He'd made it clear that her heroine, Cinderella, wanted wealth to solve all her problems.

He cringed now at the way he'd accused her— accused every little girl, which meant every woman, since they'd all been little girls—of wanting to latch onto Prince Charming for the castles and gowns his money could buy. In Mallory's version of the story, Prince Charming didn't have to be rich. *It's having enough respect for yourself to be with people you can trust,* she'd said, before he'd made her cry, *instead of people who'll lie to you to keep you where they want you.*

He'd lied from the start to keep her with him, to use her as a light in another dark night. Eli wasn't her

Prince Charming. *Choose whichever set of earrings you like* wasn't happiness in her book, but it was all he had to offer. Money, lies, and crippled emotions.

Over, under, around and around the dancers went, unweaving the ribbons until they finished with a twirl that detached them completely. The maypole stood bare. The people applauded.

Eli accepted his fate. This date was for one night only. In a few months, he'd leave Masterson and return to his usual life. He'd fly to Manhattan, he'd return to Dallas, he'd take a business trip to Tokyo, but he'd remember this one night and that one pure kiss. He'd wonder where Mallory was and how she was doing.

And who she was with.

"Tell me about this friend of yours who's coming next semester. Is he still in Ohio now?"

He felt the change in her body, an increase in muscle tension.

"My friend." She traced the seam of her jeans with her finger. With his glove. "My friend would be very disappointed in me if he saw me this evening."

"I imagine if you were my friend, I wouldn't be thrilled to have you spending an evening with another man, either. Not even on a fake date."

"It's nothing like that. He's been my coach."

Sure, it isn't. He'd bet her coach saw it differently. Eli took a moment to brush her hair behind her shoulder as if it had been caught between them. Then he put his arm back around her with a silent F-U to the guy in Ohio. *Eat your heart out, friend. Tonight, for these hours, she's mine.*

"He's very adamant that you should never put all your faults and doubts on display."

Eli shrugged, unimpressed. "That's nothing more than the code of the male locker room. Everyone pretends they'll win the game that day, even in the middle of a losing season."

She turned abruptly in his arms. "Ha. I caught you. That's just faking it until you make it. You've done it, too."

He raised an eyebrow at her, but it was hard to be supercilious in the face of her playful enthusiasm. "I said that was the code of the male locker room. I didn't say I lived by it."

"He does. I do, too, but I pretty much broke that rule five minutes after I met you. I don't know what it was about sitting on that hay bale behind you—"

"Leaning on top of my head."

He hadn't stopped her, because it hadn't felt bad, and not entirely unfamiliar—in a flash, he realized why. The sensation had been similar to carrying his little sister in a piggyback ride. He'd forgotten all about that, until this second. When he was a teenager and they were little children, his brother and sister had climbed all over him like he was their jungle gym.

"—staring at the bonfire. I guess staring at the fire is more likely to make you think deep thoughts than staring at these guys doing this slap-yourself dance.

This is the silliest-looking dance, you have to admit. I couldn't cry about anything right now if I wanted to."

He was aware she was laughing, but the images in his head were too vivid to ignore. His brother, his sister, piggyback rides... Old memories he'd buried so deep, he'd forgotten them. A black lake, a fiery explosion... New memories he wanted to bury deep, but couldn't.

"I shouldn't joke about that, should I?" Mallory sounded subdued.

Eli had to pull himself back to the conversation. Mallory had turned toward him more fully. There was a little wrinkle between her eyebrows as she waited for him to answer her.

"Joke about crying?" he asked, trying to pick up the thread of the conversation.

"I don't want you to think I'm ungrateful. You had to deal with a pretty big crying episode, and you were very kind. I think I cried so hard because I've haven't cried for two years, not since my friend explained all the ramifications of losing your composure like that."

Eli's sister used to lose it every time he had to return to college. He'd pull out of the drive as a little eight-year-old girl wept for him, and he'd feel like a monster for making her wail. He'd stopped coming home as often after his freshman year, only visiting on the big weekends like Thanksgiving, just so he wouldn't make her cry more times than necessary. To this day, he preferred anger to tears. Tonight, he'd tried to get Mallory to rant and rave at him, rather than cry.

He never cried. He hadn't even cried with relief when he'd gotten out of the plane wreck alive. He'd held Mallory to his chest tonight, though, as she'd cried hard enough for the two of them. Maybe he'd felt calm when she'd regained her calm because he'd finally stuck it out long enough to see that crying wasn't as frightening as he'd thought for so long. How could he have been so damned afraid of tears?

Man up. Big boys don't cry. Never let them see that they've gotten to you, son.

Of course, that was it.

It angered him that Mallory's friend was making her afraid to cry, too.

"For two years, you haven't let yourself cry?" he asked.

"I used to lose it over every little thing. Christmas movies. Greeting card commercials. The frustration of trying to get medical records sent to the right hospital."

"One of those things is not like the others."

"I know. But that was before I, um, I met my friend. I decided not to let myself cry about anything, ever. If I won't cry at lost-pet posters, then I won't cry when I'm under pressure to present an important paper at work, someday. I just stopped crying, cold turkey."

"That sounds wrong. What kind of friend prohibits another friend from crying at all for two years?"

"That was my idea. His was not to cry in front of anybody."

If Eli had the chance to go back and hug his eight-year-old sister before he got in his car and returned to college, he'd stand in the driveway and hold her until her tears dried up and she could wave instead of wail. He would have felt better during his drive back to Masterson for having done so. Instead, to avoid feeling bad, he'd avoided coming home to someone who'd wanted a piggyback ride.

That had been the wrong decision, and only now did he see how steep the cost had been. He looked into Mallory's eyes as the loss hit him.

Bye-bye, Eli.

Then he breathed again and cupped the side of her face in his palm. "I don't think this friend's advice is good for you."

"Why not?"

"He sounds like an idiot."

Chapter Nine

Never make the same mistake twice.
                    —How to Taylor Your Business Plan
                                        by E.L. Taylor

"He's *not* an idiot."

Mallory pulled away from Eli's hand with an angry jerk. This was her birthday fantasy. She was not going to let him ruin it by insulting yet another hero. He'd been right about Cinderella, but E.L. Taylor was different.

Eli persisted. "Your friend doesn't know what he's talking about."

"How can you say that? I told you the whole story. He taught me everything, so that I could navigate my family dynamics and get something productive done."

Eli lowered the empty hand that had been cupping her face. "Is it possible he's being manipulative with your emotions by telling you not to react, not to cry?"

"No. It's not."

He's E.L. Taylor, okay? Not an idiot. Also, he's too busy making millions to bother manipulating me.

Eli was dying to say something else, she could tell. He even opened his mouth, thought better of it and closed it.

The crowd broke into applause. The dancers took their bows. The couple beside them on the branch left, probably unwilling to let Mallory and Eli's quietly tense exchange dampen their festive evening.

Eli sounded sincere. "I'm concerned, but I don't want to randomly criticize anyone's hero. Cinderella taught me not to, earlier. It occurs to me that this guy might be your real-life Prince Charming. In that case, your fake boyfriend is jealous, and you should take his words with a grain of salt."

"Oh. That's a very sweet thing to say." Mallory realized she'd touched her fingertips to her heart, like she was a Disney princess. Goodness gracious.

"Somebody's been hitting me over the head with an oilcan all night. I'm glad to know it's working."

That was so charming. She ought to answer a sweet comment like that with a sweet kiss. The gap left by that missing kiss felt awkward to her.

Eli tapped her knee. "So, is he your real boyfriend? You so sagely pointed out that if you'd had a real boyfriend here, you wouldn't have needed a fake one.

That doesn't mean you don't have a real boyfriend somewhere else. Like in Ohio."

"I sincerely doubt he'd ever be interested in me that way."

He's E.L. Taylor. Also, he's too busy making millions to bother dating an in-home caregiver from Ohio.

She was really embarrassed now for having been too embarrassed at the beginning of the night to admit that she thought of a business book as her best friend.

"He's lucky to have someone who jumps to his defense so quickly," Eli said.

She was stuck with her little white lie now. "I defend him because he does mean a lot to me, but not the way you're thinking. His advice pulled me through a really dark time in my life. I might have stayed stuck forever, reliving my past in my head over and over. He showed me that I had to forget about all the years I'd wasted up to that point."

"That doesn't sound right, either. Don't cry? Forget about your life prior to meeting him?"

"Not *forget*. That was my word, not his." She reached up to wriggle her ski cap into place a little, as if that would get her brain working. She was making Eli more concerned. A concerned man was not going to think about her as a desirable woman. If she was going to break her rule and enjoy a hot kiss with this fake boyfriend, she wanted to make it a good one. A kiss of lust, not pity.

She slid off his lap and the tree branch. She stood and faced him, their eyes on a level, so he could see that she was telling the truth. Mostly. He wasn't going to think sexy thoughts about her if she revealed that she loved a book.

She began with the basics. "Never look back."

Eli looked at her sharply.

"That's what he actually said. Not 'forget about the past.'"

Eli came as close to rolling his eyes as a fierce man could. "That is the most overused, trite advice out there."

She glared at him. "I'm trying not to jump to his defense, but you don't have to make it so difficult with your eye-rolling and your insults."

Eli didn't so much as blink for a beat, but then that tenth of a smile touched the corner of his mouth. "Touché."

He crossed his arms over his chest, but it wasn't a negative gesture. He was giving her all of his attention, anchoring himself in place to listen until she was done, and that was a very, very sexy thing for a man to do.

"I thought his advice was wrong, too. Not just 'never look back,' but all of it. He couldn't possibly know what it was like to be me. But I had nothing to lose at that point, so I tried to do things the way he recommended."

She turned her hands palm-up and shrugged. "It worked. I used to daydream about how wonderful my senior year would have been at twenty-one, but the more I wished I could have already graduated, the more likely it was that I would never graduate.

Once I stopped looking back at the goals I hadn't met, I had nowhere else to direct all my energy, except toward the goals I wanted to meet in the future. It worked. Here I am."

Her explanation must have been better this time. Eli's scowl hadn't returned, although his smile had faded. Poor man, so grim.

"That was an excellent explanation of a frequently meaningless phrase," he said. "You should write a book."

"Ha. No." She laced her fingers together, gloved and bare. "I'm pretty sure it's already been written."

"When we sat on the hay bales, you said you aren't as happy as you thought you'd be, now that you'd gotten what you wanted."

The man didn't forget a thing she said. Sexy.

"That's what I planned to think about tonight, all by myself at the Yule log. Then Kappa Lambda and some wet sand and a stolen mitten and this growly statue that turned out to be an interesting man kind of distracted me, but I think I found my answer tonight, anyway."

She stepped closer, standing in between his knees, and placed her hands on his crossed forearms. Bodies—his was so steady, so solid. She'd been touching him all night, wanting to remind herself how to touch a body that didn't need her to fix it.

"I think the reason I'm not happy is because I'm constantly looking forward. The moment I started this semester, I started looking forward to the next semester. When I think about next semester, I'm planning how I'll manage to speak to the right people and get the right things approved, so I can move to the next goal after graduation. Looking forward is more productive than looking back, so it might be the best way to have a successful career, but it's not ever going to bring me happiness."

"What will?" His voice was a low, delicious rumble. They were standing so close that he didn't need to speak loudly at all. It was a heady feeling, being welcome in his personal space.

"Cinderella got this part right, I think. The key is finding your own people. Someone who is kind to you. Someone who enjoys being with you, maybe someone who says you're perfect even when you know perfectly well that you're not. A champion when you're down. An ally. A friend."

She ran her fingertips over the cheek she'd whispered against during the show, then let her thumb rest on his lower lip. "If this was a real date, I would have kissed you about ten times already."

The lip she touched changed shape, slipping into a smile under her thumb. "I thought you spent your real dates talking."

"I do. I spend real ones and fake ones talking. But I only kiss when they're real. It's a shame this is a fake date, because I've never kissed a man with a beard before."

"If this was a real date, I would have shaved for you."

He smiled wider when her thumb skipped across

his lip, a devilish, arrogant smile. He knew he'd flustered her.

She pretended he hadn't. "I don't know if I'd want you to shave. It's hard to imagine what you'd look like without this." She squinted one eye and pretended she was imagining him without the beard, but she was just admiring him. He did broody and untamed so well.

"Mallory." His mouth was serious now. He was going to say something she didn't want to hear.

She pressed her thumb against his lower lip again. "But if you shave for real dates, then the only way to kiss you with a beard is on a fake date. I happen to be on a fake date."

"You're toying with me, Mallory."

"If this is a game, can I choose my prize? Say, a fake kiss with a man who has a real beard?"

"If you like." He stood, and she took a step back. He was tall, strong, an alpha male fantasy in real life. He could pick her up and take her somewhere, anywhere he wanted to, but he only stood over her as she leaned her back against the tree's massive trunk. The stage lights were bright on the other side of the tree, but she could see enough of him, here in the shadows.

He placed his hand on the bark, right beside her head, and braced his arm, reminding her of the opportunity she'd missed by the hay bales. This spot wasn't nearly as private, but if he kissed her the way she wanted him to kiss her, she'd stop thinking about anyone else in the universe, anyway.

"Or," he said, commanding her attention away from his mouth, back to his eyes.

"Or what?"

"Or, you could spend a weekend in my bed. I'd pick you up on a Friday with a clean shave, because a gentleman shaves for a woman. It's much more pleasant for her when she doesn't want me to be a gentleman, and we risk that public indecency charge somewhere along the way, because she's decided she's too impatient to make it to my place. Then…"

Mallory stopped breathing.

Eli leaned in, murmuring words over her lips, her cheek, her ear. "Friday night…happens. Saturday, all of it, day and night. By Sunday evening, you have this beard once more, to do with as you please, anything we haven't done yet, or everything we already have."

Her heart pounded. "Are you toying with me?"

He paused.

"No," he said gravely. "I don't think I am."

He wanted her, genuinely. A weekend in his bed. Such a big part of her wanted it, too, but she couldn't do this for fun, extending a fake date into a weekend fling. She liked him too much. She had a heart. So did he.

"Eli, Eli." She closed her eyes against the passion smoldering in his. "Can you make this evening turn into something real?"

She felt his pause.

"No, I don't think I can."

Just as she felt her heart start to break, he said, "Not yet."

Chapter Ten

Never fall into the trap of hearing only what you want to hear.

—How to Taylor Your Business Plan
by E.L. Taylor

Mallory opened her eyes.

The man who had just whispered the sexiest words any man had ever whispered to her pushed himself away from the tree that was keeping her upright after she'd melted.

Eli shoved some of his hair back. She hadn't even gotten to mess it up—not yet, anyway.

"When?" she asked.

He shook his head like he didn't know. That was okay, because she didn't know what she was asking, exactly. When would he ask her out on a real date? When would he kiss her, unshaven? Shaven?

When would they spend a weekend in bed?

Her whole body had gone up in flames as he'd whispered those words over her skin, because damn if the part of her that would say *I'm not that kind of girl* was utterly losing the battle with *How far away is your place?*

Her place was a dorm. She had tests to study for. Classes to attend. School, that thing she'd planned for and worked for and left everything behind for— that was real. This was a one-evening fantasy, not a one-night stand. Not a weekend with a gorgeous man who'd let her do anything she wanted to with his strong, healthy body.

Eli unzipped his leather jacket and held out his hand. "Want to take a walk?"

"Please." She pushed off the tree, grabbed his hand and started walking, taking big strides, burning off some of this heat.

Was he as hot and bothered as she was? She needed to watch where she was walking in the dimly lit field, but she took her eyes off the ground to peek at him. Their eyes met, and they both laughed, more than a little sheepishly.

"Well," she sighed, "that was a dumb game to play on a fake date that forbids kisses."

"Yes, it was."

She waited a few strides. "You won, by the way. I hate to admit it, but that was exceptional. No wonder you think you're God's gift to women."

Eli threw back his head and laughed, really laughed, and it was contagious and wonderful, and this was the best date Mallory had ever been on, real or fake.

"Where are we going?"

"I'm open to suggestions," Eli said.

"We've pretty much covered the festival. I'm hot-chocolated out. Maybe there will be another musical act."

"All right."

But they kept walking away from the stage, hand in hand, leaving the crowd and the light behind until it got too dark to walk easily. Their steps slowed to a stop.

As if they hadn't been silent for the last few minutes, Eli picked up the conversation. "What were you thinking of doing with me by the hay bales?"

"I was thinking of doing the same thing I was trying to do with you by the tree, Fake Boyfriend with a Beard, but you're playing hard to get."

Mallory was just able to see his face in the starlight. She tilted her head and pretended to be coquettish, which, according to Eli's logic, meant she was actually being coquettish. She batted her eyelashes, which made her feel coquettish whether he could see it or not.

He sounded amused. "You weren't trying to kiss me by the hay bales."

"I thought about it."

"You were pissed off because I was going to kiss

you. The opposite of this moment, where you're pretending to be pissed off because I didn't kiss you."

"Pretending? I'm honestly curious about the beard, and my curiosity has been denied."

"Allow me to refresh your memory. You stuffed my gloves into my jacket, told me you had planned to show me something that didn't require any money, then told me I was a jerk, so forget it."

"Oh, *that*."

"Yes, that. If I'm back in your good graces, let's do that. What is 'that'?"

Since they were facing one another, they were holding both sets of hands now, and Mallory gave them a little swing. "I'll answer your question if you answer mine."

"Trouble," he said on a sigh.

"Allow me to refresh your memory from five minutes ago, when you said, 'not yet.' What are you going to make real, and when?"

"That's two questions—ow."

She'd squeezed his hands hard for doing that big-brother smart-aleck thing again. "But I'm cute," she added through gritted teeth, "so you'll answer two questions."

"Cute is the wrong word—don't squeeze. Pretty. Vivacious. Expressive."

"You mean talkative?"

"Indomitable."

"Ooh, good one. Is sexy in there?"

"Passionate. About many things."

"Yes, but how about sexy?"

Mallory was laughing too much to sound sexy. The darkness made her feel uninhibited. She could say anything, and if she made a fool of herself, it didn't matter because Eli would only be in her life for one night. She'd have no witness to either her weaknesses or her silliness once they parted ways.

Her laughter caught. She didn't want to part ways.

Eli brought their clasped hands up between their chests. Like a large and lazy lion, he dipped his head and ran his jaw along her knuckles.

The sensuality of him, the reality of him, called to her body and filled her mind. It was her birthday, and she was too old to be Cinderella with a sweet prince. She wanted the seduction of the dark, Jane claimed by a legendary man in the wild, Christine spellbound by a phantom.

She tipped her head toward Eli with some vague intent to nuzzle him while he savored the rub of her knuckles on his jaw, but he lifted his head and let go of her hands. She heard his calm inhalation, a steady breath, a deep voice. "Yes, sexy. So sexy, it's killing me."

She spread her fingers wide, her hands freed by his. This was not the time. This was not the place. But this was the man.

"That's excellent news," she murmured. She was rewarded with his laughter and relieved that he broke the spell for her.

She was thinking too dramatically. This one evening was enough. It was a wonderful night. They were having fun, and her life would go back to normal tomorrow. All her plans and goals would still be there, unchanged. *Happy Birthday, Mallory. Stop worrying and enjoy your party.*

She tugged at the hem of her coat, squaring it up. "Seriously, this time. What are you going to make real, and when?"

"Seriously, Mallory Ames—" of course, this man had caught it, the one time she'd used her last name "—I'm in no hurry for this fake date to end, because there will never be another night like this. But when it ends, I want it to end with a good-night kiss. And since you don't do fake kisses, it will have to be real. Me, kissing you, no games."

"I see. When will this happen?"

"When I can't stand not kissing you any longer."

It was intoxicating to be with him. "Then, when the fake date ends with a real kiss, will that be the start of a real date?"

"I don't think it can."

"Why not?"

He didn't answer.

She wouldn't let him go back to being a silent statue, not with her. She placed her hand on his hard arm. "You do see that the phrase 'I don't think it can' means it might happen?"

"It might." Those two words were said in the authoritative voice of *Never.* Subject over, move on.

"Oilcan." Mallory squeezed his arm.

Eli smiled, breaking his statue stance, but it was a sad smile, not even one-tenth sexy. "It might, but even then, it won't be the same as this. Nothing will ever be the same as this, and in the words of a pretty, vivacious, expressive, indomitable, passionate, fearless and perfect woman, this is exceptional."

"You forgot sexy."

"I'm trying not to dwell on it. Thank God you're in a thick wool coat. Take my glove, too. Cover up that naked hand."

It might. She didn't want to hear anything else, not her own voice reminding her that she'd worked for two years to get here, and *here* didn't include an emotionally intoxicating love affair. *Never abandon a good plan.*

Eli's voice returned to the amused, charmed, the perfect man of her fantasy. "Now, tell me what you're going to do to me. Or with me."

"We're going to go make a Christmas wish at the bonfire."

"That sounds very wholesome."

"I'm going to try to make you desperate to kiss me the entire time."

"That won't be very difficult."

Nothing will ever be the same as this.

But the next thing might be even better.

Mallory would find out when Prince Charming finally kissed her good-night.

The fire grew larger.

Eli kept walking closer, Mallory's hand in his own once more.

The sick feeling in the pit of his stomach made him angry. The anger was why he'd come to the park tonight. He knew why the fire sickened him, of course. He'd escaped burning wreckage as water had filled the cockpit. The death he'd faced would have been gruesome, burning up, drowning, both.

His therapist had suggested giving exposure therapy a try if this avoidance of fires continued more than a few months. He'd have Eli begin by looking at fires that were smaller, contained, limiting the exposure to a few minutes. Then a few more, until the sight of flames would no longer cause a spike of anxiety.

Anxiety. He'd let the therapist name that one.

It didn't matter what it was called, Eli was not going to spend months timidly facing little candle flames. The announcements for this Yule log lighting had been on every gas station pump when he'd filled his motorcycle after he'd driven to Masterson. He'd left his staff to deliver his Aston Martin and a more anonymous Ford pickup, but the motorcycle had been his excuse not to fly. This festival had been his excuse to face a bigger fire than he could have built himself. He'd come tonight to face it and be done with it, in one grand episode of exposure therapy.

But a woman in a pink coat and blue hat had stood next to him and started talking. She'd grabbed his arm, argued with him, and even lain on a hay bale to talk to some stars. She was so damned distracting while he was dwelling on demons. Then she'd slid down his body, and he had come alive.

So, he'd lied to keep her by his side tonight, just so she'd make him feel better. Just like her father had done. Just like her aunt and her brother and all the others who were not the key to her happiness. She thought Eli was different.

He wasn't even Eli.

"What are you going to wish for?" She sounded upbeat as they got closer to the fire.

"I'm not going to make a wish."

"You can't go back to just brooding at the fire."

Brooding was a good euphemism for coming to grips with a near-death experience. He liked it. It wasn't exposure therapy. It was brooding.

"I'll watch you make your wish," he said.

I'm going to use you as a way to associate something pleasant with fire.

He was a real prince, all right.

"The table that's selling the wishing papers is over there," she said.

"Selling wishing papers?" It sounded absurd, and it gave him somewhere else to vent his turmoil. "Someone came up with a great marketing scheme to defraud the good citizens of Masterson out of a few pennies."

"Ah, that's the fake boyfriend I first came to know and love and knock upside the head with an oilcan."

Eli chuckled. He actually chuckled as he got closer and closer to a *fire*. That was the kind of miracle Mallory was. He wanted to scoop her into a bear hug and spin her around.

He wanted to kiss her.

Not yet.

He had to tell her the truth first, but he wasn't ready to stop being Eli.

"The wishing papers are free, just to blow your skeptical mind. They do ask for a charity donation, but that's only if you can afford it."

If she only knew… But she'd know soon enough, and it would change everything for her, for him, for them.

"They make super cute blank notes, and they tie a little greenery or something organic to it, to make it easier to throw. The air's always swirling around the fire. Without the weight, everyone would fold up their papers and try to sail paper airplanes at the fire, and you'd have wishes going every which way." Her free hand went every which way, demonstrating out-of-control airplanes. She looked cute, although he'd told her that was the wrong word to describe her, but she was so cute that it took him a second to realize she was talking about fiery airplane crashes.

He needed to keep Mallory in his life. He wanted her to be the woman he made the time to see.

If you need those earrings for next week's event, get them. An arm offered in escort, a hand on the small of her back, a night of sex. *I'll be in Tokyo tomorrow, then back through LA for two days. Let the staff know which dates you'll be in Manhattan. I'll see you then.*

She would never fit into his life. He had to let Mallory go.

Not yet.

She was so into the moment. "I had a great professor my sophomore year. She went through the origins of all kinds of holiday traditions. Throwing the greenery onto the Yule log had nothing to do with weighting wishing papers. Greenery represented life, but you have to wonder, why would you want to burn up life?"

Burn up life. He ignored the roaring flames and concentrated on the little dip in the center of Mallory's upper lip.

"For centuries, you see, *life* was the polite way to refer to desire. Arousal. Sex. Animal appetites. Life."

He nodded. "I get the picture."

"I was trying to get you to picture kissing me."

"I never stop."

"Me, neither, but you're still holding out?"

"It's not time to say goodbye. I can last a long time."

They continued to walk closer to the fire.

"Sorry," Mallory said with a giggle. "A man who lasts a long time was kind of… Anyway. Where were we?"

"The Yule log." For the hundredth time tonight, he could feel a smile teasing the corners of a mouth he'd thought had forgotten how to smile.

"The burning of the Yule log was a winter purification ritual. To atone for all your carnal sins, you could speak them into the greenery, toss them on the log, burn them up and start the new year as chaste and pure as the winter snow."

"I doubt Masterson is ready to have all its residents whispering their dirty secrets into pine boughs."

They'd reached the table. There were only a few scraps of paper and those ubiquitous golf pencils left.

The donation jar was nearly full. It was about to get a one-hundred-dollar bill, anyway. Eli took a moment to fold it so Mallory wouldn't see the number on the bill.

"Don't I know you from somewhere?"

Eli froze at the too-familiar question.

"I'm sure I've seen you before," the female table attendant cooed. "Masterson is such a small town."

He kept his head down, folding the money slowly, *not yet, not like this, please don't let Mallory find out like this*.

"I'm not from Masterson." He didn't make eye contact with the woman as he placed the bill in the donation jar. He knocked a few pencils off the table and bent to get them, buying time, *not yet*.

Mallory's arms came around his neck from behind before he'd stood halfway back up. What was she doing?

"I'm ready for my piggyback ride," she announced.

Ah. He played along. It had been over a decade, but it was like riding a bicycle to stoop low, reach a hand back behind each of her knees and stand.

Mallory lurched over his shoulder awkwardly, a move that let her arm block his face while she chatted up the attendant. "He came to town just for my birthday. He's the best."

Did Mallory know he might be recognized? Did she already know?

The attendant sounded cooler. "Well, good luck."

"Let's go," Mallory muttered.

"Aren't you supposed to take a piece of paper?" Eli muttered back.

"I got one before I met you tonight. It's been in my pocket this whole time."

"Then what was the tip for?" Not that he'd miss it, but he only had so many hundred-dollar bills on him.

"I didn't tell you to put money in the jar. If you don't want to make a wish, just grab some greenery. I'm sure you have a carnal sin or two in your past you can whisper into it."

"Nothing to repent."

"Sounds boring. You can wish for a more exciting year." She reached down and grabbed a pine bough. "Giddy-up."

He carried her closer to the fire, relieved, exasperated, loving the weight of her on his back, hating the blinding yellow blaze in the night. It was hard to ruminate over it—or anything—with Mallory's arms around his neck.

"You're choking me."

"Sorry." She let go and slid down his back to a stand.

He turned around to face her the second her toes touched the ground. "Why did you do that? Hide my face?"

Please, God, let her have known all along.

He would kiss her right this second if she said she hadn't wanted the public to recognize him, if she'd known all along he was E.L. Taylor—if *that* man was the one she meant each time she said *You're mildly funny.*

"I was trying to substitute for your coffee cup."

"You...what?"

"Whew. This fire is really putting out some heat." She twirled the pine bough, peeking up at him as she spoke. "You used your cup to hide your face tonight, more than once. You didn't want to walk down the row of booths. You kept leaning back on the branch to keep your face in the tree trunk's shadow. When you knocked those pencils off the table, I knew you weren't comfortable with someone seeing your face. It's not a big deal to me. I wanted to help."

She didn't know who he was.

"That was—" It was so hard to keep the disappointment out of his voice. "That was very thoughtful of you."

It had been very generous of her to use her own body to shield him through an imagined phobia.

It was the wrong type of anxiety: he was using her to feel alive in the presence of a bright fire and a black night. He was using her to avoid being E.L. Taylor, the man who'd so ruthlessly killed off all the parts of his life that hadn't fit his vision of being the man who had it all.

He didn't.

Eli had more. Eli had piggyback rides. One-dollar cocoa. Tree branches and silly conversations. Darkness and seductive conversations. The ability to soothe a friend when she felt so sad, she cried. Eli had received a single, real kiss. But it was all too new, too fragile to hold on to if he lost her. He would fall right back into being E.L. Taylor.

"I don't know why you hide your face," Mallory said, brushing his cheek with the pine bough to catch his attention. "It's a very handsome face, and even the thickest beard and shaggiest hair can't change that. Your eyes will always be Paul Newman blue. I hope you add laugh lines. Not frown lines."

She did not know just how fake of a fake boyfriend he was. He was going to have to tell her and kill a perfect night. But, before they parted ways, he was going to kiss Mallory—*he* was, not this imaginary Eli.

Me, kissing you, no games.

Unless she slapped him in his handsome face, called him the liar he was and walked away.

He did have a wish, after all.

I wish this evening could have a better ending than I deserve.

Chapter Eleven

Never abandon a good plan.
> —How to Taylor Your Business Plan
> *by E.L. Taylor*

There was a crowd around the white picket fence.

The adult crowd took turns pelting the Yule log with their wishes—or trying to. The heat of the fire created its own little wind system, which caught the ribbons and leaves on the papers and diverted them from their target. People lingered after throwing their wishes to watch the crazy acrobatics their neighbors' wishes performed.

Eli would have to snake his way through the crowd to get Mallory up to the fence for her throw. He felt the danger of it. *Don't I know you from somewhere?*

"I don't want to join their reindeer games," Mallory said. "Let's go around the sandpit to the other side. It's too hot this close to the fire, anyway." She unbuttoned her pink coat and started walking, certain he wouldn't disagree, probably certain he would be relieved.

Eli gritted his teeth at her thinly veiled attempt to shield him from a weakness he didn't have. But, since he did need to avoid the crowd if he wanted to have her all to himself, he could say nothing.

He escorted her along the long line of volleyball courts with a hand at the small of her back. Her coat was unbuttoned, but the double-breasted peacoat style didn't fall open. Still, he got a glimpse of a thin, white sweater underneath, a delicious peep, as erotic as catching a glimpse of lingerie.

"You know..." She was uncharacteristically hesitant. "My friend who's coming to MU next semester...? He's got a lot of good tips for how to make plans to handle obstacles when they arise."

That bastard. Eli prayed he never saw the two of them together, her and her little Ohio friend strolling across the campus.

"Like what?" he asked. "Don't cry? Forget they're there?"

She snapped her mouth shut at his caustic questions.

Damn it. He hated that guy.

"Does he even have any accreditation in psychology or psychiatry?" Eli asked. *Never take advice without considering the source.*

"No. Do you?"

He frowned at her petulant tone. "I'm not the one who is advising people on how to deal with their families and handle their emotions. If he doesn't have credentials, then he's a quack with all that 'Don't cry' stuff."

"Yes, you are advising me how to feel. You just advised me to distrust his advice, although his advice is working for me. I think it could help you, too."

"The face thing isn't what you think it is. I'm okay there." He had issues everywhere else.

"He wrote a book," Mallory said, an earnest disciple defending a god. "I hate that I called you a man without inspiration. I hate that you agreed it was true. Maybe you'd be inspired by the same book that inspired me."

Eli stopped and looked at her closely, wanting to see every nuance in her expression. He had a memory for detail, and he knew how she'd looked just before she'd pitched that crumpled cup at the barrel and cried over Cinderella. She looked almost as frustrated again, now.

"This guy is your hero, isn't he?" Eli was jealous. Flamingly, blazingly jealous.

"His book changed my life. He's going to be a featured author this semester. You don't have to be a student to go to a book signing. You could come with me and meet him, too."

"Meet him, too? You've never met him?" All that searing jealousy was smothered so quickly that Eli laughed in relief. "Who is he? Dr. Phil?"

She rolled her eyes.

He reached out to tug down her ski cap. "Never meet your heroes. It's one of the oldest adages around for a reason. He can't live up to your expectations. He's going to disappoint you. It always happens that way."

Ask any entrepreneur who couldn't convince me to invest in his start-up.

She fixed her hat as if he hadn't straightened it right. "I'm not going to meet him as my hero. I'm going to meet him as his equal."

"You're Dr. Phil's equal?"

She turned on her heel and marched off, a complete ninety-degree turn from where they'd been headed.

"Whoa. No, no, no—I didn't mean it like that." He caught her and turned her in his arms to look into her eyes, because if he'd made her cry again, he was going to hate himself.

She looked furious, thank God.

"I don't appreciate you laughing at me."

"I wasn't, I swear I wasn't." He caught her to him in a quick hug, then held her just a little way from himself, cupping her face in his two hands. He ran his thumbs over her perfectly beautiful, perfectly dry cheeks. His thumbs had to feel cold to her, because her cheeks were warm, like her heart. Her personality.

Warm. It wasn't an emotion. It was this woman.

"I'm laughing at the idea that he could be *your* equal. Nobody can compare to this person I'm looking at right now. You're like a bright piece of a star in this world. I was standing alone in the dark tonight, and this star just dropped out of nowhere and landed right beside me, and I'm so damned lucky that I got to be with you." He kissed the cold cheek under his thumb. He kissed her nose, he kissed the corner of her eye, which should only earn laugh lines in her life.

"Eli." She said his name like a litany. "Eli, Eli."

It's Taylor. He froze as he was, cupping her face in his hands. *It's Taylor, the man who's been lying to you. The man who divides his time between Manhattan and Tokyo, not a college town. The man who wears suits and ties, who has a sharp haircut, a shaved face. I have no friends. I've lost touch with my family. I've been crippling myself emotionally to fulfill my business goals, and I didn't realize it until I plunged from the sky into a lake.*

"Eli." She had stars in her eyes as she touched his face, too. "It might work out? It might? There is no way you can say these beautiful things to me and think that I wouldn't change my plans to be sure they included you."

The stars in her eyes were the reflection of the bonfire at his back. It could warm him, or it could burn him.

It's Taylor.

He rested his forehead on hers. "I don't know how to make this night turn into something real."

"You know how. You said it yourself. You just kiss me, and I'm yours. Me, kissing you, no games."

She was right. The game was over. To hell with Eli and screw Taylor, he was just himself, a man who wanted this woman. Now.

"Come with me." He grabbed her by the hand and headed into the darkness.

"To where?"

Somewhere private. He was going to have to tell her who he was, and then he was going to kiss her with everything real he had, until she couldn't think about his lies or his money or anything but him.

Afterward, he was never going to let her go. He had money, damn it. He could get anything he wanted, even a girl who thought Prince Charming would still be her choice if he were poor.

There was nowhere private to go in this park. Every tree had a couple under it, every bench was being used by the adults of Masterson, who weren't as wholesome as he'd thought. The hay bales were too far away, but it was a sure thing that another couple had already found dark privacy behind them, anyway.

"Right here." He stopped in the open field and turned to her in the dark, stepping close, ready to give her his real identity in the quickest and most passionate confession he could manage, but she didn't wait for the first word.

Mallory kissed him. She pulled him close, holding him tightly, stepping on his foot in her rain boot.

He didn't care. Her coat was open, so he could slip his arms around her waist for the first time. After a night of thick denim and thicker wool between them, this was so much more access, so much more to touch, that it felt like a great intimacy to feel the curve of her waist under the softness of a white sweater.

They deepened the kiss, mouths opening, tongues mating, tasting, wanting more.

"All right, folks. That's enough. Park closes in half an hour."

They broke the kiss and turned toward the voice, still clinging to one another tightly. Eli cursed in disbelief. A uniformed officer was walking toward them with his arms wide open, herding all of the kissing couples out of their cozy hideaways.

"Take it on home, everybody. We're closing this part of the park. Head toward the main gate, folks. Last call at the beer tents. Don't drink if you're driving."

"Oh, my God." Mallory squeezed Eli so hard her voice came out in a squeak. "We're going to get arrested for public indecency."

With a burst of laughter, Eli picked her up and spun her around under the stars.

"Don't make me dizzy. I've never tried to outrun a cop before."

"Let's go. I know a place we can use as our hideout." He set her down and took her hand. He'd take her to his rented house. He'd tell her everything there, and then he'd make love to her for hours in a fourposter bed, until the sun rose over the lake. Someday, when they made love by the Aegean Sea, they'd agree the lake had looked more beautiful.

Mallory tugged him in the direction of the bonfire. "I don't care where we go, as long as I get to make my wish first."

"As you wish."

"You're getting funnier."

They stopped at the edge of the sandpit to the side of the fire, away from the crowd, and she pulled her paper wish out of her pocket, holding up a folded square with a pine cone tied to it. "You'll notice I don't have any greenery on mine." She lowered the paper and said in a stage whisper, "Very boring year." Then she held up the pine cone again. "I wrote this when I first got here, hoping for a more exciting semester, because my friend would be on campus and everything."

"Yes, the inimitable Dr. Phil."

"Very funny." She bumped him with her shoulder, a move he hoped she repeated ten thousand more times in his life. "But I can tell it's going to be a more exciting year than I dreamed. I've already narrowly escaped the cops."

He wanted her in every way, all at once. He wanted her body under his hands—*hurry up*. He wanted to stay here and flirt over wishes—*take your time*. He wanted her, full stop.

"Does the pine cone represent any other type of overindulgence in your near future?" he asked with a wink.

"A pine cone means I passed my science classes, and I understand the concept of aerodynamics. Those green boughs are like fans. Everyone's missing when they throw tonight because they're trying to throw fans. This will make a better missile."

The air near the sandpit was swirling as the fire's heat hit the cold air. One of those swirls took the paper right out of Mallory's hand. She tried to grab it. Missed. The pine cone pulled it down to land with a thunk in the sandpit.

"Serves me right for bragging," she said.

"I've got it." Eli crouched down and reached for it, only one corner close enough to touch with his fingertips. He snagged it and shook the sand off, making it unfold. As he turned toward Mallory, her handwriting was clear in the firelight, simple words written in dark pencil lead.

I hope E.L. Taylor will like me.

He stared at it.

His first thought was *Of course, I do.*

But he hadn't told her his real name yet.

His second thought was *She knew all along, thank God.*

But she hadn't. She would have told him when she'd helped him hide his face.

He finally saw the truth. Her hero was him. Her book was his book.

It couldn't be. He didn't mention families. He didn't tell anyone not to cry. What the hell would that have to do with business planning?

Never show your doubts to the world.

He'd written that, yes, but he hadn't meant that she shouldn't talk about her worries with her own grandfather, for God's sake. She was going to be so embarrassed when he taught that chapter. He'd seen the two years of tears she'd bottled up by mistake. He'd touched them with the fingertips that held this paper.

She snatched the paper away. "You didn't read it,

did you? If you tell anyone your birthday wish, it won't come true. It's not that I'm superstitious, but I want everything to go just right next semester. Two years is a big investment." Mallory was blushing now, her color high in the bonfire's light.

If she only knew... But she'd know soon enough, and it would change everything for her, for him, for them, even more harshly than he'd known it would.

She folded the strip of paper and wrapped the pine cone's ribbon tightly around it. "I'm still going to throw it. If the birthday wish mojo is gone, I've still got the Christmas thing going for me."

She raised her arm, took aim, and threw it hard at the Yule log.

Bull's-eye.

It turned to ash almost instantly, becoming part of the smoke that carried it out to the universe.

"Well, that's that." Mallory sighed beside him, her face turned up to the smoke and stars. "I guess we'll just have to see what happens next."

Chapter Twelve

The End.

—How to Taylor Your Business Plan
by E.L. Taylor

Eli lingered under a pecan tree near the main gate.

Mallory was happy to linger with him. This particular pecan had been strung with multicolored Christmas lights. They looked beautiful in the night, and they didn't cast much light on the two people below. That was probably why Eli had stopped here, to keep his face in the shadows, waiting for the bulk of the crowd to clear the main gate before he took her… somewhere. With him.

She remembered his seductive words, his husky

voice when he'd spoken over her skin under the massive oak tree. *And then, Friday night...happens.*

She'd melted into a puddle then.

She could melt so easily now, if only Eli didn't look so grim.

"The crowd will clear out soon," she said.

He remained silent.

"Are you worried about something?" *Because I am.*

Eli was studying her as if she were some exotic bird who had landed near him.

No, I'm your very own piece of a star.

He broke his silence with words that sounded portentous. "I meant what I said, that you had no equal. This man who wrote a book you believe in—"

"I won't get a complex over Dr. Phil, I promise." She tried to lighten the tone.

"You're determined to meet him, although conventional wisdom tells you not to."

She didn't know if he was asking her or telling her this. "The rest of 'never meet your heroes' is 'wait until they are your equals.' I think we're equal enough. He has a college degree from Masterson. I almost have a college degree from Masterson. He also has a Harvard MBA, but still, we're equal-ish. When he was twenty-nine, he owned dozens of companies and sat on the board of dozens more. Now I'm twenty-nine, and I have the idea for a company."

"I wasn't aware of that."

She clapped her hands together, ready to break this strange mood. "Look. I know you read that wish, so we both know who I'm talking about. It might seem like a long shot, but I think I can convince E.L. Taylor to invest in me. I told you I'm faking it, but only some of it. There's no way I'd want him to know that my family was able to manipulate me into that huge gap between my junior and senior years. He'd be concerned that I could be that gullible again about something that would affect a new company, but I absolutely know I won't be. Everything else, all the research, all the numbers I've run, everything will be solid. I have a good chance."

Eli's intense scrutiny was unnerving.

She tried for humor. "Nobody needs to know I'm wearing my grandmother's clothes or my sister-in-law's shoes."

When that didn't get even one-hundredth of a smile, she slipped her arm around his waist, just to prove to herself that he was no longer that remote man who'd first shaken her touch from his sleeve.

"It was a dumb wish, wasn't it? I should have said I hope he'll give me a specific amount of venture capital. I was feeling emotional, I guess. But if you think about it, nobody invests in someone they can't stand to be around."

"Your goals aren't dumb." Eli stepped away and turned to face her squarely. "Why did you trust me with all of this tonight? A perfect stranger?"

"Eli, what are you talking about, exactly? I feel like I'm missing something here."

"You told me your doubts. You let me see your tears."

"The tears happened despite myself. Then I told myself that it wouldn't hurt anything if you saw me at my worst, because you were going to disappear after tonight. I'm so glad you're not going to disappear now, because you've brought out the best, too. I didn't know I could have as much fun as I've had tonight."

"But it was fun for one night," Eli said. "A fake date from the start."

"Yes, but now that we've ended our fake date with a real kiss…" She trailed off at his expression.

"That was the goodbye kiss, as we knew it would be."

She stepped close and put her hands on his chest. "It was real. You, kissing me, no games." She tried for a smile. "Until the cops came."

He softened the tiniest bit. "We said 'it might' turn into something real, and I'm very sorry it didn't."

She slipped her arms around his waist, locking him in tight. "We've been happy together, all night. Talk to me. Tell me what happened."

"Fearless Mallory." He reached behind his back, grasped her wrists and freed himself, but he didn't let go of her. He bent his head and rubbed his cheek along her hand, just once. A farewell.

A whisper was all she could manage. "You're breaking my heart. Don't disappear. Won't we see each other again?"

"If we do, you won't see me the way you do now, not the way you have tonight. You may not like me at all. I want you to know, I'll never forget the perfect date that Eli had with Mallory. There will never be another night like this. Thank you."

After a brief, hard squeeze of her hands, he let go and walked away.

"Eli!"

He kept walking.

What can I do? What should I do?

"Wait. I have your gloves." She held out her hands, palms up, begging him to come back and get them. "Eli!"

He glanced back over his shoulder. "Keep them."

Then he merged into the crowd and left her under the pecan tree, all alone.

Taylor straddled his bike wearily. Every limb of his body weighed a ton. It didn't matter. The next time he saw Mallory, she would hate him.

He wouldn't be Eli. He'd be Taylor. *E.L. Taylor.* Mr. Taylor.

He wasn't anyone's hero.

The farther he drove from the park, the darker his thoughts got. No Mallory, no light—there was nothing to distract him any longer from cold reality. He was the empty, callous son of a bitch who stared at fires and couldn't sleep. And when Mallory Ames came to find him in January, she was going to be devastated to learn that her hero was nothing more than that. *Never meet your heroes* might have been the only intelligent advice he'd ever given.

He came to an intersection and stopped. To the right was Greek row, the street where most of MU's fraternity and sorority houses were located. A little flicker of something came back to life inside him. It wasn't joyful, but it made him feel alive. He turned right.

It was obvious which house was Kappa Lambda. They'd erected ten-foot-tall Greek letters on their lawn to identify themselves. Judging by the crowd on the lawn and the number of people with red Solo cups in their hands, the odds were that at least one of those letters would be knocked flat on its face before the night was through.

Taylor killed the engine and took off his helmet. Then he just sat, one foot on each side, keeping the bike balanced, waiting until he saw them.

Mallory had asked him if his peripheral vision was a superpower. Others in his past had remarked on his ability to recall visual details. He just had to recall the scene, and it was like looking at a photograph. He could zoom in on different details, like the three fraternity brothers in burgundy hoodies, one in corduroy pants, one in khaki board shorts, one in jeans. White sneakers on all of them.

There they were.

He waited, knowing he was out of place, knowing the people closest to him on the lawn were starting to point and whisper. When the three boys spotted him, Taylor kicked the bike's stand into place and dismounted. The three lacked his ability—and Mallory's ability—to fake being cool and calm under stress. The moment they realized where they'd seen him tonight was comically obvious.

Taylor walked directly toward them. The party-goers in his way scattered like minnows as a shark swam through their school. Girls then stopped at a safe distance to devour him with their eyes. The boys pretended they didn't notice him, so they wouldn't have to challenge his right to walk where he wanted to walk.

Taylor stopped less than an arm's distance from the three he'd come for. "Allow me to introduce myself. I'm E.L. Taylor."

They were mute.

"This is how it's going to go down. First, you're going to hand me my girlfriend's mitten. Second, we're going to have an educational conversation about the appropriate way to ask a woman to spend her time with you. Lastly, and this one will be in effect for the rest of your time at this university, when you see me anywhere on campus, including your own fraternity house, you'll get out of my sight. Are we clear?"

They exchanged nervous glances with one another, quickly coming to the correct conclusion that they should go along with anything E.L. Taylor suggested. After all, he was known for his plans.

"Let's begin. Step One."

He watched as two of them scrabbled in their pockets while the third hissed, "Do you still have it?"

Taylor held out his hand, and the mate to Mallory's lonely mitten was placed in his palm. "Step Two. How many times should you invite a woman to spend the evening with you?"

They looked at one another again. The one in corduroy ventured a timid answer. "None?"

"Once, boys." Taylor gave them the same look he gave someone who was about to be fired for gross incompetence. "You invite her out once. If she says yes, you have the chance to show her your best side, such as it is. If she says no, then leave her the hell alone. Don't be a pain in the ass and ask her out ten more times. Don't be a criminal and stalk her. Once."

They mumbled some *yes, sirs*.

"Step Three," Taylor said.

They stared at him. He gave them a minute to let their beer-soaked brains recall the itinerary he'd laid out.

He unzipped his jacket and tucked Mallory's mitten into the inner pocket. Then he zipped it up and looked at the boys who were still gaping at him.

"I said *three*."

They turned tail and ran.

Eli returned to his bike, put on his helmet and checked his gas gauge. He already knew he wouldn't sleep tonight. He might as well burn up another tank of fuel.

The cursor blinked on Mallory's computer screen.

She changed it from a white arrow to a black one.

She watched it for a moment, a stationary thing, unexciting. Uninspiring.

It's not supposed to be inspiring. It's a cursor.

She changed it from a black arrow to a hand.

Eli, where are you? Are you okay? What happened?

She'd gone to the Yule log three nights in a row, Sunday, Monday and Tuesday, hoping he'd be there. He hadn't been. She shouldn't go tonight.

She changed the cursor back to a white arrow.

She probably would go, anyway.

"Is that him?" The woman in the cubicle to her right, Gladys, was a full-time employee, not a student. Her whisper was full of excitement, like she'd just spotted some juicy gossip. That was how Gladys always sounded, because she always sought out juicy gossip when she should be working.

Mallory stared at her screen glumly. It wasn't like she had room to criticize. She'd been staring at cursors for ten minutes.

"It can't be." The answering whisper came from another cubicle. "But whoever he is, I'm glad he walked in the door."

Mallory ignored her coworkers and got back to typing. This basic data entry was simple drone work that did nothing to divert her from reliving a goodbye under Christmas lights. And reliving it. And reliving it, daily, during the longest week of her life.

"Is he in a motorcycle gang or something? Say yes. That look is hot."

"He's hotter than a man has a right to be, already. He doesn't need to dress it up in leather, but I'm not going to complain, either."

"Oh, I hear you. Totally agree."

Mallory looked around. The excitement spreading from cubicle to cubicle was almost tangible. Everyone had stopped working, men and women, both. At the end of the row of cubicles, even Irene, the senior administrative assistant, had opened the glass door of her office and come out to see…something.

Mallory gave up and stood. Whoever had just walked in was causing enough of a stir that it might take her mind off *him*.

It was him.

Eli had found her. She must have said enough about her job for him to deduce where she worked. He'd *searched* for her.

With a little skip of happiness, she headed down the row of cubicles. He was walking toward the dean's office, his expression deadly serious. She wanted to head him off before he asked her boss if a woman named Mallory worked here.

His profile was just the same as when she'd first seen him. Stern, even grim. Silent, even while he was being greeted by the dean, shaking the hand he was offered.

Shaking hands with the dean?

Mallory stopped.

Irene stepped away from her glass door with her most gracious smile for—for *Eli*. She gestured toward the door of a currently empty private office, the one that was reserved for January and the arrival of the Executive-in-Residence.

The woman sitting in the cubicle where Mallory had stopped reached up and tugged on her sleeve. "Don't you dare go ask for an autograph. Irene will kill you."

The warning was unnecessary. Mallory couldn't

go anywhere. She was sunk shin-deep in quicksand, and going under.

Her Eli, her rugged and sexy and unsmiling Eli, who could be so charming if he only had a little oil-can for that rust, *that* Eli walked down the hall with Irene and the dean. As the dean kept up his effusive welcome, Eli turned his head and looked right at her. No flicker of surprise, no jolt of recognition crossed his face.

He hadn't needed to look her way at all, because he'd probably seen her just fine in his peripheral vision. But he'd turned his head; he wanted her to be certain that he knew she was there. Then he turned away.

Eli had no intention of acknowledging her, for he was a multi-millionaire, and she was a student working part-time to pay off her tuition.

They were not equals. He had already known that on Saturday night. She had not.

E.L. Taylor followed the dean into his new office and shut the door.

Chapter Thirteen

*Learning Objective: Establish the parameters
within which the business will operate.*
                        —Senior Year Project *by Mallory Ames*

"I quit."

Mallory hissed the words under her breath.

The pointing-hand cursor blurred with her tears.

*You must continue to play when the game isn't fair,
or you'll never win.*

There was no game left to play. She'd wanted so
badly to meet him—a man who'd written a book
which stated that she should never meet him, not unless she waited until they were equals. She'd been so
determined to break that rule. For two years, it had
inspired her to take action.

Meet E.L. Taylor? *Meet him?* She'd kissed him, damn him.

It was so horrifically clear. She'd been open and honest with him, more than she'd been with anyone, even with her grandpa. She'd confessed to everything, from being a fool for her family to raiding her dead grandmother's closet. He was the one person who knew that every detail about her, even her appearance, was a lie.

She'd babbled to the stars about birthdays and wasted years, while he'd sat silently on the next hay bale over. She'd drunk hot chocolate next to him— oh, what a fool she'd been, saying she'd buy him a cup if she could. She'd been so careful not to make him spend too much. *Just the hot chocolate. I don't need a cookie to go with it.*

It had amused him, no doubt. He'd enjoyed spending an evening with a woman who was too dense to realize who he really was.

He was the hero whose philosophy she'd passionately defended throughout the evening, and he had egged her on, challenging her to explain his own rules. But after he'd read her wish, his mood had changed. He must have realized his little masquerade had gone too far. He'd left her under a pecan tree before she could fall in love with him and slobber all over him like a loyal Labrador.

I quit.

She wanted to scream it.

She couldn't. She had nowhere else to go, nowhere else to live, no way to get there if she did. She'd given everything up to be here at Masterson University, right here, right now. She couldn't quit. She'd starve.

Those were real-life stakes which the great E.L. Taylor had never faced. His *face*. She'd helped him to hide his face from a perfectly nice charity volunteer who'd started to recognize him.

Why hadn't Mallory recognized him?

She dove under her desk for her backpack, jerked the zipper open and dug for her book. His book.

She flipped the book over. The photo on the glossy book jacket was so familiar to her. Eli didn't look anything like it. Even now, she had to know what she was looking for to see any resemblance. His eyes in the black-and-white photo weren't that startling silver blue, of course. Just a dark gray. Too dark—the photographer must have touched them up so they wouldn't appear too light or white.

That smile—so polite, so empty. Nothing like Eli when he threw back his head and laughed.

She glared at the photo, her eyes blurring again, of course, because she was upset, damn it. She had seen this smile on Saturday night. Early on, when he'd stiffly suggested she return to her friends and family at the festival, this practiced, cold smile had given her a moment of déjà vu. Through the beard and shaggy hair, through the flames reflected in his eyes and the bitter set of the lines in his face, she'd recognized that empty smile.

Yoga breaths. She couldn't freak out in her cubicle.

She shoved the book into her backpack and placed her hands on the keyboard. She was on the clock;

she'd better work. She needed this job, because she needed the financial aid package it was part of. She needed the financial aid to cover her tuition and discount her dorm, because she needed to finish her degree, because she needed the clout it would give her when she met with investors. It was all a cascade of steps. E. L. Taylor had taught her that.

The very last step was supposed to have been his investment in her new business. She'd designed a better way to match caregivers and clients, a better way to meet the needs of both, but there was no conceivable way she could present it to him now. He'd be able to point to every part she'd already told him was weak. He'd laugh at her.

No, he wouldn't laugh at her. She wouldn't give him the chance. She would never speak to him again.

One minute later, without having pressed a single key, she dove under her desk again for her backpack and pulled out her book. The man in the photo was different in more ways than being clean-cut and clean-shaven. His expression was untroubled, unconcerned as he paused to look into the camera. It was the same expression she'd seen in his photos in business journals.

Nobody else in her family enjoyed *Shark Tank* and its discussions of valuation and equity, but Mallory had watched clips of her hero's guest appearance on her cell phone. He'd been polished, remote, somewhat amused.

The man she'd met last week was hardened. It had been a struggle for him to interact with her at all, at first. She'd left him to his brooding, but he'd come after her, offering to buy her hot chocolate, wanting a chance to speak in complete sentences to a fellow human being. His sense of humor and his charm had gotten rusty with disuse. Because...

Why? What had made the man in this photograph turn into the angry man she'd run to for protection?

I don't care. He lied to me.

She tossed the book onto a stack of completed paperwork in the corner of her cubicle.

That pile wasn't going to get any higher today. Mallory couldn't sit here until quitting time, waiting for the office door to open and Eli to walk out.

Eli. Had that been a joke, too? E.L. sounded close to *Eli.* That must have made it easier for him to keep up the pretense.

She was a dunce.

Mallory logged out of her work profile. Students were allowed to modify their work hours for academic necessities, when exams needed to be studied for and special projects were due. She had a special project: find a new hero.

She zipped up her backpack and headed for the door, leaving her book behind.

"Mallory. Mallory!"

Mallory jumped a mile at the tap on her shoulder. She'd started wearing headphones after last Wednesday, when *Mr. Taylor* had surprised everyone by appearing weeks ahead of schedule. The music prevented her from listening for office doors opening and closing down the hall as the bigwigs like Mr. Taylor came and went at their leisure. This had made her a little less tense throughout the workday. She blended right in with the other interns who'd been doing it all semester.

Still, she was embarrassed that her supervisor had to physically tap her on the shoulder to get her attention, even if her peers had to be tapped all the time. Her peers were generally nineteen.

Mallory tugged on the string to her earphones, letting them fall into her lap with a little plastic clatter. "I'm sorry, Irene. Could you repeat that?"

Irene handed her a set of forms. "I need you to complete this, print a fresh copy and deliver it to Mr. Taylor."

"Oh…no. I can't. I'm busy."

Irene looked at Mallory's monitor. "Busy doing what? Processing transcript requests? For goodness's sake, take care of this first. Mr. Taylor is waiting."

Mallory dutifully spread the forms out on her desk, but the moment Irene's office door clicked shut, Mallory opened a desk drawer and pulled out her mini cosmetics bag, the one she kept for touch-ups throughout the day to maintain her professional appearance.

She'd been having huge debates with herself every morning on what to wear. Nothing as mundane as deciding which blouse would go with which skirt. Instead, she'd had to decide if she should wear business attire at all. She changed her mind daily.

Eli—Mr. Taylor—knew she wasn't required to

wear it. He knew it was her silly way to pretend she had a job that required her to dress like an executive. Since he knew she was faking it, she should no longer try to fake it.

On the other hand, she was so angry with Mr. Taylor for all the wisecracks he'd made about not meeting her hero if they weren't equal, she was going to dress like an executive if he was going to dress like an executive.

The daily debate gave her an outlet for her angry emotions. She pulled things out of her microscopic dorm room closet, tossed them on her institutional twin bed, made a mess and blamed Eli. She was afraid if she stopped dwelling on the trivial and started remembering how he'd hugged her while she'd cried, her tears would start again and never stop.

This morning, dressing like an executive had won. She completed the forms in a ridiculously easy five minutes, hit Print, and touched up her powder and lipstick.

Ready to enter the lion's den? You can do this.

Mr. Taylor kept the blinds on his glass door closed. She hadn't seen him since he'd walked into the office last Wednesday and given her the shock of her life. She braced herself for the sight of him, then knocked.

"Come in."

She hadn't braced for the sound of his voice. Her heart fluttered like a wounded bird in her chest. *Come in* was spoken by the same voice that had said *There will never be another night like this one.*

She couldn't think about that. She had to deliver these forms.

There was nothing to it. She merely had to turn the doorknob, walk steadily across the carpeting in her sister-in-law's cast-off classic pumps, place the forms on the corner of the executive desk, refuse to think that it was about as wide as the space between two parked pickup trucks in a dark field, turn around and leave.

She did it.

"Miss Ames."

She had her hand on the doorknob, ready to pull it shut behind herself.

"Stop."

She did not.

The door shut.

Taylor threw his pen onto his desk, cursing under his breath.

Now he was going to have to come up with yet another stupid task to get her back in here. He couldn't walk out to the open reception area's cubicles and strike up a conversation. Everyone would be listening. Everyone would wonder how in the world they knew each other, which was precisely what they needed to talk about.

He glared at the door that hid her from his view.

He knew she hated the sight of him, but he did not hate the sight of her. It had been a week since he'd first walked into the offices of the university's school of business. In that week, Mallory had stayed hidden in a cubicle that was almost in the back corner of the open reception area. He hadn't managed to be within speaking distance until now, when he'd manipulated her to make it happen.

He stared at the door. For perhaps six seconds, she'd been here, live and in person. He could recall the image now, every detail, an image so different from the others he had of her.

She'd been so very pretty in the park while dressed in pink, but she was stunning in a professional environment. Her hair was smoothed into an updo. Her trim skirt and tailored blouse looked as good today as they had in the days of Jackie Kennedy and *Mad Men*. If he hadn't known they were her grandmother's clothes, he never would have guessed.

She wore black high heels. Red lipstick. It wasn't a high-maintenance look, but a professional, powerful look. Stud earrings—pearls. A ring on her right hand, a blue stone, a tiny chip of a thing, nothing like the rocks he could provide. It was probably her birthstone. She'd turned twenty-nine this December, and he had been there for it, her fake boyfriend for one night. He wished it could have been more.

You knew from the start it was only one night. So did she.

Yes, so had she—but she was furious with him, anyway.

In his mind's eye, he focused on her face, looking for the nuances, until he had to admit that she did not look furious. Fury was an emotion that required effort and energy. He'd paid his therapist enough to buy a sports car to spell that out for him. Mallory had been only going through the motions just now.

He couldn't unsee the straight line of lips that should be curved, the flat affect on a face that should be expressive, the dead eyes of someone who was performing a chore solely because they had no choice. That was the very definition of servitude.

That was Cinderella.

With a groan, Taylor put his elbows on his desk and dropped his head into his hands. He couldn't force her to perform tasks as if he were the wicked stepmother and she was the scullery maid.

For the entire coming semester, he was going to be aware she was perhaps forty feet away from him, but he might never catch another glimpse.

He picked up the forms that had wasted her time and dropped them into the trash can.

Chapter Fourteen

Learning Objective: Given an unexpected scenario, explain how the business will remain operational.
—Senior Year Project *by Mallory Ames*

The janitor would unlock the inner office.

Mallory would know it was time for her mission to commence when she heard the vacuum sweeper shut off. Wrapping up the cord would take the janitor a minute, then he would pick up the trash can, bring it out to the main office space and empty it into his large bin on wheels. Since he cleaned the Executive-in-Residence office last on his rounds, he'd roll the large bin past the cubicles and out the main door, then return to fumble through his keys, relock the inner offices and leave for the day.

While he rolled the bin out, Mallory would have two minutes to sneak in and out of Mr. Taylor's office, like Tom Cruise stepping over laser beams, *Ocean's Eleven* trimmed down to *Ocean's One*.

She needed to return a pair of gloves without seeing, speaking to or in any way interacting with their owner, the liar who had amused himself by watching his devotee break every rule in his book. Unfortunately, the man she wanted to avoid had begun working late hours. He was always still at his desk when she left for the day.

Not today. He'd left just before the janitor had arrived. The moment he'd walked out the door, Mallory had taken the gloves out of her backpack and hidden them in her lap. It was time for her to get rid of her last trace of Eli.

Closure.

The vacuum sweeper went quiet. Mallory gave the buttery leather one last caress. The bin rolled past her. She made short work of the distance between her cubicle and Taylor's office, walking with confident strides, even if their length was clipped by her pencil skirt. She set the gloves on his desk—but they looked too obviously out of place there. The janitor had just dusted. He might notice that they hadn't been there two minutes ago.

She picked them up and looked around, but every surface was clean and uncluttered. The gloves would be obvious anywhere.

The desk chair wasn't pushed in all the way. She ran around the desk to drop them on the seat, pushed the chair in, and turned to leave. No, the chair shouldn't be pushed in. She pulled it out to where it had been, rushing now, then turned to the door—which Irene was blocking.

"Hello," Mallory said, faking calm confidence like her life depended on it. "I was just leaving for the day, unless there's anything else you need from me."

"I need you to come up with a good explanation for whatever it is you're doing in Mr. Taylor's office."

It sucked, having a sharp boss.

Never be afraid to speak the truth.

Shut up, Mr. Taylor.

But Mallory followed the advice. "I was putting Mr. Taylor's gloves back where they belong."

"I saw you pick them up from his desk just now. I haven't had the staff sign the nondisclosure agreements yet because we weren't expecting Mr. Taylor until January, but not entering his office after he's locked it is common sense. You cannot go poking around an office after its occupant has left for the day, especially when that office is occupied by a celebrity."

"I'm just returning his gloves." Mallory picked them up. "Look. They're just gloves."

"How did you get his gloves, if you didn't just pick them up off his desk, which I'll remind you I saw you do? Why would you have his gloves in the first place?"

The park, the hand-holding, the bonfire, the wishes—Mallory hesitated a moment too long. Irene lost her patience.

"There is no circumstance that excuses this. I'm

sorry to see you go, but I have no choice. You'll need to get your personal belongings from your desk. Your belongings, not anyone else's."

Mallory's life crumbled before her eyes. "Please. I'm begging you to believe me. I had his gloves legitimately. Without this job, I will lose my dorm. I will literally be out on the streets."

A male voice interrupted, slightly amused, supremely confident. "I didn't see the memo that there would be a meeting in my office after five."

Irene was as flustered as Mallory, but Mallory hoped she hid it better.

"Mr. Taylor," Irene said, getting out of his doorway by coming into the office, allowing Mr. Taylor to enter as well.

"Irene." He acknowledged her with a nod as he walked to his desk and picked up his mail. "How are you doing, Miss Ames? I hope the gloves were warm enough."

Her heart was pounding as hard as it had when she'd faced her family and negotiated a salary. She faked the same calm confidence now. "Yes, they were."

He held out his hand.

She put the gloves in them. "Thank you, Mr. Taylor."

"Anytime. I did try that table-side guacamole, by the way. Great suggestion." Then he held up his finger as if to stop her from answering, when she had absolutely nothing to say, and he gave Irene one of those *don't waste my time* looks. "Did you have anything for me?"

"No, Mr. Taylor."

"Thank you." He said it like *you're dismissed.* "And Irene, I trust Ms. Ames is still gainfully employed? I didn't overhear everything, but there's no reason to fire someone when it was my idea for her to borrow my gloves. I was going into a restaurant as she was coming out. It was a cold enough night that I had come in my car. I noticed she had no gloves and she was going to walk somewhere on campus." He questioned Mallory. "Your dorm?"

"No, it was the library." She could pretend with the best of them—which would be him.

He turned back to Irene, seeming to be supremely bored with the detail he'd asked for to add some authenticity. "She told me to get the guacamole, and I told her to wear my gloves and give them back once she found hers. Any questions?"

"None."

"Good." He turned his back on Irene. "Can you stay a minute, Ms. Ames?"

Irene left and pulled the door shut.

Eli's—Mr. Taylor's—blue gaze was piercing. "Why are you avoiding me?"

The panic she'd just endured left a fine tremor in Mallory's hands, in every muscle. She wanted to collapse. She couldn't. She was speaking to her hero like they were equal.

Equal-ish.

She leveled her own no-nonsense gaze on him.

"Let's see if I can remember. You lied to me about your identity, kissed me, then dumped me and walked away without a word of explanation. That sums it up."

"It wasn't the best time for an explanation. I knew I would see you again on campus, and I had every intention of having this conversation with you when we were neither outdoors, cold, nor emotional."

"How nice for you to know that you'd be speaking to me later, but *I* didn't know that when you walked away." She stabbed herself in the chest with her own finger, right over her heart, right where it had hurt so badly that night, and every night thereafter, when she'd wondered where he'd gone and fretted over how he was feeling.

"Mallory, I am so sorry."

She hadn't intended to let her pain show. She reached for her anger, instead. "You're so sorry for what? For stringing me along? For enjoying an evening pretending you weren't a multi-millionaire, so you could get your kicks as Joe Average, putting dollar bills in donation jars? You stood there in the parking lot and watched me *cry*, and then had the nerve to give me that pep talk about how I wasn't pretending all these wonderful traits, while you were the one who was pretending the whole time."

"For that, I am not sorry, because nothing about that conversation was pretend."

"You know I'm faking my way through life at the moment, but it's because I'm aspiring to a better standard of living. You don't do it to sink to a lower level. You aren't supposed to fake that you're enjoying a

cup of hot chocolate at a stupid small-town festival."
With a stupid small-town girl.

"I did enjoy the hot chocolate."

"You're obscenely rich. Astronomically rich."

Eli—Mr. Taylor, damn it—paused for a moment
before answering. "I'm at a loss here. What does
being rich have to do with my enjoyment of a cup of
hot chocolate?"

"Because you're used to better. You've probably
had the very finest handcrafted chocolate, melted just
so by a pastry chef at a Michelin-starred restaurant."

He looked irritated at that. She'd guessed right.

"You must have thought I was such a naive little
girl, championing the quality of the nuns' hot chocolate, as if I'd ever traveled to France or Switzerland
and knew how it compared to what the world has to
offer."

"Is hot chocolate the issue you want to discuss?"

"Why didn't you tell me who you were? It seems
cruel to string me along when you knew that I was
your—your *fan*. A fan of your book."

"How could I have possibly known that? Be fair.
It wasn't as if you were wearing an official fan club
T-shirt. That doesn't exist, by the way."

"You're not funny."

Something flashed across his expression, something like surprise or…or hurt. She couldn't possibly
hurt the great E.L. Taylor.

"When did you figure out that I was your biggest fan? Because you most certainly knew when you

ditched me." The moment she asked, she knew the answer. "My wish. You saw my wish."

He nodded. "And up until that moment, I didn't know your friend and hero was me."

"It wasn't you. It was an image of you I had invented in my head."

"The timing is important. When you remember that night, remember that everything before you threw that wish happened before I knew you were a fan."

"No wonder you wouldn't kiss me."

He came around the desk to stand in front of her. He didn't touch, didn't reach for her, but he stood quite close, with an intimate quiet to his voice. "I distinctly recall kissing you. It was the kiss of a lifetime."

She felt it all again, that hum of arousal, the way joy and hope had made everything feel like magic, but she was standing before a supremely confident E.L. Taylor in his natural environment, a businessman conducting an after-action review of a transaction. He was no rusty Tin Man. He didn't need an oilcan. He needed nothing from her at all.

"I meant that you wouldn't kiss me goodbye after that wish. That earlier kiss wasn't for you, Mr. Taylor. It was for Eli, a man who never existed. The joke's on me."

"Fearless." He said it more to himself than her.

She turned away and walked to the door.

"Mallory."

Her hand was on the doorknob, but this time she paused.

"Your wish did come true, you know. I do like you."

She walked out of his office and stopped at the first place she could, the kitchenette. Her hands were still shaking. She fussed with the coffeepot, although it was empty and clean for the night.

It was over. That had been it, the closure everyone touted. One big conversation to tie it all up with a bow. She'd tuck it away with the rest of her life that she couldn't allow herself to look back upon.

She needed to think ahead. She had bigger problems than a lying millionaire. This morning, dressed for work, she'd been stopped at the dorm building's exit by a simple fluorescent green paper taped to the door, the notice that her dorm would be closed during the winter break.

All the buildings on campus would be closed for sixteen days over the winter break, from the offices to the classrooms to the dining halls, a cost-saving routine on most college campuses across the country. No dorm supervisors, no janitorial staff, no electricity to heat a six-story building for over two weeks. When Mallory had made her budget two years ago, she'd forgotten all about the need to find alternate housing during the winter break. She'd flown home for Christmas, the cost of the ticket split by her separated parents, so she hadn't paid any attention to the dorm closure as a freshman, sophomore, or junior.

This year, it was an issue. She had no way to get back to Ohio, not after selling her car. Her grandpa needed every penny of his retirement funds to pay for the assisted-living facility. Her brother would make her grovel if she asked for plane ticket money, and then there was a fifty-fifty chance he'd say no, anyway. Mallory needed to find a local place to stay—a free place to stay, because free was the only thing in her price range.

She heard a private office's glass door opening. Who else was here after hours, besides Irene and Mr. Taylor? Her poise was razor thin. If Mr. Taylor came into the kitchenette, her ability to stay calm and confident would fail the test.

She escaped to the ladies' room, which was nicer than her dorm's. Really, the office had almost everything except a bathtub and a bed. Too bad she couldn't just move in here for the winter break, but the office buildings were closed during break, too. Besides, Irene would flip.

Mallory poked her head out of the ladies' room to be certain the coast was clear. She went back to her cubicle, put her pumps in the backpack that no longer held a man's gloves, pulled out her old ballerina flats, and left to walk across campus to her lonely room in the dorm. Instead of looking back on those moments of closure with the man she'd known as Eli, she began to plan how she'd locate free living arrangements.

What was one more obstacle? Her Taylor-built plan was made of little else.

Chapter Fifteen

Learning Objective: Given two alternatives,
choose one and justify its benefit to the business.
    —Senior Year Project *by Mallory Ames*

"There's this woman…" Taylor tapered off.

He shouldn't have brought her up. Mallory had
nothing to do with the plane crash. Nothing to do with
nightmares. Nothing to do with the brother and sister
he ignored or the fortune he paid attention to, nothing
to do with the fame that came easily and the friend-
ships that didn't, nothing to do with teaching a book
he no longer believed in. It had nothing to do with
goddamned anything else in his goddamned world.

But God, he wished it did.

His therapist, whom he was supposed to address as

Scott, like they were friends instead of doctor and patient, prompted him through the encrypted video connection on his phone. "There's a woman who does what?"

"She…she's…interesting." Taylor would not wince at his own wimpy reply. He shifted his position in his armchair, a ridiculously easy-to-spot bit of body language that made him wish this was an audio call, not video. He'd chosen to sit in the master bedroom's bay window for this session. There'd been no need to go into the office on campus today. There never had been a need, other than checking on Mallory.

"Is she new in your life, or is she one of the people in your past?" Scott asked.

"New."

Mallory would have made that rolling gesture and whispered *oilcan*.

The therapist accepted one word as a complete sentence. "I'm assuming this woman has the potential to be a romantic connection?"

Taylor gave a grunt of agreement. That was one way to put it. The other was that he was crazy about her. She was special, unique, unequaled in his world. He wasn't thinking about a polite dinner; he wanted her in his bed, to lose himself repeatedly and to discover her continuously, for that weekend he'd described as she'd leaned against an oak tree in the dark. For more than a weekend, more than a week. For as long as he lived.

He was insane. He and Scott had already established this, although Scott chose other words.

"Breaking out of the social isolation you built is

the goal, of course. But this is a risky time to imagine yourself in love. Your social isolation has been long-standing. The traumatic event only revealed it. Choosing a new companion is one of those life decisions that should be avoided during a period of grieving and recovery after any trauma. You've done excellent work in identifying your emotions. Now is the time to rebuild the earlier, essential relationships you allowed to lapse, rather than creating new connections."

Apparently, the psych world didn't approve of multitasking. Taylor did. His new connection to Mallory had helped him recognize how far he'd distanced himself from his siblings, why he'd done so, and what the consequences had been. Being with her for one night had been as productive as ten therapy sessions.

"Love can come later," Scott said. "You need to focus on the issues you've already uncovered since September."

Taylor didn't label anything *love*. That was his therapist's word, along with *the traumatic event*, which sounded complicated. Taylor had to remind himself they were talking about a plane crash, horrific but simplistic. A machine had stopped working while he'd been in it, nothing more, nothing less.

He challenged Scott's theory. "Love should wait? And yet, you encourage me to get my brother and sister to love me again." He immediately held up a hand to correct himself before the therapist could. "You're encouraging me to be better at loving them." *After ten years of neglect.* "If love and connections are what the traumatic event revealed I was lacking, what's the difference? Being better at loving is being better at loving."

"The difference is that you already love your brother and sister. You've loved them their whole lives, even if you were burying that emotion for much of that time. This new woman would require you to create a new emotion. I recommend that you acknowledge to yourself that she is interesting, but now is not the time. A symbolic gesture of farewell can close that side road, and you can keep driving in the right direction. A note, flowers, whatever seems appropriate, based on how much you've already invested in the relationship."

It had been a fake relationship from the beginning. Taylor wanted to ask if he should send fake flowers, but he knew it would sound snide.

Bitter. That was an emotion.

As Scott congratulated him for attempting to contact his siblings yesterday, Taylor looked out the window. The entire lake was empty, not one boat for the half mile he could see. The water was flat, ideal for crew, but it was too cold to row. The only craft available to row were a cheap plastic kayak and a clunky fiberglass rowboat, anyway. He should buy himself a racing shell.

"Your text messages to your siblings successfully opened a channel of communication. At our next session, I'd like to discuss your comfort level with trying to reach them live, either through a phone call or video chat. It's unfortunate they'll be in Monte Carlo with your parents for Christmas. If you want to attempt the plane flight, I'll support you."

No way in hell was Taylor getting on an airplane.

"That's a low priority." Taylor sounded so unconcerned. Mallory would say he was just faking it until he made it. She'd be right.

Maybe one day he'd genuinely be unconcerned about flying. If not, he'd fly, anyway. Sooner or later, he would have to travel somewhere beyond the reach of his motorcycle.

"Our next session will be in January," Scott said. "If you feel isolated over Christmas, volunteering at a soup kitchen or other charitable activity can be rewarding in a different way than making a financial donation."

Taylor's security team would love that. With great wealth came the greater risk of being taken hostage by those who wanted that wealth. His private security detail gave Taylor a wide berth at his direction, but he knew they were on the perimeter of his home. If he should obey a sudden impulse to pop into a soup kitchen on Christmas Day, they'd scramble and keep up, but it would be unfair of him to do that to them—and to the soup kitchen. Why should they let him take over someone's job after walking in on a whim?

Scott was in earnest. "Giving the gift of yourself is a gift to yourself."

Such flowery nonsense. Worse than Taylor's own published platitudes.

Scott recapped the issues. Taylor focused on the lake rather than on a brother who didn't text back, a sister who did, and an interesting woman who no longer saw anything in him to admire. He wanted to be on the lake. He wanted to taste the cold water in the air. He craved the feel of a perfectly balanced oar in his hands, but a cheap plastic one would do. In the kayak, he would be the machine that created the speed—not a motorcycle's engine, not a sports car, not a plane. He'd be a machine that would not break. He needed only his own two arms.

Only two arms—those were the limbs that the pilot still had use of. Taylor had reviewed the hospital bills for the month. The wheelchair costs were unchanged from the previous month. No new charges for crutches or a walker. No improvement, then, despite the cutting-edge methodology that the pilot was going through to regain the use of his legs.

Crew required the full body to row, arms and legs, but a kayak was all about the arms. Taylor would send the pilot a kayak, so he could be the machine that flew over the water. Taylor would text his sister back and try his brother again. He would give Mallory real flowers to close an interesting chapter they'd stopped writing on the first page.

He ended the call and tossed his phone onto the nightstand. It knocked a knitted blue mitten askew.

He wouldn't fall in love with his one-night-only fake girlfriend. He'd been through a traumatic event. Now was not the time.

He straightened the mitten.

Not yet.

He'd send those flowers, but he wouldn't say good-bye. *Not yet* meant it might happen, still.

It was time.

"You can do this," Mallory told herself. She swung her backpack over her left shoulder. Nothing new there. She always carried her backpack, just like every other student of every age. It wouldn't arouse any suspicion.

Then she picked up the bedroll she'd made, Girl Scout style. She'd laid her clean clothing out on her warmest blanket, then rolled it up and tied it in place with her belt. It might look odd on a security camera, but she knew the chances of anyone pulling security footage from the dean's office were slim. She'd carry it low by her thigh, just in case.

Lastly, she picked up the grocery bag of granola bars and all the other nonperishables she'd eat while she camped out in her cubicle, looking for a better place to stay. When she found it, she'd leave the ad-ministrative building through a fire-escape door. Those opened from the inside, even when locked on the outside. If she failed to find a place, then staying in a chilly building without electrical power was not going to kill her.

All students had to be out of all of the dorm build-ings by seven. Mallory had timed her departure so that she'd arrive at the office building just before five. With luck, everyone else would have already skipped out early for the holidays. If not, she'd hide in a toi-let stall when security made their final sweep before locking up the office building. It was far from ideal, but desperate times called for desperate measures. Having her plans blow up at the last second qualified.

Mallory had aced her last exam this morning, then she'd caught up with her new friend in her microeconomics class, Jacinda. She was a younger woman—wasn't everyone?—who'd assured her that her parents would love to have her use their spare bedroom for the holidays. Jacinda had a car, too, so Mallory had a free way to get there. It had been a perfect solution for the winter break housing situation.

"Hey, good news," Jacinda had said, just hours ago. "My parents will refund the cleaning fee in January."

The cleaning fee? That was how Mallory had found out that the spare bedroom was listed on a room-share app. She'd misunderstood what Jacinda meant by *Sure, my parents have a spare room, if you need one.*

Mallory was expected to pay $30 a day, plus the $50 cleaning fee.

She didn't have $530. If she did, she wouldn't give it to anyone's parents. She'd buy a plane ticket to Ohio and go see her grandpa. Everything that could go wrong in December had gone wrong, and she was tired of surmounting obstacles. She needed a friendly face. She needed to be with somebody who loved her.

Mallory breathed through the tears that threatened as she stepped into the dorm's elevator and pressed the button for the lobby. She would not cry, because she'd returned to her no-crying-at-all-over-anything policy. The doors opened with a chime. Mallory walked confidently to the front desk, signed her name on the dotted line and officially checked out of her room until January.

There was no turning back now.

She crossed the almost deserted campus and walked into the office building like it was just another day at work. The cluster of cubicles was a ghost town. She headed down her row with her groceries and her bedroll, telling herself the emptiness wasn't creepy at all.

It was her first time in the office in over a week, because students were not allowed to work during final exams. She'd been grateful to spend a week without listening for the nerve-racking sound of a private office's glass door opening. Final exams were less stressful than dodging E.L. Taylor.

There were dead flowers on her desk.

Mallory set her grocery bag on her chair, kicked her bedroll under her desk and dropped the heavy backpack on the floor without taking her eyes off the flowers. The arrangement must have been stunning when it was first delivered. Nothing ostentatious, but a variety of small, unusual blooms arranged in a petite crystal vase. The card was still tied to a ribbon around the vase. No plastic pitchfork, here. This was luxury that fit in a cubicle.

She only knew one person who could afford luxury. Dead petals showered her desk as she lifted the vase to untie the ribbon. The vase was shaped like a pine cone. That seemed—that seemed romantic. Sentimental, at least. He remembered that she'd carried a pine cone in her pocket that whole night.

She tore open the vellum envelope and read the single sentence: *Because I had the time to buy you flowers.*

Every detail of that night was etched on a piece of her heart that she didn't know how to erase. When he'd tossed her up to the top of the hay bales—to safety—she'd told him that wasn't how he should act on a date. He'd said, "There wasn't time to buy you flowers." It had been her first hint that he had a heart and sense of humor trapped underneath that hard exterior.

Oh, Eli, Eli. Why couldn't you have been real, instead of Taylor?

"Mallory."

She whirled around, hiding the card behind herself.

There, straight out of the pages of *Forbes*, stood the country's most successful venture capitalist, E.L. Taylor.

The beard was gone. His hair was styled very well, shorter, devastatingly perfect for his strong features and newly revealed jawline. He wore impeccably tailored slacks, a bespoke dress shirt—it had to have been tailored for him, to fit the width of his shoulders and taper to his waist so well. His watch was understated, for a Rolex.

The last trace of Eli was gone.

"What are you doing here?" he asked curtly.

She did not know this man. In voice, in demeanor, in appearance, he was *the* E.L. Taylor. This was the legend she'd toiled for two years to meet.

Be careful what you wish for; you might get it.

Mallory challenged the one and only E.L. Taylor. "You first. What are you doing here?"

"They're locking up the building tonight for the rest of the year. I came to get my gloves." His voice was flat. He owed no explanations to a peon in a cubicle.

"If you'll excuse me," she said, trying to sound unemotional and flat, just like her former hero, "I have things to do."

"Do you need a ride this evening? You have extra bags."

"No, thank you. I'll—I'm just going to leave them here until next semester."

It had been the smallest hesitation, but he narrowed his eyes for a moment. He took in her casual clothing—more comfortable for sleeping in—and the grocery bag. Then he crouched down, a flex of masculine thighs and backside in those civilized slacks, and looked under her desk.

"You decided to keep a bedroll in your cubicle until January, with a stash of granola bars. Why?"

"It's none of your business."

"Answer me."

"I already did." Mallory found that very satisfying to say. She'd have to adopt that *unnecessary question* thing from her hero. Former hero.

"The dorms close today, too, I assume. Most people who find themselves homeless would choose to sleep in their cars. Why don't you?"

She laughed at his audacity. What did he know about homelessness? "I would have to own a car. My grandfather's car was my one-way ticket to school from Ohio. Then it became a year's meal plan at the dining facility."

"The dining facility which will be closed until January."

She owed him no explanation. He could glare at her all he wanted to. She would not flinch.

But then, to her shock, he smiled that one-tenth of a smile. "Mallory Ames, you are not the paragon I thought you were. You are stubborn to an asinine degree, and you need to learn how to ask for help."

"I'm doing very well. I don't need help."

"Don't prove my point so quickly." His lips quirked—*quirked*, the jerk. "You have nowhere to stay, and I'm renting a six-bedroom house just outside town. I won't make you ask. I'll just answer you. Why yes, I do have a spare room. You're welcome to use it. I happen to have my car today instead of the motorcycle, so grab your stuff. Let's go."

She didn't move. "That would violate a fraternization policy."

"You're not my student. You haven't even signed up for one of those mentorship coffee-and-donut gigs. I suspect that when it's my turn to be the speaker for the Thursday guest lecture series, I will stand behind that podium, and you will not be in the theater."

The mentorship coffees were exclusively for graduate students and well-heeled alumni. Mallory had volunteered to serve the coffee as a way to be in the room where it happened, as the saying went. She'd un-volunteered after the dean had shaken Eli's hand.

"The semester hasn't started. I'm not on the faculty yet. Do I need to keep demolishing your stubborn opposition to the offer of a place to sleep for the winter break? A place, I might add, that won't be having its electricity shut off? Winter is cold, even in Texas. The house is big enough that you can continue to avoid me with very little trouble."

Mallory tried to come up with a brilliant counter to his offer, but that tenth of a smile made him look like Eli, distracting her from the debate.

"If you don't accept this offer, then, at some point in the next week, you will be caught by a security guard on his rounds. Being charged with trespassing is not nearly as good a story as being charged with public indecency."

"You're not funny."

"But I am right."

"I can't live with you. Let me be the one to point out that we've kissed. It's too personal."

He tipped his head to the side, looking more relaxed, not less, now that she'd addressed the elephant in the room. "Kissing generally is."

"This isn't going to be that weekend in your bed you described."

"There are six bedrooms, Mallory. I won't go into any but my own. Since we're being refreshingly blunt here, if you choose to go into mine, I won't kick you out."

"Don't hold your breath."

"I'm not." He picked up her bedroll, grocery bag and backpack. That tenth of a smile took on a shade of sadness. "I told you that you'd never see me the same way again."

Chapter Sixteen

Learning Objective: Identify the similarities and differences between an established business entity and your own prospective company.
—Senior Year Project *by Mallory Ames*

The house wasn't the grandiose palace Mallory had been expecting.

It was a sprawling split-level which spread along its piece of the lakeshore from one wooded boundary to another, taking up almost all of its cleared lot the way a teenager stretched out on a twin bed that was just a little too small for him. There were formal living rooms, two of them, as well as a more casual family room, a sunroom, a game room, two offices, a home gym and a massive back porch. Stairs led up to some rooms and down to others. Passages connected the wings that had been added as the house had grown over the years. Just as he'd promised, Mallory was able to avoid her host without any effort at all.

The only indication he was aware of her presence was a note she'd found on the kitchen counter: *Eat something besides granola bars. Help yourself to anything. The kitchen gets restocked on Wednesdays.* She'd made herself an omelet and left the handwritten note on the counter, aware that just a month ago, she would have been thrilled to have an E.L. Taylor autograph, let alone an entire note. Now, it was just a note from a guy who'd left half a pizza in the fridge.

He'd written on the cardboard box, too. *Yes, I have had pizza around the world, and yes, this one is very good. Reheat in the oven. Don't microwave. Ruins it.*

On her third night in the house, in the middle of a thunderstorm, the power went out.

Mallory took the book she'd been reading—a sweet Christmas novel, a respite after reading so many textbooks this semester—and her cell phone to use as a light, and tiptoed out of her bedroom. She began making her way to the downstairs family room, the one room in the house that had any holiday decorations, for a little ambiance while she finished her novel.

The family room was divided from the kitchen by a breakfast bar with eight barstools. The kitchen and family room combined to make one open space, but it still felt more cozy than the rest of the house, particularly because there was a fireplace in the family room.

The mantel had been decorated with ornaments and garlands that exuded all the holiday warmth of a department store display. Mallory was certain the decorations had been part of the kitchen restock. Some enterprising company probably included it with their regular December deliveries: a dozen eggs, a gallon of milk, a six-foot garland, four bows.

The fireplace had also been stocked with kindling and a charmingly photo-ready pile of logs. This storm was the perfect time to use it. The fire would provide light to read by, so she could save her cell phone battery. If the power stayed out for a long time, the fire would keep the room from getting too chilly. Besides, Mallory hadn't had the chance to build a real log fire in years. If she was going to live here for two weeks, she might as well enjoy the amenities.

She reached the half staircase that led from the hallway with all of the bedrooms down to the family room. Her flannel nightgown covered her from her neck to her toes, so she was warm. More importantly, the nightgown was super modest. If she encountered the other resident of this massive house, she wouldn't be embarrassed by anything other than the flannel's pink bunny print.

She stopped on the stairs. There was already a fire burning, but nobody was around.

It was irresponsible to light a fire and leave. It didn't seem like something the brilliant E.L. Taylor would do. She took the last step down and tiptoed toward the kitchen, thinking he might be there, but it was only a black space. All of the appliances with their glowing digital clocks and touchpads had died with a crack of lightning.

"What are you doing?"

Mallory spun around with the book clutched to her chest. She could see over the back of the couch, now that she was in the room. Taylor was stretched out on it, staring at the fire, not at her.

"You scared me to death," she said.

He didn't say anything, so after standing there awkwardly for a moment too long, Mallory turned to go back up the stairs.

"You should stay and read by the firelight." He hadn't taken his eyes off the fire, but he'd seen her book with that super peripheral vision, apparently.

"I don't want to intrude," she said.

"Please. Intrude."

There was something in that *please* that made her step closer to get a better view of him over the back of the couch. "Are you okay?"

He shut his eyes, blew out a breath, then turned his face toward her and opened his eyes. "Yes."

She looked at his face and thought, *No.*

She should go. She was trying not to dwell on either Eli, who'd never been real, or Mr. Taylor, whom she avoided like the plague, but she never stopped thinking about this man, for better or worse. Sharing this room with him wasn't going to make her think about him any more than she already did, so she might as well stay near the fire. Her bedroom was pitch-black and would soon grow cold.

She held up her book. "The couch is the closest to the light, and you're kind of hogging it."

He sat up.

Mallory sat down.

They remained side by side in silence for an eternity. Mallory went through the motions of reading her book although she was far too aware of *him*, the physical presence of the man next to her, his body strong and healthy, his whole demeanor unhappy.

"You're staring," he said, without looking away from the fire. His five-o'clock shadow was just enough to add a touch of Eli to his appearance.

"My book is boring. There's nothing else to look at."

Do you miss being Eli? Do you miss holding hands with a girl in a blue ski cap?

She needed to stop thinking like that. It was like asking an actor if he missed being a movie character. E.L. Taylor had given an Oscar-worthy performance, but he was not Eli.

"I don't know what to call you," she said. "Mr. Taylor in the office, of course. What should I call you here? E.L. Taylor is a mouthful. Do you go by E.L.?"

"Just Taylor."

"Okay."

"You can call me Eli."

She closed her book. "I don't think you're trying to be mean right this moment, I really don't, but it's not nice for you to remind me what a sucker I was. I'm not going to keep calling you by a fake name. It's not cute."

"It's not a fake name. I was Eli growing up. I still

am, to my immediate family. If I see them." He closed his eyes and turned his head from the fire toward her again, such an odd way to look from one thing to another, but the end result was the same, Paul-Newman-blue eyes gazing into hers.

"I don't know why I told you Eli when you asked me my name, but it wasn't intended to trick you into being a sucker. You weren't one, anyway. A sucker gets taken advantage of and loses something of value. Their money, their car. There has to be something they get suckered out of."

"I didn't know who you were. You took advantage of that by staying anonymous."

"To get what from you? What did I trick you out of?" *My heart*.

With the firelight on his face and the shadow on his jaw, he looked so much like Eli, it hurt. She wished she didn't still like him as Taylor.

She pulled up her feet to sit cross-legged, smoothing pink flannel bunnies over her knees. "You amused yourself at my expense."

"Mallory." He said her name with such disappointment, like she was a student he'd expected to give a better answer. "When I read that wish and saw my own name, did I strike you as being amused?"

"Can't you see what a fool you made of me? I told you all my plans and all the flaws in my plans, all the mistakes I made. I laid it all out for the man who wrote 'Never divulge more details than necessary.' Your book taught me to anticipate what might go wrong, so I would never be taken by surprise. How did my face look when I realized which office you were being shown into? I'm floundering now. I broke all the rules that had been working for me, and I don't know how my plan is going to turn out."

"That book wasn't intended to dictate your life."

"Yes, it was. It's an advice book. You can't conduct your business one way and your personal life another. Either you believe in moving forward, or you don't. You believe in setting goals, or you don't. You make hard choices, or you don't."

He sat forward, elbows on his knees, and scrubbed his face with both hands. "I wish I'd never written that book. It's caused me nothing but grief."

How could he hate a book that had been so important to her? A book that he wrote?

"It made you a lot of money. It made you famous enough to be on TV, and that made you even more money. You dated beautiful, famous women. A rock star. A supermodel."

"Like I said, nothing but grief." He kept his head in his hands, but another smile touched his lips. "I see you've been doing your research."

Busted.

For two years, she'd only researched him by reading articles and interviews in her local library's copies of *Forbes* and *Harvard Business Review.* She hadn't been interested in his personal life. That would not help her move forward with her plan, and she'd been so very strict with herself about putting all her effort toward her goals.

But after Eli had walked into the dean's office and

shocked her to her core, she'd made up for lost time. The first candid shirtless photo she saw had made her jaw drop. How unfair that the one day of her life she'd gotten to sit on his lap, they'd been in winter coats.

Tonight, he wore long plaid pajama bottoms and a close-fitting, short-sleeved T-shirt, exposing his arms to her sight for the first time. He looked great in photos, but being only a couch cushion away as those defined muscles bunched and flexed and stretched the sleeve of that T-shirt was something else—the difference between looking at a photo of a tropical ocean and actually standing on the shore with her toes in the hot sand. She didn't touch the water either way. But, in person, the possibility was right there, if only a wave would lap a little higher on the shore.

Most of the photos had been taken at black-tie events. The man looked good in a tux. So did the women who got to be by his side. He didn't need a caregiver from Ohio as a girlfriend.

Pretend you're equals.

She shrugged and waved one hand, a princess in pink bunny print. "Feel free to research me back."

"How?" He dropped his hands and sat back. "I can't just look at a thousand photos of you on the internet. I tried."

"You tried?"

"Of course. I came up empty. I have to do my research some other way." He turned sideways on the couch and laid his arm across the back of it, giving her all of his attention, while she split hers between his blue eyes and those incredible arms.

"I have to look at you whenever I can in real life instead of photos. It's not often enough." He tapped his temple. "But I've got pictures up here of Mallory crossing the campus in her blue jeans. I see Ms. Ames killing it in the office in her pencil skirt. I can tell a lot about the kind of day you're having by the way you walk."

She frowned. "When do you see me walk?"

"When you leave the office, you take the sidewalk that goes past the east side of the building. My side. On the days I pretend I have a reason to come into the office, I wait for you to walk by before I leave, except that one night. You were still there, but the janitor had started cleaning the offices, so I finally left, but I sat in my car a while, waiting for you to come out. You didn't. I went back in and found you and Irene in my office."

Mallory could still taste the fear that she'd been on the brink of losing everything. "I was being fired. You were very smooth with your excuses."

"You played along flawlessly. I thought it was better to give her a story she could accept. I know how the rumor mill would have worked if I'd told her it was none of her damned business how you'd gotten my gloves, which is what I wanted to say."

"I didn't thank you then. Let me thank you now. Without that job, I would have lost my financial aid package. I would have had to drop out."

"You will never have to drop out."

"What does that mean?"

They stared at one another through one lightning flash. Another.

Taylor dropped his gaze to his thigh and flicked imaginary lint from his plaid flannel pants. "There's money in your student account, if you need it. If you don't, let it sit. The school will give you the remaining funds when you graduate and they close out the books."

"I *don't* need it." She'd worked for two years to achieve success on her own terms, and now the man who'd inspired her to do so was telling her she could give up, take some free money and be just fine?

Aren't you proud of me for doing this, E.L. Taylor? I made a plan exactly the way you taught me to. Do you think I can't complete it?

"I can do this," she said. "I *am* doing this."

"It's just twenty grand." He spoke evenly, but he sounded angry.

"Twenty grand?" It was a breathtaking amount. She could move out of the subsidized dorm, rent an apartment, and still have enough to buy a used car and more. "I can't accept that much. I can't accept any amount."

He laughed, sort of. "You're consistent. You didn't want me to give you money for hot chocolate, either. Take the money. It won't hurt me. Good God. I hit the half-billion mark this year."

She sucked in a quick breath. Five hundred million dollars? It was an unfathomable amount of money.

"And still, people I care about won't take my money. I have to pay bills for them when they aren't looking." He drove his hand through his hair. "Why won't any of you take the money? It isn't tainted. I haven't made it by doing anything illegal or immoral. I won't miss the money."

"The point isn't that the money won't affect you," Mallory said. "It affects me."

The rain pelted the windows, a force of nature that dumped water whether the people below wanted or needed it. She'd be a fool not to use the money, but it didn't make her instantly happy. Twenty thousand was a sudden deluge in a land where she'd painstakingly constructed irrigation ditches in the sand.

"'Never let anything take you by surprise,'" she quoted. She laid her hands in her lap, palms up, empty. For now. "I failed to predict the possibility of an influx of cash at this stage of the plan. I'm a terrible student of E.L. Taylor, it turns out. He tested me, and I wasn't ready for it."

Taylor sounded resigned. "You'll modify your plan, and you'll use it to its best effect. That's the way you are. It's been refreshing to know a woman who'd prefer college tuition instead of another set of earrings."

"Twenty-thousand-dollar earrings?" She sounded sour. Jealousy was not her best self. "Be real."

He lifted the hand that had been resting beside her shoulder, tucked a strand of hair behind her ear, then gently touched the shell of the ear he'd bared. "Yes, for real. But those women have slept with me."

"Unlike me." Her voice was supposed to sound firm, not husky. Not jealous.

"You and I are something different. What's between us isn't courteous, consensual sex."

"What is between us?"

She wouldn't have dreamed she'd be asking this even a half hour ago, but this storm, that *Please, intrude*, his frustration that money wasn't a simple gift for her and for others—*people I care about*—combined to make an invulnerable man seem vulnerable. It crept into her heart just enough to make her feel a little vulnerable, too.

"I don't know what we have, Ms. Mallory Ames. I haven't put a name to it, have you?"

"No, Mr. E.L. Taylor, I have not."

His voice was quiet, reflective. "If we shared a bed, I think we'd be lovers, not people who date and have sex when their schedules allow. We'd want each other every night. We'd share our days, a meal, a conversation, anticipating those nights." He leaned closer and gently pressed his thumb on her lower lip, the way she'd done to him as they'd shared the tree branch. It was, she realized now, a touch that was more intimate to receive than to give.

"I can only learn so much from seeing you on a faraway sidewalk. If I want to know more about you, and I do, then I have to talk to you on stormy nights. I have to listen to what you say, and what you don't, and watch the expressions on your face as you do and don't tell me about yourself. I need to learn you differently than I've learned anyone else in my life, because there's more here, and it's very real. I want to be with you just like this tonight, to talk with you like a lover, even if you never become my lover."

His fingers trailed over her hair. Her heart tripped and her skin heated, a familiar sensation, so like her night with Eli when she'd fallen under his spell in the shadow of the massive tree, when he'd told her she could do with him as she pleased. *Anything we haven't done yet, or everything we already have.*

It had sounded so sensual despite being in the middle of a park, no place for a seduction, so they'd broken their mood with a laugh, agreeing that it was a bad time and place to play that game. She hadn't known there was another game being played simultaneously, that the man toying with her had been E.L. Taylor, pretending to be someone else.

He touched, very precisely, the imitation pearl stud in her earlobe, one he could and would so easily replace with a real pearl, for any lover.

He was toying with her again. She knew for a fact he could manipulate others, he could sound sincere when he was not, he could fake anything.

She stood and snatched up her book. "I've had enough of that game. You're very good at it. Stop practicing on me."

"No—Mallory, stay."

"Really, Eli?" *Damn it—that shadow of a beard.* "I mean, really, Taylor? Good night. I leave you to your fire and all of the abject misery that comes with writing a wildly successful book and hitting the half-billion mark and—and having sex with glamorous women you shower with twenty-thousand-dollar earrings. You poor man, it all sounds so grim."

As she headed for the stairs, her peripheral vision was just good enough to see Taylor fall back on the couch to resume his sprawling position in defeat.

She made her way back to her bed by the flashes of lightning, pushed open the door and dove for the mattress, landing facedown so she could muffle her cries in the bedding, and nobody would know how weak she was, except herself.

Chapter Seventeen

Learning Objective: Describe the effect which a volatile market would have on your business.
—Senior Year Project *by Mallory Ames*

Taylor jackknifed upright, awakened by the hideous crack of thunder. He tried to get his bearings in the darkness. He was still on the sofa. The room was black except for the orange glow of a few dying embers. There was no storm outside the window, but he'd heard thunder.

Not thunder. There'd been an explosion. He was supposed to be doing something, a task that meant life or death. What the hell was it?

Water was part of it, he knew that, so he stumbled in the darkness from the couch to the kitchen island to the sink, knocking over a bar stool on the way. He couldn't stop to pick it up—he needed to do something with the water.

He cursed out loud, and the sound of his voice was real. He held on to the edge of the sink and turned on the tap. The water felt real. The dream—it had been the dream again, of course. It always started the same, with him in the air, unable to muster any vestige of awe at the dark landscape below as he watched the headlights of miniature cars traveling in straight lines, exactly as he'd felt on a real September night.

Then a propeller had stopped spinning, black water had come rushing into focus. *Terror.* He'd seen clearly—too late, too late—that he'd lost everything important to his soul years before he'd lost his life in a single second of deafening impact. *Regret.*

Only he hadn't died.

He'd come to just seconds later. Water had been pouring into the broken cockpit, bringing with it a rush of cold, clean-washed air, which he'd been so desperate to inhale below the toxic smoke of the burning fuel that had cost him $150. He'd clawed his way out of his seat belt and ducked under the water.

He cracked his head on the plane's controls, reached out blindly, felt a human body, a leg in jeans. The pilot was here. The pilot wasn't moving—was he dead, this supposed friend, this person from his past? Taylor couldn't let the body burn up.

He groped frantically in the dark, lungs bursting under the water, but there was no air above the water, either, so he kept going until his hand hit the pilot's seat belt buckle. He could feel the heat of the fire right through the water. *God—God, I'll boil alive.*

With an explosive effort that drew out every last bit of energy remaining in every last cell of his body, he launched himself over the controls toward the pilot's missing door. His head broke the water's surface, his lungs sucked in the unbreathable black smoke, and he rolled onto his back, dragging the pilot's body with him. Taylor's arm was his oar, his hand was the blade. Catch, stroke, recover, catch, stroke, recover— the rhythm must be kept while muscles strained. *Ignore the pain, cross the finish line, break that record, more, faster, take the pain, winning is everything.* The air became breathable, the fire more distant, with every stroke of the oar, every pull of his shoulder muscles.

Then the fire went out. Through the grit in his eyes, he strained to see the plane, but it had vanished. The water was black, the air clear. The plane must have sunk, and Taylor would sink, too, if he stopped for even one stroke, weighed down by the lifeless body he was dragging along. Catch, stroke, recover.

His ears were ringing from the sound of metal sheering on impact. He couldn't hear the sound of his own strokes, his own grunts of exertion. He didn't hear the woman in the canoe until she was on top of him, a little grandma who paddled like hell while Taylor hung onto a rope she'd wrapped around his arm, once they'd both realized he was too exhausted to lift the pilot's body into the boat, too exhausted to climb in himself without letting go of the pilot.

"Are you okay? I heard you crash into something and shout."

Taylor gripped the edge of the sink. He could hear. He could hear the woman speaking.

"Taylor, do you hear me? Are you sleepwalking? Hey, Eli. It's me."

The ringing in his ears cleared instantly, for it was only a phantom from the crash that had left him deafened for days. A phantom could not exist in reality, and reality had just walked up to his side, a barefooted woman wearing a nun's habit made of flannel with pink bunnies.

Pink bunnies. Mallory. *Oh, thank God.*

He let go of the sink and grabbed Mallory for dear life, hauling her against his chest and burying his face in her hair. The long strands tickled his nose as he breathed in too hard, too fast. They stuck to his wet cheeks—damn it, his cheeks were wet—and he welcomed that nuisance, he craved that touch that could do him no good, except to bring him back to his body and his place in the world, in this kitchen, holding Mallory.

He was alive.

Now, what was he going to do about it?

"You're doing a shot of tequila?"

The disbelief in Eli's voice sounded better to Mallory than the anguish had.

She kept an eye on him as she sliced a lime into quarters. She'd picked up the toppled bar stool and pushed him onto it a little while ago, after he'd told her the terrible story about the plane crash. She'd stoked the fireplace to get some light and heat in the room, hurrying because she didn't want to leave him at the cold breakfast bar, alone.

As soon as she was within arm's reach, he'd pulled her close to stand between his knees, and he'd kept his arms looped around her waist. He'd watched the fire as he'd told her about the pilot who couldn't walk. She'd felt his crushing guilt in every word, and she'd held his head in both of her hands as she'd pressed her cheek to his, smooth against rough. The warm tears had been hers, that time.

"You're really doing a shot of tequila?" he asked again.

Mallory pushed aside the lime slices and plunked a bottle of very high-end tequila on the breakfast bar. "I assume that is a rhetorical question."

She watched Eli's face, but the fire was behind him, so it was hard to see if she'd gotten even a tenth of a smile.

Relax. Smile. You need to loosen up.

If she wasn't able to help him smile, that was okay. He was allowed to feel any way he wanted to feel as far as she was concerned. He'd survived a wreck, a fire, a near-drowning.

She felt raw enough just hearing about it, just holding him through the memory of it. This man, who'd been so important to her in one way for two years, might never have become important to her in a different way this December. He could have ceased to exist. She would have spent her twenty-ninth birthday hiding in a festival crowd she didn't want to be in. She would have had no one to tell her Cinderella wasn't as self-reliant as she was. She wouldn't have known what it was like to kiss a man with her heart wide open under a starry sky.

He was right: it had been the kiss of a lifetime. She'd almost never had it. That alternate Mallory wouldn't have known what could have been.

She sat on the bar stool next to his and put her head on his shoulder. He didn't move away or shake off her touch.

"Why haven't I heard about this? Wasn't it in the news?"

"I kept it out. It's not good for business."

She picked her head up. "How do you keep something like that a secret? Aren't there official investigations?"

"There are. Money fixes things." He put one finger under her chin and gently closed her mouth. "Legally. Reports can be redacted for the public for all kinds of excuses that lawyers are paid well to come up with. It's a business investment to have them do it. The news would have hurt a dozen fledgling companies who are depending on my reputation in order to get off the ground."

She'd accused him of not knowing how to correctly *fake it 'til you make it*, but he knew how. He had to do it, or other people with dreams like hers would suffer.

She ducked her chin, embarrassed that she hadn't seen this before. "'Never show weakness.' You have to appear invulnerable all the time."

"E.L. Taylor does, yes. That's part of my job, but I've been just the same as you."

She raised her head at that. "I'm embarrassed I ever tried to say we were equal-ish."

"We're two peas in a pod. I told you my book wasn't intended to apply to your personal life, but I was applying it to mine, too. I was so focused on creating E.L. Taylor and then maintaining E.L. Taylor that I lost touch with my family. I can barely remember people I was friends with when I was younger. Eli Taylor forgot that being the invincible E.L. Taylor was a job, not a life."

He laced his fingers in between hers. "This girl in a blue ski cap sat on a hay bale next to me once, clapping her boots together to get the sand off them, and she said she was pretending all the time, too. But she's not my equal. She's wiser. Already cautious about spending an entire life pretending to be someone she isn't. She told me that being who you really are, flaws and all, might be a better way to live, but if you never try it, you'll have wasted your only chance to find out."

She nodded, too touched to speak. He remembered everything she said. He paid attention to her. He treated her like a lover whether or not she ever slept with him.

"The moment before I knew I was going to die, my thought was, 'I wasted it.' I'd gotten to live for thirty-two years, but I'd wasted them. I wasn't leaving behind anyone who would grieve for me. I know that sounds selfish, but that means I hadn't invested myself in other people. Their businesses, yes, but not people. No one would miss me at a family dinner, because I never visited my family anymore, anyway. No one would miss my sense of humor, because I never relaxed enough to be even mildly funny with anyone." He picked up their joined hands and rubbed her knuckles along his jaw as if it were the greatest luxury in the world to do so. "No one would miss holding my hand. I'd wasted my life."

"But now you won't."

"You'd think I'd be like Scrooge after the ghosts visited. He saw the error of his ways, threw open the windows on Christmas morning and everything was fixed, just like that. I'm afraid it doesn't work that way. But I found a decent therapist. I'm making progress."

"Progress? Even when I didn't know you were E.L. Taylor, you were very E.L. Taylor-ish. How are you going to stop being that?" She used their hands to push him in the shoulder. "You're not going to swagger into the office and leave all the women sighing in little melted puddles anymore?"

"You're kidding."

"Not kidding. You definitely have swagger. You should keep that part." He had the sexiest tenth of a smile she'd ever seen, and she was getting to see it right now. It made her heart hop and flutter. She didn't waste any energy trying to stop that unstoppable hop.

"I made progress because I made contact with my sister. We've texted this week."

That was sobering. "That's the first time you've talked to her since September?"

He let go of her hand and picked up a lime slice, evaluating it in the firelight. "The first time in more than a year. They're almost eleven years younger than I am."

"They? Two sisters?"

"A brother and a sister. Twins. When I went off to college, they were starting third grade. They turned twenty-one in October. Decided to do it in Vegas."

"That sounds like fun."

"I didn't go. It was after the crash, but…" He set down the lime. "See? It's not like a magic wand just fixes everything."

"Cinderella never knew how easy she had it."

"You're mildly funny," he said, and she smiled, since he couldn't. "I didn't want to fly. The therapist said that was normal. It won't be an issue unless I get to the point I think I'll never fly again, but for now… normal. But that wasn't the only reason I didn't see them. It's awkward to be around them. I don't know how to make up for so much neglect.

"They're twins, so they're extra close. I told myself they didn't need me, so it wasn't that bad if I didn't go home and spend time with them during college. Those visits got more rare as I began being the businessman instead of the person. It's hard to suddenly say, 'Changed my mind. Let's be family again.' I'm making progress, though. Thank you for that."

"What did I do?"

"You cried on me. You made me feel like I had

some potential to be... I don't know. To be there, if somebody needed me. After Eli had a perfect night with Mallory, he knew that even if the twins no longer needed him, he still needed them to know he was around, in case they ever did. So I texted them. She answered. He didn't."

Mallory put her head back on his shoulder. His definition of progress was so paltry. *This poor man, so grim.* "What else did your therapist tell you?"

"If I stare at enough fires, they won't make me feel sick anymore. And I should be very careful to not fall in love with you."

She closed her eyes, one moment of pure emotion, not good, not bad, just an intense pulse, the inseparable blend of hope and fear, love and grief.

Then she picked up her head and picked up the bottle of tequila. "That's enough for now. I don't know about you, but if I'm going to spend the rest of the night watching a fire until it burns itself out, if I'm going to do that while someone I care about talks to me like a lover, even though we're not supposed to become lovers, I definitely am going to need a shot of tequila first."

She poured one glass and picked up a lime slice. Eli—because he'd always been Eli, deeply buried but abruptly freed by a terrible crash—pushed the second shot glass toward her with a smile that was at least two-tenths of a full smile.

"Hit me up, bartender."

She poured while he made his way through the dark to the stove, coming back with a shaker of salt.

He kissed the back of her hand, then sprinkled salt where he'd kissed. He licked the side of his finger with a wink that brought back all of that buzzy, aroused feeling she'd gotten accustomed to on her twenty-ninth birthday, then he salted that spot, too.

Eli began the traditional toast. "Remember, life is always easier when you take it with a grain of salt."

They licked the salt.

"And a shot of tequila."

They threw back the shots.

Mallory finished the toast as fast as she could. "And-a-slice-of-lime." She shoved the lime in her mouth to ease the tequila's burn.

Then she and Eli sat on the floor in front of the couch and stared down the fire, together.

Taylor woke up on the floor.

He could tell it was daylight because the sun was trying to come in through his eyelids, but he wouldn't let it. He kept his eyes shut, and drifted back to sleep.

He drifted awake a minute or an hour later. With his eyes shut, his brain cataloged all the spots on his body that had been in contact with the hard floor for too long. In every house he owned, every interior designer scattered luxury pillows on a carpet in front of a fireplace for comfort. Taylor knew from hard experience that pillows were never that damned luxurious after an hour on a floor, let alone a whole night. He preferred a bed, always, with or without a bed partner.

Speaking of which...there was a woman, breathing softly, using his chest as a pillow.

He cracked open one eye and saw pink bunnies.

Mallory. Holy smoke. *Mallory.* It all came back to him. She'd spent the entire night with him. How had he gotten so damned lucky?

There'd been no sex, of that he was certain. His body would be flying from the endorphins, still. His heart would be—well, he didn't know how his heart would feel once it got its heart's desire, because that had never happened before. And it hadn't happened last night, because when it came to Mallory, he hadn't found the names for the emotions he felt toward her.

He opened both eyes and looked up at the Christmas decorations peeking over the edge of the mantel. There'd been a shot of tequila. Before that, the dream. He hated that dream. Hated it every time. But this time, it had ended with Mallory to hold on to. Talking. Tequila. A fire that hadn't transformed itself into anything except a couple of small logs in a modest fireplace. A woman falling asleep with her head in his lap while he wrapped a strand of her hair around the finger he'd used for the tequila salt. He'd unwrapped the strand, wrapped a different strand, over and over, until he'd fallen asleep, too. All in all, a damned good night.

Would have been better on a bed. This floor was hard.

Mallory was soft. In her flannel, she felt like the ultimate teddy bear, so wholesome, even with her thigh thrown over his. He reached down to move her leg and encountered her bare knee. He lifted his head an inch—a reflex—and saw Mallory's very bare, very sexy thigh draped over him. Her nun's habit of a nightgown was completely bunched up around her waist. If he picked his head up higher, he'd probably see what she wore below the waist, under her clothes—so hell, yes, he lifted his head.

Nothing. She wore nothing, unless one counted a scrap of black lace that didn't begin to cover the round curve of her backside, the very last thing he would have guessed lay under pink bunnies, a pink coat, a blue ski cap, a *thong*, good God, he'd never been so hard in his life.

"Yoo-hoo. Anybody home?"

What the hell? A female voice. Was it Wednesday? Had they come to restock the kitchen?

"Eli, are you here?"

Eli. The only woman who called him Eli was sound asleep in his arms. Except for his mother, who was in Monte Carlo. Or his sister, who lived hours from here, but sounded like she was in the hallway.

"This house goes on forever. Have we been down this hallway yet? This must be the last of the bedrooms."

His brother's voice. He hadn't even texted back.

Eli couldn't believe they were here, his brother and sister. He couldn't believe they were about to walk in on him—him and Mallory, sleeping together. At least he was dressed a T-shirt and pants, and Mallory's nightgown was modest—oh, *crap*.

It was instinct to try to cover her up as his siblings burst into the room, which was how he was caught with his hand spread over Mallory's bare backside as his sister jumped off the bottom stair and threw her arms open wide. "Ta-da! Merry Chrisss...oops!"

Chapter Eighteen

Learning Objective: Define the term "rapid-growth firm."
— Senior Year Project *by Mallory Ames*

"I was shielding you from their view."

"By putting your hand on my butt?"

"Yes. Your underwear is too small."

Mallory rolled her eyes. This was absolutely, positively, the worst possible way to wake up, ever. She was never going to recover from this, *ever*. She was going to be beet red from now until the day she died.

Eli had taken her aside to give her a quick update on just who these people were, but it had quickly become a hissing match between the two of them. His brother and sister were pretending to ignore them while sitting at the breakfast bar with their backs to the cold fireplace.

"I thought you'd only just exchanged your first text message in a *too small* eternity. How did you not know they'd stop by? Do they live in Masterson?"

"We live in Dallas," his sister said cheerfully, turning around in her seat to address her older brother. "We came in your jet. You said we could use it in your text, so we're using it."

Mallory was startled. His sister had heard their angry whispers from across the room.

Eli cursed softly.

"Heard that," his sister said. "Oh, look what's for breakfast. A bottle of tequila. Good thing I turned twenty-one. *In Vegas.* You should have been there."

Eli grimaced. "I forget how good her hearing is. It's freaky."

"So, you have freaky wide-angle vision or whatever, and she has freaky hearing." Mallory addressed his little brother, who was also six feet tall. "What freaky sense do you have?"

"None at all. I'm just normal." He said it with a smile, but it was subdued. Perhaps he felt like the odd man out in this trio of siblings.

"Good. Then I like you best." Mallory marched her bare-footed self over to the bar stool next to him and sat down. "I'm Mallory Ames, by the way, and I am never going to recover from this first impression. I'm very sorry for…it."

"I'm TJ," he said. "You were asleep. He's the one who should be very sorry for…it."

"I didn't let you onto the property unannounced," Eli said drily. "The security guard is the one who'll be very sorry for…it."

TJ scowled, which made him look more like Eli. "He's the guy you sent to Vegas to keep an eye on us. He knew who we were. Don't fire him."

"I'm Eli," his sister said. "My name is really Eleanor Elizabeth. You can call me Eliza. But Eli is pretty close, and when I was little, I wanted to be just like my brother." She made a face at TJ. "My cool brother, so I made everyone call me Eli, too."

"That's so cute." Mallory turned to check on Eli— her Eli. He looked baffled, as if he had never seen any of the three people who were sitting at the breakfast bar before. She had to make a *get over here* motion with her hand behind TJ's back.

Eliza was perfectly capable of carrying the conversation if everyone else was too embarrassed, subdued or baffled to do it. "I got named after two great queens. Eleanor Elizabeth. Lucky me."

TJ sighed. "You do this every time."

"TJ got named after Roman emperors. Tell us what TJ stands for, TJ."

"Tacitus Jovian."

"Wow," Mallory said. "I've never met a Tacitus Jovian before. What does E.L. stand for?"

"He wouldn't tell you?"

Everyone looked at Eli.

"She never asked. It's Erasmus Leonardo. I got the Renaissance geniuses."

Everyone looked at Mallory, who tried valiantly

to nod as if that was a perfectly ordinary baby name. "Well. Now that we've all been introduced, I'm going to slink away in humiliation and find something to wear that might be a little more dignified in case our paths cross again. It was nice to meet you. I'm sorry the power's still out. I hope you three have a good time together." She headed for the half staircase.

Mallory's hearing wasn't amazing, but Eliza wasn't trying to whisper, either. "She's not leaving, is she? Your date ends first thing in the morning after a fun night of tequila? I like her. You should try talking to her when you're not in bed."

"I do talk to her. She's staying here for the holidays."

Eliza sucked in a happy-sounding breath. "Oh, that's exciting. Go get dressed, too, so you can both show us around. Hurry up. No hanky-panky. We're only here until seven tonight. Then TJ and I are taking your jet to Monte Carlo. We're not as good as you are at getting out of Christmas with the parents."

Eli knew he was doomed the moment the twins spotted the two-person kayak.

"You have to race us. Rowboat versus kayak." Eliza turned to Mallory to keep her in the loop. "If there are Taylors and boats, there must be a race."

TJ picked up one of the oars and gave it a spin. "If we're not competing, we're not a family."

Eli wasn't imagining a touch of bitterness there. Or was he? He turned to Mallory.

She only smiled at him as if they were a happy

little couple, because they were faking it once again. They'd discussed it out of Eliza's earshot, which meant they'd had to go to another room and shut the door.

Mallory had objected: *You only have one day. I'll be in the way.*

He'd begged. *I need you to hit me upside the head with that oilcan if I screw this up. I don't want to screw this up.*

The oilcan reminder had softened her up a little. *We'll just behave like friends, right? I mean, we are just friends. Not lovers.*

Mallory, they're going to think it's weird if we're all stiff and formal with each other, old buddy, old pal, considering how the day began.

I can't do fake kisses with you.

How about real hand-holding?

Deal.

Since the power was still out, they'd all eaten Mallory's granola bars for breakfast. Nobody had washed theirs down with tequila. Then they'd all started their tour of the house, worked their way outside, skipped past the empty stable, and zeroed in on the dock.

"Do you need to do some warmups?" Eliza asked him. "Given your advanced age?"

"Athletes always warm up." Eli swung his arms, big swings to loosen up the shoulders, as Eliza stood still. "The smart athletes do, at any rate. If you capsize, it's not my fault that you have to fly to Monte Carlo tonight in wet clothes."

TJ handed his sister a life vest. "Mallory has to get in the rowboat."

Mallory didn't think so. "There are oars only for one person. I'd just be deadweight. A rowboat is slower than a kayak, already."

Eliza snapped her life vest shut. "Exactly."

They agreed to row and paddle out to a buoy, which gave everyone a warm-up. They'd race from the buoy back to the dock.

Eli made sure Mallory was situated, then he pushed off, put the oars in the oarlocks and set his feet. It was like riding the proverbial bicycle, although he hadn't been on the water in years. Easy as pie.

Until he took the first real stroke. Catch—put the oar in the water at just the right angle. Stroke—pull the oar through the water. Release—lift the oar out of the water, bring it back to the start position. *Catch, stroke, release.*

This was not his first time on the water in years. He'd been on the water, in the dark, in September. *Catch, stroke, release.* Dragging a pilot whom he'd thought was dead. If he'd released his hold on what he'd thought was a corpse, the pilot would have drowned. Eli would have murdered him without knowing it. *Catch, stroke—*

He let go of an oar. It started to slip out of the oarlock. He caught it. Too many years of training didn't abandon him, even now, while he was out on the water where explosions made him deaf, where he couldn't hear the voice of the woman in the canoe.

"I can row us back to the dock," said a different voice.

Mallory.

"You don't have to be out here if you don't want to be out here. I'm on your side, whatever you want to do."

It was the voice of the woman he loved. Eli could hear her, and thank God, he could hear her, because he loved her.

Can you name that emotion, Mr. Taylor?

He was so done with that. The emotion was love, as obvious to him now as the oars in his hands, but naming it, knowing it, wasn't enough. He wanted to act on that emotion. He needed to get over *the traumatic event* before he could do so, or else he might drag Mallory under, too. He was sick, literally sick, and very tired of waiting to recover.

His therapist had been good, setting him on the path, pointing him in the right direction, but that pace wasn't going to work any longer.

He was E.L. Taylor, damn it, and he gave advice to people, too. He advised those who were ready for change to determine their core question and use that to make their plans. For Mallory, it had been *Are you going to finish your degree?* Eli knew his core question now. *Are you ready to recover?*

The answer was yes.

He looked into Mallory's eyes, and he started rowing.

The rowboat was nothing like a racing shell, clunky instead of sleek, but the basic motion was the same. The resistance of the water against the blade, even the sense of creating speed were there. It felt good. Then it felt great. Then Eli won the race.

His sister pouted while he gave her a hand to pull her up onto the dock. "You are such a show-off."

"Show-off? *Show-off?* You forced me to row."

Eliza smirked at him. "Oh, I read this great book. It says 'Never say someone made you do it. You and only you control your actions.'"

Eli trapped her arms in a bear hug from behind and picked her up before she could react. "It does not say that. You lost the race. You're going in."

She put up a good fight, he'd give her that, and when he held her over the freezing water, she got in a really good kick on his left shin, which hurt like the devil and also made him proud. She was still as feisty as she'd been in third grade.

But a lot bigger. He set her down on the dock. "If it wasn't December, you'd be going in. Watch out when the weather gets warmer. When you least expect it, I'll be collecting this debt."

Her face lit up. "This summer? I can come and live with you here this summer? My master's degree is a year-round program, but I get almost the whole month of June off. I could bring my horse. That stable's just sitting empty. I'll bring two. We could ride."

Eli felt terrible—and honestly, a little claustrophobic at the thought of having his family moving in with him, bringing their animals, consuming his time. "No. That won't work. I'm just renting this house for a few months."

There was a terrible moment of silence.

Eliza shrugged. "It was just a thought."

But she looked like a six-year-old whose Barbie had just lost an arm. Eli knew that, because she'd once brought him her Barbie and its arm to fix. He'd laughed at the sight, and she'd immediately pretended she didn't care if it ever got fixed, because it was just a dumb doll. He'd fixed it, but she'd never brought him another broken toy. It was shocking, how much damage one could do in a thoughtless moment.

Eliza started to leave the dock. He'd told her no, that he wouldn't spend the summer with her. He hadn't meant it that way, just like he hadn't meant to laugh at a plastic doll with one arm.

He tried to explain. "I have Tokyo on my schedule almost every other week this summer. I don't have any reason to rent this house in June. It's nothing personal."

Eliza kept walking. It was too late, the damage had been done.

No, damn it. I have to fix this.

"The rental agreement is only through May," he said to her back. "I couldn't stay through June if I wanted to."

Eliza turned around. "You could own this house by June. If they didn't want to sell it, you could make them an offer they couldn't refuse. You have the money to do anything you want. The only reason you won't have this house in June is because you don't want it. You don't think it's worth what you'd get in return."

She walked away.

Damn it.

He turned to his brother. "I don't know what she means."

TJ only shrugged and walked off the dock, too.

Eli watched them go. They didn't need him. He felt the loss, but he also felt the fairness of it. How many times had he walked away, back to college, back to Wall Street, leaving them behind, making them feel unwanted? If he'd known how it felt…

It felt terrible.

A hand took his. "I don't know what that was about," Mallory said, "but I'm so sorry." She laced her fingers with his, and stayed by his side. His friend.

I love you.

He couldn't say it, not yet. He needed to figure out where he kept going wrong in his other relationships.

"It's about money. I screwed up something with money again." He had to laugh or else he'd cry out of sheer frustration. "I paid for their whole Vegas party, anything they could wish for, but they seem pissed off every time they mention Vegas. You're pissed off that I gave you money. Nobody ever seems to want it when I try to give it to them, but now Eliza is pissed off that I won't buy this particular house. She said I would think it wasn't worth what I'd get in return. What in the hell would I get out of owning this house besides a place for her to stay in… June… I'm an idiot."

He turned to Mallory, appalled at himself, relieved to have cracked the code, embarrassed not to have done it sooner. "It's her. What I'd be getting in return if I bought this house is *her*. I'd get her company for the summer. But I told her I wouldn't buy the house, so she thinks I value her less than a house. Than a house. That's crazy."

But that was it. From a very young age, Eliza must have thought every decision he made reflected her value to him. She wasn't worth the cost of a trip to Vegas to see her on her birthday. She wasn't worth the financial loss if he left a business consortium in Berlin to be at her high school graduation. Every time he hadn't shown up, she'd assumed something else had been worth more than she was. What else could she have thought?

"Would she be happy if you bought it?" Mallory sounded doubtful. "You won't be here in June."

"I don't know her very well anymore. She was so little when I moved away from home. She just wanted piggyback rides from me. She wanted…my time."

Mallory bit her lip.

"Do you think that's still it? That's—that's amazing. Does she still think I'm cool to hang out with?" The thought made him laugh. Mallory thought he was funny. Could Eliza think he was cool?

"She could come to Tokyo with me in June. It's a little crazy there. These executives, these icons of industry, do karaoke for hours. I don't, but God, it would be great to have her come with me. She'd love it. I think she would, anyway."

Mallory was absolutely beaming at him. He was blown away by her beauty in the December sunshine.

He squeezed her hand. "What are you so happy about?"

"I'm smiling because you're smiling."

He was smiling, wasn't he? "I need to go talk to my sister."

Mallory gave him one of those little shoulder shoves. "Go get your sister back," she said.

So he did.

This was the most bittersweet date Mallory had ever been on, real or fake.

The sun was setting, but the front porch faced west, capturing enough warmth for them to sit there, all four of them, waiting for the car that would take the twins back to the airport.

"Are you going to come in June as well?"

Eli was speaking to his brother, not to her.

Mallory could have melted at the effort Eli was making to reach his brother, it was so touching. But the question made her wonder where she would be in June. She looked at the trio of Taylors sprawled on the steps, and tried not to picture herself here.

A wistful pang was still a pang.

TJ only answered Eli with a shrug.

Eli looked at his watch. "You know, we're running out of time. There could be a half-dozen good reasons for you to be giving me the silent treatment, TJ, but I wish you'd give me one to work on. What's going on?"

TJ heaved a sigh. "I don't have a problem with you. You followed in Dad's footsteps. Did what was expected of you. I'll have to remind him he got at least one son to stay in the family business."

"When you tell him what? What are you planning to do?"

"I'm teaching. By June, I'll be teaching in India at a boarding school for girls. It's been in operation for years now. I saw a documentary on it when I was a freshman, and I'd never forgotten it, so I applied for the job. They provide top-notch educations to girls in the most poverty-stricken communities. It's astonishing how much impact there is on the whole community by educating just one girl. There's a socioeconomic ripple effect that—" TJ cut himself off.

"It sounds fascinating," Eli said, and Mallory could hear the sincerity in his voice. "If you need anything at all—"

"Nope. I'm sure they need money. I'm just not here to ask for that."

Mallory remembered their stormy fireside chat. *People I care about won't take my money. I have to pay bills for them when they aren't looking.* A school in India was going to be the beneficiary of some major grants very soon. Poor Eli—it wouldn't bring his brother any closer to him, but it was all Eli thought he could do. TJ didn't want to travel to Tokyo or even stay in this house in June. He had plans.

TJ flicked acorns off the steps. "You know Dad. It's going to be a merry Christmas when he finds out. He doesn't approve of teaching. There isn't a lot of money in it."

"I approve of teaching." Eli made the announcement, and the twins both looked at him in surprise.

Mallory gave Eli their signal, making that rolling motion with her hand. *Keep going.*

"Do you know what I'm doing here? Either one of you? It was in the Masterson alumni news."

Eliza threw an acorn at him from her seat on a lower step. "If you don't know that neither I nor TJ went to Masterson, I'm going to throw you in the lake."

Eli put his hand on her head. "Vassar." He nudged TJ with the side of his shoe. "Columbia. Of course you don't know what I'm doing, because I didn't tell you, and that's my fault. I'm working on it."

Mallory could have laughed at the matching expressions of shock on the twins' faces—but they weren't her siblings, and this wasn't her family. She needed to remember that.

"I'm teaching at the university. Only for a semester, but I'm going to have MBA students in a classroom. Between you and me, TJ, teaching is now part of the family business. If Dad's unbearable about it, you've got my jet at your disposal. Go have a merry Christmas somewhere else. Or here. You could come here."

Eli glanced Mallory's way. She knew he wanted to know if that had gone well. It sure seemed to her like TJ wanted someone to back him up on his career decisions. Eli had figured that out quickly, once TJ had started talking. She nodded at Eli and tapped her heart lightly.

Eli winked back.

Mallory felt more in her heart than bubbly champagne. She felt like she belonged.

Except she didn't. She liked Eli's brother and sister. She liked Eli so very much, and he liked her. But that was where it ended.

Before his waking nightmare, he'd spoken to her about talking like lovers, but not making love. She'd told him to stop seducing her, and she'd stormed out of the room. That had been the end of that. After his terrible nightmare, he'd held onto her for a long time, but he'd flat-out told her he was being careful not to fall in love, that it would be bad for him, psychologically, right now. She'd fallen asleep watching the fire with him, but there'd been no kisses. No more attempts at kisses. They'd held hands today, but only because he wanted to put on a good show for Eliza and TJ.

January would come, and they'd see each other in the office now and then. Maybe a lot. But she wouldn't be his girlfriend, and she wouldn't be part of his family. There was no point in sitting out here now, watching them like a child with her nose pressed against a toy store window, getting a glimpse of what she could not have.

Mallory excused herself as she should have done more firmly at breakfast. "I'll let the three of you have a few minutes to say goodbye."

"Wait a minute." Eliza, of course, had something else to talk about. "I think it's amazing that you didn't know my brother was a stud when it came to rowing and fencing. What did you first see in him? Where did you guys meet?"

Mallory implored Eli silently. *I told you I didn't want to be your fake girlfriend. Don't make me lie.*

Eli turned his palm up. *What's the problem?*

At their silent exchange, Eliza's face fell. "Dumb question, huh? I always forget that he's famous now. It was bad enough when he was rich. Rich and famous? Everyone he meets is already predisposed to like him. It's too easy for him."

Mallory was offended. "Not me. He didn't tell me who he was at all. I had to find out the hard way."

Eli settled back on the stairs. "I think we should tell them the truth, Mallory, my dearest, darlingest cupcake."

He did?

"Okay," she said, not knowing if it was okay or not. "You go first."

"I met Mallory at the annual lighting of the Yule log in the town park. She walked right up to me and started talking. Must have been something she liked about the way I looked."

Mallory shook her head at Eliza. "It was really dark, and he was doing this whole wild-man thing with his hair, and he had a beard. I didn't know who he was. He said his name was Eli. Not Taylor. He bought me hot chocolate, which cost one dollar, so you can't say I was dazzled by all the money he spent on me."

"Actually, it was one hundred dollars. I only had one-hundred-dollar bills on me."

"You—you paid one hundred dollars to drink a cup of hot chocolate with me?"

"I bought you two cups."

"Two hundred dollars?" Mallory was appalled. It didn't matter how much money Eli had. Two hundred dollars for hot chocolate in a paper cup was outrageous. "Don't do that. It's crazy."

"The nuns would beg to differ, I'm sure."

His sister looked between them like they were playing ping-pong. She settled on Mallory. "So, if it wasn't the money or the fame, what did dazzle you?"

"Yes," Eli said, clearly enjoying himself. "What did dazzle you?"

"We talked."

"You talked," he corrected her. "I listened."

"Really? It was hard to tell you were listening when you were doing that whole statue imitation, staring at the bon…fire. Oh."

The look they shared was one of a kind. Only the two of them knew what he'd been going through when she'd walked up to him. Only the two of them knew how they'd spent last night, staring that fire down together. It wasn't sex or even a kiss, but it was an intimate bond.

"We both talked, and some of the topics were serious, and he was very patient and kind when I got all choked up." She was getting choked up now.

Eli looked away, all nonchalance. "She wept like a waterfall on me. Very sexy first impression."

"He refused to shake my hand when I introduced myself."

"She got mad at me after she finished crying, because I wouldn't tell her that she looked bad."

Mallory crossed her arms. "He picked me up and set me on top of a hay bale without even asking."

Eli huffed out a sigh. "So, I'm not supposed to buy her things, and I'm not supposed to tell her she's pretty. She's really hard to date."

Eliza and TJ both stared at their big brother.

Eliza recovered first, turning to Mallory with a beaming smile. "Well, I love you!"

Chapter Nineteen

Learning Objective: Define the term "mature firm."

—Senior Year Project *by Mallory Ames*

"How long did your therapist say that reconciliation should take?"

Eli smiled at Mallory's pert question. "I don't want to be too smug about it. The fact that Eliza and TJ showed up on my doorstep probably accelerated the timeline by six months. The fact that they seemed pretty...open? Is that the word for it?"

"Openhearted. Your brother and sister are very openhearted people."

"Good word. The fact that they are so openhearted with me, even TJ, probably skipped another six months. They get the credit. I'm grateful, though. Today was a really good day."

"You didn't wake up with strangers looking at your bare butt."

Ah, this woman made him laugh. Eli looked down at Mallory's pretty face as she lay with her head on his thigh, looking at the fireplace.

He stretched one leg out as he sat on the floor, virtually in the same position as the night before. Nothing seemed harrowing tonight. The power was on, and they'd found a string of twinkling lights in the garland on the mantel and plugged them in. They'd done a shot of tequila for the fun of it, instead of hoping it would ease strained nerves. The fire looked like a fire to him, although they'd been smart about it and were burning only one log at a time. If he should start to feel anxious, it would be easy to extinguish. So far, he felt great.

And, yeah, his brother and sister didn't hate him. What a difference a day could make.

"He wanted you to spend twelve months reconnecting with your siblings? What kind of snail's pace is that?"

Eli brushed a strand of hair off Mallory's forehead as she frowned. "Want to guess how long I was supposed to look at little fires before I moved on to medium fires?"

Her sleepy eyes opened wider at that. "You showed him. You went to the biggest bonfire of the year, you rebel."

"That didn't exactly work. It was kind of hellish, actually, until you showed up."

"Mmm. And then you did it again here, anyway, by yourself."

"Also hellish, until you showed up."

"So, which one of us is not the paragon we thought the other one was? Someone around here was labeled 'stubborn to an asinine degree.'"

"I told you, we're two peas in a pod."

He was smiling down at her when she looked up at him and said, "I really like you."

Game over. This was the woman. His one and only.

A piece of a star just landed next to me. I'm so damned lucky that I get to be with you. He wanted to say that out loud to her once more. And this time, he didn't want any of his own insecurities to mar their happiness under a starry sky.

She was almost asleep, her whole body going slack. His whole body was not slack.

"One thing left," she mumbled. "Your pilot."

Eli's drowsy desire was doused as effectively as if he'd jumped off the dock into the December lake water. The pilot was in a wheelchair because of him, trapped.

Eli was trapped with him; he could see that now. He'd been waiting for the wheelchair to disappear, hoping that he hadn't permanently injured this distant friend. That day might never come. The wheelchair might never go away. If he couldn't face that, if he allowed that piece of *the traumatic event* to fester, his heart would never be whole.

He needed it to be whole. It could be cracked and patched, because scars made things stronger, but it had to be whole. His to give. God willing, Mallory's to receive.

He sighed and lay back on a luxurious pillow that wouldn't feel luxurious by morning. But he had a sleeping Mallory in his lap, a fire burning safely in front of him and a long night ahead of him.

He needed to make a plan to see—not the pilot. Owen. Owen Michaels. He needed to drive down to Houston and meet with Owen in person. He owed it to the man to give him the chance to give him hell for the damage he'd done.

Eli was ready to recover, and baby steps weren't his style. Forget the drive. He might as well fly to Houston.

Eli swept into the hospital, his open trench coat flaring out behind him, a man on a mission in a suit and tie, his armor for battle.

He'd just defeated one obstacle. Completing the flight from Masterson to Houston hadn't been much of a challenge. The luxury jet was nothing like the tiny prop plane that had bounced on every air current. Either that, or Eli had just been too keyed up about facing the man he'd put in a wheelchair to spare any energy worrying about the airplane. It had been anti-climactic, in its way.

Mallory had poked about the cabin, once she'd realized he wasn't particularly fazed by the flight. She'd been amused by the luxurious bathroom with its shower. Delighted with the pastries that had been arranged for their breakfast. When she'd made a joke about joining the Mile High Club, he'd completely forgotten he had any problems in the world for a minute or two.

Some day...

But they were in the hospital now. Owen Michaels was expecting them. Eli wished he knew what to expect in return.

"Slow down." Mallory pulled back on his arm. "These pencil skirts limit my oh-so-confident strides. How do you swagger into a hospital and know which way to go?"

"My assistant sent a floor plan."

He slowed his strides for the woman by his side. He'd worn business attire, because he wouldn't lose his composure as E.L. Taylor. He knew how to meet the expectations others had of him when he wore a suit and tie. Mallory was wearing a skirt and heels to match his business attire, because...

Because she was his friend. He hoped the journey from friends to lovers would be brief, because he wanted her more than he'd ever wanted a woman in his life.

He paused outside the correct room. Mallory had her hand tucked in his elbow. She squeezed his arm. "He's probably apprehensive about this meeting, too."

For once, Mallory turned out to be wrong.

Owen was unabashedly glad Eli had come. Mallory stayed awhile, a star by his side, and then she stepped out. Eli shut the door after her and walked back to Owen. The time for real talk had come.

Looking down at the man in a wheelchair got to him. They'd been about the same height on the airstrip, two big men buckling into a tiny cockpit, oblivious to how they'd get back out.

"Owen. Let me say this. I appreciate your courtesy this morning, but I don't know how you can even talk to me. The guilt is mine. I know it."

"Whoa. Hold up. What are you guilty of?"

Eli gestured toward the wheelchair. "This. All of this."

"Sit down, man." Owen rolled his wheelchair over to a table.

Eli sat. Eye to eye, he saw that Owen was still the same formidable man who'd once pushed hard to make his crew team.

"You got me out of that cockpit alive. You swam me to safety. You may think it's terrible that I'm sitting here, but it is the God's honest truth that it's a miracle I'm sitting here at all. You saved my life. You were a hero that night."

Eli wasn't impressed with that assessment. "I'm a good swimmer. I'm in shape. That doesn't make me a hero."

"No, it doesn't. Look at Adrienne. That canoe-paddling angel is in her late seventies and barely five feet tall. She pulled us both to shore."

"Exactly. That's a hero. She had no quit in her. She could have called 911 and waited on the shore, and nobody would have thought poorly of her. She jumped in a damned canoe and tried to get to the plane before it sank, just in case anyone had survived."

She'd refused Eli's financial reward, too, saying she'd only been doing the right thing. He'd paid off her mortgage, anyway.

"One-hundred-percent agree," Owen said. "But that's you, too. You could have escaped from that cockpit and swum to shore, and nobody would have thought poorly of you. You didn't do that."

Eli took a slow breath, the same kind Mallory had taken so many times in difficult moments. *Two peas in a pod.* He needed to match her determination.

He gave voice to the worst truth. "You wouldn't have been in the air in the first place if it weren't for me. You only flew me because I'm E.L. Taylor."

Owen laughed at that. "Sorry, I'm not a big fan. On the crew team, I didn't even like you that much. You didn't know who the heck I was that day, did you?"

It was not the response Eli had expected, but he rolled with it. "Actually, you did look vaguely familiar. That's unusual. A thousand times, I don't know the person who swears they know me. I looked you up in the yearbook, after. I remember you now. You were a sophomore when I was a senior."

"Don't worry about it. I couldn't name the sophomores on the team when I was a senior, either. You didn't make me fly you anywhere that day. I only flew you because I needed someone to cover the fuel costs. I wanted to log some more hours."

Then it was Owen taking the big breath, bracing himself. "I was the pilot. I don't think you really get what that means. It was on my shoulders to make the flight as safe as possible. Sometimes, it's not possible, and then it's still the pilot's job to preserve life."

"Your skill set us down in one piece, mostly. Thank you."

"Your skill pulled me out of that wreckage. Thank you."

They looked at each other a moment longer.

Owen shook his head. "Well, look at us, a couple of heroes sitting here at a table without a damned beer in sight."

"I'll bring the whiskey next time."

"You do that. Seriously. This is far from over, and it's been brutal, but I'm going to walk again."

If sheer willpower could do it, Eli knew Owen would walk. If not, that wouldn't stop him from having a good life.

Eli might even be able to help out in more ways than paying hospital bills. "It's come to my attention that I have a bad habit of just dropping gifts on people whether they want them or not. While you're working on your recovery, would you want to give a few top of the line kayaks a test run?" Eli barely hesitated. "With me? I need someone to race against."

He didn't make friends in his line of work. That didn't mean he couldn't make friends at all.

"Hell, yes." Owen held out his hand.

Eli shook it, fully aware that a friendship was an incredible gift to receive in the face of a tragedy. "In that case, I look forward to giving you a new kayak for Christmas and then immediately kicking your ass in it."

Owen laughed. "You can try. Merry Christmas."

The private plane was posh.

Mallory could appreciate it, but she couldn't enjoy it. Not with Eli sitting next to her silently, concentrating deeply on something she wasn't part of. The private jet seats were full-size recliners, so being next to him wasn't as close as she wished it were.

He'd tossed his suit jacket aside and sat, looking out the window, his chin resting on his fist, Rodin's *The Thinker*—or just a man who'd done a lot this week to think about.

"How are you doing?" she asked in her most gentle, most positive tone, the one she'd used with the people whose bodies were so very sick and in need of comfort. She craned her neck a little bit, trying to see what had him so entranced.

Eli dropped his hand and looked her. Blue skies reflected in his blue eyes. "It's beautiful out there. This isn't as comfortable as a tree branch, but you could sit with me, and we'd be able to see everything together."

He really was okay. She'd thought so, but it was good to know he thought so, too. Because if everything else was good, there was one thing that could be better.

Once she was in his lap, she told herself to take a deep breath—and went for it. "Excuse me, Mr. Taylor?"

That took his eyes off the view. He looked at her with one eyebrow raised. "Yes, Miss Ames?"

Oh, he did deliciously bossy so well.

"I would like to review my policy on kisses."

That made him set his hands on her waist. "Please do."

She fiddled with his loosened necktie for a moment. "I want to redefine a real kiss, because as you know, that's the only kind I allow."

He settled back in the seat, a powerful man at leisure, but under her hands, she could feel the rise and fall of his chest. Under her thighs, she could feel the tension in his.

"From now on, the criteria is simple. I have to want to kiss the person badly, and he has to want to kiss me, too. I have been dying to kiss Eli for days. He bought me a hundred-dollar cup of hot chocolate and told me I met all his standards."

"I told you that you exceeded them."

In his voice, she heard everything she could have wanted to hear. Warmth, admiration, affection—desire. This was going to be wonderful. He wanted her as much as she wanted him.

She ran one finger over his shoulder, over the polished cotton of his dress shirt. "Eli kissed me only once, but it was the kiss of a lifetime. I'm not sure what happened, but he hasn't tried to kiss me again. I'm going to have clarify that all kisses from him qualify as real and are quite welcome. But in the meantime, while we're on the plane, I wondered if you, Mr. Taylor, would like to kiss me? Because I don't really care which name you go by. You are always you, and I would like to kiss you, oh, so badly."

"Ms. Ames. *Mallory.* From now on, and I do mean for the rest of my life, I'm Eli Taylor. Both names. And all of me would very much like to kiss *all* of you. But I'll start with your perfect mouth."

She could hardly kiss because she could hardly breathe, she wanted this so badly. Their lips met, softly. Pulled away again, slowly. She kissed his lower lip, which had smiled under her thumb, and she kissed the corner of his mouth, which was far too busy returning her kisses to smile at the moment.

He tapped the center of her upper lip with his finger, then kissed her there reverently. Then her cheeks, her eyelashes.

With a little breath, she turned so she would be chest to chest with him, one bent leg against his hard stomach, which was only possible to do if she let her pencil skirt ride up very high. Her breath was all shivery as she ran her fingertips down the smooth shirt that hid his hard chest from her view—for now.

He placed one hand on the side of her neck, his thumb on her jaw, and held her head steady as he stared her down, not angrily—oh, no—but seriously. His other hand drifted over her hip and her bunched-up skirt to slide over her backside, finding mostly bare skin and a little bit of lace.

The breath left his body. The fire burned in his eyes. He was putty in her hands, a glowering, gorgeous man at her mercy.

"Please tell me, Eli Taylor, that the pilots don't leave that cockpit."

"They don't."

"Please tell me that we aren't landing soon while you take me wherever it is we're spending the night."

It seemed to take him a great deal of concentration to look at his wristwatch. "We have at least two hours."

"In that case, this would be the ideal time and the most elegant place with the most beautiful view for us to stop talking like lovers and actually become lovers."

Chapter Twenty

Final Grade: A+

—Senior Year Project, *Mallory Ames*

She'd never seen Eli so anxious.

She'd expected him to be very, very relaxed after welcoming her to the Mile High Club, but instead he was at the mirror over the sink in the jet's spacious bathroom, fixing his hair and straightening his tie. Then he turned around and eyed her critically, head to toe.

"Um…" He looked at her updo. "Maybe you better re-twist that bun. Your lips are a little puffy. I don't suppose we can do anything about that."

"*Eli.* Why are you so worried about our appearance?"

He cleared his throat and looked a little sheepish. "It's Christmas Eve. This is supposed to be your Christmas present."

"I loved it. Can I have another?"

He tapped her on the nose. "You'll notice we've been in the air awhile—or maybe you were too busy to notice—but we've been heading north this entire time. You were looking for a place to stay for your winter break, and I thought you might want to spend your time off with your grandpa. In Ohio."

"Grandpa? We're going to land in Ohio?" She threw her arms around Eli and kissed his cheeks soundly, feeling more like a little girl and less like the *femme fatale* she'd just so successfully been.

Eli was kind of holding her off, like she was an exuberant, large puppy. "Yes. He's expecting us. I just had no idea I'd be meeting him after so thoroughly messing up his granddaughter's hair. And makeup. And clothes." He looked chagrined. "This is not a good look. I mean, this is a fantastic look, but it's not a good look for Grandpa. I'd like to meet him, if that's okay with you. I have to leave tomorrow, Christmas night. I always line up business in Asia over the holidays, but this will be the last year for that. Christmas should be family time, now that I have a family again. But you have a family, so I thought you'd like to be with them."

He sounded nervous. Mallory was stunned, but this was as close to babbling as she'd bet E.L. Taylor could get.

"I can send the jet to bring you back to me on January sixth. I know that's a long way away, and I only asked you to pack an overnight bag for this trip. I thought I was being clever that way, to get you to pack your personal makeup and stuff, but I know you need more clothes and coats for a couple of weeks in Ohio. I'm not trying to dump a big gift or a lot of money on you without checking with you first, but in this situation, it wouldn't be much of a gift if I sent you somewhere with only one change of clothes."

He *was* nervous. It was unbearably sweet.

"There are suitcases on board, ready for you. Nothing crazy, just two weeks' worth of clothes and shoes and whatever, just to get you by. I kept my word and didn't go into your bedroom, but I sent the housekeeper in to get some clothing sizes for my assistant. Anything that doesn't fit or that you don't like you can get rid of. Maybe your sister-in-law would like your hand-me-downs."

"Are you done?" Mallory asked.

"Yes."

She launched herself at him and kissed him over and over. "You're taking me to see my grandpa for Christmas. Thank you, thank you, thank you."

"If that's too expensive, I have another gift that didn't cost me any cash." Eli reached into a pocket of the coat he'd hung on the door and pulled out a blue mitten. "The boys of Kappa Lambda were very cooperative when I stopped by their party that night."

She pressed the mitten to her heart. "I can't believe it."

"I'm sorry."

"For what? This is a wonderful gift. It cost you

more than money. You spent your time and—and I'd bet your swagger and everything else you have that isn't money to get this back for me."

"I'm sorry because I shouldn't have kept it so long. It was all I had of you for a little while. It's been my lucky charm. It worked for this flight, didn't it?"

He cupped her face in his hands and kissed her passionately, because her lips couldn't look *less* kissed, anyway.

It was Epiphany, January sixth, and the last of the Yule log was being burned tonight to officially end the holiday season.

Tiny tots ran wild around the park, unable to contain themselves while waiting for the Three Wise Men to arrive with a real camel and bags of candy.

Mallory could hardly wait to see Eli. The last time she'd seen Eli had been Christmas Day. He'd given her one more gift: he'd set up indefinite payment for her grandfather's assisted-living apartment. Eli had asked her grandfather's permission to do so. Grandpa had insisted that he had funds to last through September, so it wasn't necessary. He'd worry about September when September came. Eli had explained that Mallory would be at ease if she knew her grandfather wouldn't have to move from a place where he'd made so many friends. It wasn't charity for Grandpa, but a gift to make Mallory happy. That had been a winning argument. E.L. Taylor was a very good negotiator.

After her grandfather had fallen asleep in his recliner during the football game on TV, Mallory had been truly sorry to whisper to Eli that she had nothing to give to him.

Eli had winked. "You could give me an interesting new start-up to invest in."

They snuck out to have a second round of pumpkin pie in the dining room, and she'd pitched her caregiver-client matchmaker concept. She'd asked him for twenty-thousand dollars in return for a twenty percent share of her company. Eli had countered with twenty grand for thirty percent. They'd shaken hands on twenty-five percent.

Eli had needed to leave for Japan. Mallory had ridden with him to the airport. Limousines were private enough for making love, she'd learned. If her lips had been a little puffy and her hair had been a little messy when the limo returned her to her grandfather's apartment, Grandpa had been kind enough not to say anything. He'd just patted her hand and said her new fellow seemed to be smart and respectful. He approved.

Her father hadn't quite believed she was dating somebody as rich as her brother kept claiming E.L. Taylor was, despite the fact that she and Eli had talked every day by phone. Her brother had been even less polite to her than usual, because jealousy didn't become anybody. Her sister-in-law, however, had swallowed her pride and graciously accepted the cast-offs from Mallory's new wardrobe.

Mallory was glad to be back in Texas, gladder still when the chauffeur took her from the tarmac to the town park. "Mr. Taylor said you would know where to meet him."

There could only be one place Eli was waiting. She headed for the bonfire at a brisk walk, taking confident strides. She skipped the crowd and headed for the darker side of the sandpit. When she caught sight of Eli, she ran.

He scooped her up and spun her around under the starry sky.

"I missed you," she said between kisses. "Take me home and make love to me. Hurry, or we might get caught for public indecency."

"I don't care where we go, as long as I can throw my wish first." Eli pulled a folded piece of paper out of his pocket. He held up the pine cone that was attached to it by a ribbon. "Aerodynamics."

Eli threw the wish up in the air, straight up toward the stars. It came fluttering down, spinning in a little helicopter motion as the pine cone pulled it down to earth. He caught it and held it out to Mallory.

"You're supposed to throw it onto the Yule log," she said.

"You need to read it first, or it won't come true. I read your note before you threw it one month ago, and it came true. E.L. Taylor likes you."

Mallory unfolded the wish.

I hope Mallory Ames will like me.

"Oh, Eli. I like you. So much more than that."

Eli kissed her, because he could. Because he needed to kiss her, to hug her and hold her hand, to live the rest of his life with her touch.

For just one more minute, though, he needed to let go. He stepped back and pulled another folded wish out of his pocket. "Once upon a time, I wrote a book that said you should never meet a hero, somebody who inspires you, unless you were their equal. You inspire me, Mallory. I want you in my life, which means we need to be equals. That means you would have to love me, because I love you. With all of my heart, Mallory, I love you."

"Oh, Eli, Eli. Yes, we're equals. I love you with all of my heart, too."

He'd never wanted to kiss a woman so badly. So he did.

She kissed him back as the air swirled around the bonfire, until he whispered over her perfect, beautiful lips. "I want to spend the entire weekend in bed with you, but I have one more wish in my pocket. Let's see if this one comes true."

He stepped back and threw it up to the stars, higher than the one before.

Mallory caught it on its way down. She unfolded it with trembling hands. In the firelight of the Yule log, she read, *I hope Mallory Ames will marry me.*

One perfect, happy tear rolled down her cheek, because a dream was coming true. She lowered the note and saw E.L. Taylor, her very own Eli, down on one knee with a ring in his hand.

"When I came to see this Yule log on the first day of the season, I was a man who had nothing. Money, yes, but nothing worth living for. Then a star fell from the sky and landed right next to me, and I've been so incredibly lucky to be with her. Mallory Ames, you are my light and my happiness. I hope you are my future. Will you do me the honor of becoming my wife?"

"Yes, yes, yes."

He slid the ring onto her finger and kissed her hand.

"Please stand up, Eli. I'm afraid I'm going to cry very hard in about two seconds, and I'm going to need a hug."

Eli stood and wrapped her in his arms. "That's what I'm here for. I'm going to love you forever, Mallory Ames."

She nodded her head and sniffed back happy tears. "That's excellent news."

* * * * *

*Don't miss the rest of the books in
the Masterson, Texas series:*

The Bartender's Secret
The Slow Burn

Available now from Harlequin Special Edition!

**WE HOPE YOU ENJOYED
THIS BOOK FROM**

Believe in love. Overcome obstacles. Find happiness.

Relate to finding comfort and strength in the
support of loved ones and enjoy the journey
no matter what life throws your way.

6 NEW BOOKS AVAILABLE EVERY MONTH!

#2809 HER TEXAS NEW YEAR'S WISH
The Fortunes of Texas: The Hotel Fortune • by Michelle Major
When Grace Williams topples from the balcony at the new Hotel Fortune, the last thing she expects is to find love with her new bosses' brother. Wiley Fortune has looks, money and charm to spare. But Grace's past makes her wary of investing her heart. This time, she is holding out for the real deal...

#2810 WHAT HAPPENS AT THE RANCH...
Twin Kings Ranch • by Christy Jeffries
All Secret Service agent Grayson Wyatt has to do is protect Tessa King, the VP's daughter, and stay low profile. But Tessa is guarding her own secret. And her attraction to the undercover cowboy breaks every protocol. With the media hot on a story, their taboo relationship could put everything Tessa and Grayson have fought for at risk...

#2811 THE CHILD WHO CHANGED THEM
The Parent Portal • by Tara Taylor Quinn
Dr. Greg Adams knows he can't have children. But when colleague Dr. Elaina Alexander announces she's pregnant with his miracle child, Greg finds his life turned upside down. But can the good doctor convince widow Elaina that their happiness lies within reach—and with each other?

#2812 THE MARINE MAKES AMENDS
The Camdens of Montana • by Victoria Pade
Micah Camden ruined Lexie Parker's life years ago, but now that she's back in Merritt to care for her grandmother—who was hurt due to Micah's negligence—she has no plans to forgive him. But Micah knows that he made mistakes back then and hopes to make amends with Lexie, if only so they can both move on from the past. Everyone says Micah's changed since joining the marines, but it's going to take more than someone's word to convince her...

#2813 SNOWBOUND WITH THE SHERIFF
Sutter Creek, Montana • by Laurel Greer
Stella Reid has been gone from Sutter Creek long enough and is determined to mend fences...but immediately comes face-to-face with the man who broke her heart: Sheriff Ryan Rafferty. But as she opens herself up bit by bit, can Stella find the happily-ever-after she was denied years ago—in his arms?

#2814 THE MARRIAGE MOMENT
Paradise Animal Clinic • by Katie Meyer
Deputy Jessica Santiago will let nothing—not even a surprise pregnancy—get in the way of her job. Determined to solve several problems at once—getting her hands on her inheritance *and* creating a family—Jessica convinces colleague Ryan Sullivan to partake in a marriage of convenience. But what's a deputy to do when love blooms?

Love Harlequin romance?

DISCOVER.

Be the first to find out about promotions,
news and exclusive content!

f Facebook.com/HarlequinBooks

t Twitter.com/HarlequinBooks

◉ Instagram.com/HarlequinBooks

p Pinterest.com/HarlequinBooks

ReaderService.com

EXPLORE.

Sign up for the Harlequin e-newsletter and
download a free book from any series at
TryHarlequin.com

CONNECT.

Join our Harlequin community to
share your thoughts and connect
with other romance readers!
Facebook.com/groups/HarlequinConnection

HSOCIAL2020